STANDING THE FINAL WATCH

THE LAST BRIGADE, BOOK ONE

WILLIAM ALAN WEBB

δ
Dingbat Publishing
Humble, Texas

Standing the Final Watch
Copyright © 2016 by William Alan Webb
ISBN 978-1537048888

Published by Dingbat Publishing
Humble, Texas

All rights reserved. No part of this book may be reproduced in any form or by any means without written consent, excepting brief quotes used in reviews.

This book is licensed to the original purchaser only. Duplication or distribution via any means is illegal and a violation of International Copyright Law, subject to criminal prosecution and upon conviction, fines and/or imprisonment. No part of this book can be reproduced or sold by any person or business without the express permission of the publisher.

Thank you for respecting the hard work of this author.

This is a work of fiction. Names, places, characters, and events are entirely the produce of the author's imagination or are used fictitiously, and any resemblance to persons living or dead, actual locations, events, or organizations is coincidental.

Prologue

October 12th

Lake Tahoe sparkled under a high sun in a cloudless sky. From the warmth of the tour boat's passenger lounge, Mary Buffer giggled as her chubby husband Winslow braced against the bow railings and turned his face into the wind. They had not vacationed since Emily's birth three years ago, and Mary intended to enjoy every moment.

The red-haired toddler stood on tiptoes and waved at her father, then knocked on the window to get his attention. Her warm breath steamed the glass. Winslow grinned at her despite the cold spray and waved back.

Out of the chill and sipping hot chocolate from a foam cup, Mary watched Winslow acting like a little boy and her giggle turned into a laugh. He often painted with words his fantasy of cutting the clear waters of the Caribbean, wind blowing his sparse hair, as he stood at the helm of his own sailing ship. He even confided that those daydreams cycled in an endless loop in his mind. She hoped so; starting a practice as a new CPA required long hours and hard sacrifices, and he deserved time to dream and play.

The muffled buzz of a speedboat grew louder as it neared. Mary glanced left, but milling people blocked her view as the smaller boat throttled down near the port bow. She looked back at Winslow in time to see something metal hit the deck and bounce, stopping near his feet. The egg-shaped object seemed familiar, but her mind did not recognize it before the blast of the grenade ripped him apart.

His right arm smacked into the lounge window and left a bloody smear as it slid to the deck. His right shoe, and most of the foot and shin, remained upright on the deck. The rest of Winslow Buffer swirled astern.

Inside the large cabin Mary Buffer watched her husband's arm slide from view. Stunned, she dropped the foam cup and covered her mouth for almost two seconds before she screamed and grabbed Emily. Panic flooded her with adrenaline and the instincts of motherhood took over. Getting away from the horror on the bow drove her to claw and elbow through her fellow tourists, headed for the stern while dragging Emily behind her.

Another woman followed with a toddler under each arm, yelling for her husband, but panicky screams drowned her out. Mother and children fell when a large man shoved through, and they disappeared in the tangle of feet. Two men fought to shield their families from the stampede as everyone made for the starboard door. Mary stumbled, but a lithe middle-aged woman with blonde hair caught her left arm, and a girl who could only have been her daughter grabbed her right. Together they got Mary back to her feet. The two women exchanged a brief glance and Mary drew strength from the older woman's nod of confidence.

A moment later the crowd shoved Mary against a window, Emily behind her and the women on either side. Outside, the speedboat bobbed on the waves. Three of the four men jumped aboard the tour boat and fanned out. They wore black shoes, gloves, and three-hole balaclavas, and all carried machine pistols. One of the attackers locked eyes with her through the window. His were green, but she could see no humanity in them, no spark of empathy, nothing except cold indifference. He turned as a deck hand rounded the stern corner of the lounge and hosed him with 9mm rounds that chewed his chest into a red slaw of bone and lung. As the crewman toppled over the side, the killer met Mary's eyes again. This time he smiled.

Mary screamed and his smile widened. Pinned against the glass with Emily, she could not move no matter how much she struggled.

Forward of the lounge, the pilothouse overlooked the entire boat from a height of ten feet. The port door opened and the ship's captain stepped out, aiming a large pistol in shaking hands. Mary's breath caught. The terrorists on board had their backs to him, but the fourth man, still on the speedboat, spotted the danger and sprayed the pilothouse doorway, grinding up both the captain and the door frame. She watched as shells ejected from the gun and bounced on the boat's deck in a shining stream of metal.

Mary tried to squirm away as the terrorists burst in through the nearest door. Several men without families dove over the starboard side.

Stopping next to her, the smallest of the three black-clad killers pointed with his machine gun and another killer charged back outside. After clubbing and punching his way through hysterical women and children, the gunman emptied his magazine into the swimmers' backs.

The leader, short but exuding authority, stood next to Mary. He scanned the lounge and spotted Emily huddled behind her. He leaned over and tousled her hair. Emily's face reddened as she sobbed louder, gulping little breaths.

"What a pretty little girl," he said. "You should be very proud."

Mary could not speak. The man's accent strongly hinted of New England. She smelled something fragrant, shampoo, or maybe cologne. Deep creases in his face resembled knife scars and a large mole dominated his upper lip. She edged away, hoping he would not notice, but he pointed at her and shook his head.

"Everybody shut up and stand still!" he yelled.

He repeated it three times before the terrified tourists quieted, except for Emily, who kept crying. Mary whispered, "Don't cry, sweetheart, Mommy's here," and stroked her forehead. Sliding sideways, she interposed herself between Emily and the gunman and buried the toddler's face in her shoulder to hush her. At the first opportunity, she would run for the door and not stop; she would take her chances in the water. If she dove deep enough, maybe the bullets wouldn't hit her.

Two young mothers clutching babies fell to their knees, begging for mercy. The leader motioned them to their feet and patted the air as if reassuring them all would be fine. He scanned the terrified crowd and examined each face, as if selecting a steak for dinner, and stopped when he spotted the slim blonde hugging a twenty-ish version of herself, the same mother and daughter who'd kept Mary from falling moments before.

"Those two." He pointed with his gun again. "They're the ones. Take care of them first."

The biggest attacker grabbed the women by their arms and dragged them, kicking and biting, to the port side bulkhead, and jammed his machine pistol against the younger woman's temple. Mary watched them with horror and relief, assuming those two had been the target of the attack, but shame kept her from looking at them.

Following a burst of gunfire, the leader pointed his machine gun at her. Mary froze.

"Sorry, lady," he stage-whispered. "Allahu akbar," he said, much louder. It came out as 'Allayhu ak*bah*.' He squeezed the trigger. Mary saw the flash, then nothing more.

SECTION 1

Chapter 1

The Dark Man whispered in my ear,
He came last night at Midnight clear.
"I bring you news, but not of cheer,
I bring no cheer, but only tears.
I bring the tears to drown your fears,
I bring the fears of all your years."
    Sergio Velazquez, *"The Dark Man"*

43 minutes later in real time
Democratic Republic of the Congo, Africa

"Ground fire, mission abort!" The words coming over the radio were frantic but the voice was calm. "I repeat, mission abort. XP—" *extraction point* "—compromised. Have taken damage. Returning to Zombie on emergency flight path Alpha. Have wounded aboard."

"Nick?" Norm Fleming said. "There's still time to call it off."

Sitting backward in the rough chair, staring at nothing, Nick Angriff remained silent for what seemed like hours. "That's Green Ghost's call," he finally said. "I won't overrule the man on the spot."

"It's suicide."

"It's still his call."

Fleming grimaced. "Normally I'd argue, but..."

"I'm glad you agree, because I'm going after them. Takeoff in five minutes."

"That's an act of war."

"This whole op is an act of war, but the DRC isn't going to declare war on America."

"But America may declare war on Nick Angriff. Take a second to think about it."

"You're always the voice of reason, Norm. We leave in five minutes. Link their GPS feeds to me and the pilots."

At the designated time, two Russian-built MIL Mi-26 helicopters lifted off from the base in eastern Kenya and headed due west.

Four hours later, a sergeant sitting across from him got Angriff's attention. "Zombie time, Saint."

Angriff nodded and glanced at his wrist-mounted GPS. It was time for the strike team to go in. He walked the length of the cargo bay to the cockpit and tapped the co-pilot on the shoulder. Even leaning down, he almost had to shout to be heard over the roar of the engine. "We're out of time!"

"Throttles are wide open, sir. This is all she's got."

Angriff returned to his seat and said a silent prayer they would be in time.

Four hours earlier

"That's it, boys," Green Ghost said to the eleven men surrounding him. He slapped a mosquito on his neck. "You heard it for yourselves. Pickup ain't coming; the XP is overrun. It's our call what to do next."

In the dense jungle they could melt away and never be noticed. That detail Ghost didn't need to mention.

Vapor spoke first. "You're the boss, but I came here to kills burps." *Butt-ugly raghead pricks.* "It's fucked up to leave without doing it."

"You know what you're saying, right?" Green Ghost said.

Vapor shook the ammo belt stretched over his shoulder. "I don't wanna hump this ammo back through the fucking jungle."

"I don't know about the others," Wingnut chimed in. "But what the hell. Let's do what we came for."

The vote was unanimous, except for Green Ghost.

"You guys are idiots," he said. "We don't have a chance in Hell of pulling this off." Then he raised his arm. "What the fuck. Let's do what we came for."

Current time

The three-vehicle convoy plowed through elephant grass and onto a dirt ribbon marked on their maps as a road. Rifle fire echoed in their wake as fire suppression teams fanned out to secure the landing zone.

Refueling crews got to work. The pilots of the two giant Russian helicopters did not power down, but kept the rotors turning.

"Saint!" the armored personnel carriers' commander called through cupped hands. "Open channel abort order from Centcom! Do I respond?" He waited, standing in the turret, half afraid of the answer he expected to receive.

"Negative—we're dark!" Standing in the APC's forward hatch, the man code-named Saint Nick half-turned to face him and made a twirling motion with his index finger. "Wind her up! Get this bucket moving!"

The lieutenant gave the order and the APC gathered speed, two others rumbling behind as they left the encampment. Saint Nick, famous worldwide as Lt. General Nicholas T. Angriff, gave him a thumbs up then turned back to the front, staring down the jungle path.

Until that moment, the lieutenant could have made a legitimate case of just following the legal orders of a superior officer. Receipt of the abort order changed all that. Now he risked his career by ignoring a direct order from the highest headquarters in the U.S. Army, yet he trusted no officer's judgment more than Nick Angriff's. Many soldiers considered Angriff lucky... somehow, things always worked out for him, even when they should have been FUBAR, and subordinates loyal to him got his loyalty in return. That was worth a lot. So, with his heart beating hard against his chest, the lieutenant ordered his driver to speed up and the radio shut down.

"Just had catastrophic radio failure!" he called. "All comm. gear is down."

Angriff smiled. He loved moments like that, when adrenaline sharpened his senses and quickened his reflexes, filling him with a euphoria found nowhere else, only when leading brave soldiers in close proximity to the enemy. He sniffed the overwhelming scent of rotting vegetation, like a death adder flicking its tongue to find prey.

Checking his wrist-mounted GPS, he saw the distance between him and his men had closed to nine clicks. Racing through the Congolese jungle in an eight-wheeled APC, down a muddy strip that passed for a road, Saint Nick did not give a tinker's damn what happened to him. He would not, however, abandon men who'd gone to battle on his orders. The price of his loyalty might be death or court-martial, but if so, he would pay that price. As the APCs skidded down the narrow path, he braced himself and called for still more speed. Seconds mattered.

Distant gunfire echoed through the jungle, faint but growing louder the deeper they sped into the green depths. Somewhere ahead, twelve

Americans fought for their lives, men who had volunteered for a high-risk, high-reward strike designed and authorized by Angriff. He'd tried to dissuade one of them from what amounted to a suicide mission, because he considered the strike team leader to be the son he'd never had, but that leader knew the risk-reward far outweighed his own life and went anyway. With him and his team trapped and under fire, Angriff faced a stark choice: let them die, or risk his life and career to save them. He'd ordered a communication blackout before the rescue mission kicked off, because, in theory, the enemy could track them by their radio transmissions. CentCom knew that and radioed orders anyway, so insubordination now bordered on abandoning his post in time of war.

"Go, go, go!" He banged on the metal hull with the palm of his hand.

Overhanging branches whipped at the APC and Angriff ducked to avoid being decapitated. Sweat blurred his vision as he scanned the undergrowth in search of targets, and he wiped his eyes on his shirt sleeves. Twin fifty-caliber Desert Eagle semi-automatics hung crisscrossed in shoulder holsters, one under each armpit.

Angriff's plan gave the U.S. plausible deniability in a clear violation of another country's sovereignty by cloaking the mission in deception and disinformation. All the equipment came from foreign manufacturers, from the three Swiss APCs to the belts holding up their Iranian uniforms. Deception underpinned every detail of the operation. Even their M16 rifles bore Singapore manufacturing marks.

Assembling the necessary gear without using U.S.-sourced equipment had taken Angriff months, but the covert attack on a summit meeting of leaders from Boko Haram, Al-Shabaab, Al-Queda, and five other African Muslim terror groups could not be tracked back to America. Operating in a hostile country without permission constituted an act of war, after all. The strike survivors exchanging fire with angry terrorists could not be associated with the U.S. military, because their special unit existed to be non-existent. The team members used nothing but code names, even to each other. Officially they were Strike Team Zombie, but the few people cleared to know of their existence called them the Nameless.

Nothing could be traced back to the American armed forces or government, with one exception: Nick Angriff himself. Three-star generals could not be denied if they were killed or captured. Angriff knew that if the worst happened, he would be disavowed as a rogue general leading an illegal operation against the direct orders of a superior officer. He did not care.

Without warning, bullets ricocheted from the metal hull with loud whangs, zipping in from different angles while cutting leaves that fell like rain. Angriff raised his left arm to block a vagrant shaft of sunlight. He drew his right-hand pistol and searched for a target as the APC sped on, bouncing and splashing through the mud. The familiar weight of the Desert Eagle was reassuring.

Twenty yards ahead, a huge banana plant shivered and the tip of a rocket propelled grenade launcher nosed through, pointed right at him. Aiming the Desert Eagle with both hands, he guessed the gunner's hiding spot, calmed his breathing, and fired two rounds. Despite the roar of the APC, Angriff heard a scream. The rocket canted upward as the dying man fell, toppling backward, and when his dying trigger finger tightened as a reflex, the missile whooshed skyward like a Roman candle. As they passed the spot, Angriff saw the man twitching in the swampy soil.

The APC topped a small hill. Two men in ragged green uniforms stood in the road, aiming rifles in the other direction. His brain identified them as enemies and in quick succession he fired the last five rounds from the pistol. One of the huge bullets missed, two hit the man on the left in his neck and head, blowing away the left side of his skull, and the other two struck the man on the right in his lower spine. The man's stomach exploded, spewing gore into the mud. He staggered forward, pushing internal organs back into the huge hole just above his navel, and then he fell, face down.

The pall of smoke rising from the jungle marked the pyre of a lot of terrorists, but the rest wanted revenge and Green Ghost knew a dumpster fire when he fought in one. Outgunned ten to one, they killed as many as possible and took off. Explosions rippled through the jungle as the Bulgarian PM-79A anti-personnel mines they'd laid out were triggered. Sometimes screams followed, sometimes not.

Bullets dug chunks out of a tree by Green Ghost's head. A splinter struck his eye. He ran through the jungle as fast as he could while hauling a dead man. Twice he dropped to return fire. Ahead of him Vapor did the same. Wingnut covered them both from behind the sweeping bole of a sycamore fig tree, eye to the scope of his M16.

"I'm the last," Green Ghost said. "Hug my six and gitfoh." *Get the fuck out of here.*

Wingnut followed, scanning for targets. He knelt, prepared to fire, moved back, knelt again, until they got back to their three Mercedes-made Unimog Dingos. Once there, Green Ghost helped load the casualties, five dead out of twelve.

Without warning AK-47s opened up, hitting the door and ricocheting. Wingnut returned fire and then jumped in the passenger seat of the lead vehicle. Vapor drove and Green Ghost sat behind them, firing at the dark figures hovering in the jungle shadows. Vapor stepped on the gas. They bounced through holes in the dirt track, heading for a fork in the trail. In the distance they heard trucks starting up.

"Which way, Ghost?" Vapor said.

"Left! Head for the emergency XP."

Leaving swirling dust and clumps of grass in his wake, Vapor fishtailed onto the track heading east. He kept a death grip on the steering wheel, keeping the Dingo from slamming into a deep hole and flipping over. He blinked away sweat.

"Eighteen clicks, people!" Green Ghost said into his head-mount walkie talkie. "Anybody on our ass?"

The voice that answered was the newest member of the squad, a husky guy called Neon. "Somebody back there, boss, but we're throwing up a lot of dust."

"We're headed for the secondary XP. If nobody's there, we keep going until we hit the Ugandan border. Everybody roger that?"

They'd gone eight clicks and just topped a low rise when Vapor yelled "Shit!" and jammed the brake pedal with all his strength. The Dingo spun and slid sidewise, stopping just short of a giant kapok tree lying across the road.

"Everybody out! Form up on the other side of the tree and set your demo charges," Green Ghost said into the headset.

They had only just spread out behind the tree when the first enemy vehicles sped into their sights on top of the rise. The first one, a Toyota pickup filled with men, was hit by a stream of .223 rounds that killed the driver. The truck rolled into the undergrowth and exploded. No other trucks came over the little hill, however, and soon enough they heard men advancing through the jungle.

With their escape route blocked and enemies on all sides, the seven surviving Americans had nowhere to go. They abandoned their Dingos after setting booby traps, and then dove behind the tree's massive bole. Using the vehicles as cover would have just gotten them shot up. This way, if they found a chance to run for it, they still had transportation and just had to disable the traps.

"This is a fucked-up place to get killed," Vapor said. "I knew I was gonna die one day; I just didn't know I'd be covered in monkey shit when it happened. KMAG-YO-YO." *Kiss my ass, guys, you're on your own.*

"FISHDO—" *fuck it, shit happens, drive on* "—brother, you volunteered for it," said Green Ghost. "Don't try and pin this on Saint Nick."

Bullets chewed up the far side of the tree and both men squatted lower.

"I thought you said there was gonna be pussy," Vapor said.

"The only pussy here is you."

They deployed behind the tree. The men on the far left and far right slipped into the bush as flank protection, with no words needed. Their fire discipline would conserve ammunition and kept their enemies pinned down—but only until the ammo ran out. When it did, so did their lives.

"Here's the plan," Green Ghost said while reloading his M16. "Flanks stay where they are. I hold here. Vapor, you and the others pull back a klick and set up covering fire. If we're not there in ten, we're not coming."

"Go tell the Spartans," Vapor said.

"Something like that. Go!"

The four pushed off from the tree and sprinted down the road. Green Ghost rose to his knees and sprayed the brush. He could hear the others doing the same thing on either side. Bullets buzzed by his head and smacked the tree. He fired until his ammo ran out, and then he slumped behind cover again, only to see his men running back toward him.

"It's a shit sandwich, Ghost," Vapor said, panting. "We're cut off. Burps all over the place back there."

"Fuck," Green Ghost said. "How did they flank us so fast?"

He sent two men to reinforce the rear flank and tried to think of some way out. The terrorists moved in without hurrying, avoiding casualties. Everyone knew they would run out of ammo sooner rather than later.

"Just what I wanted—another Fallujah," said Vapor.

Green Ghost clenched his teeth. He knew better than to expect rescue. He had nurtured the secret hope that somehow, someone would rescue them anyway, but that looked ever more unlikely. Faced with the inevitable, the stark reality of impending death made his men fight even harder.

The firing came in bursts now, sometimes nothing for thirty seconds, then a cascade of automatic weapons fire, followed by another lull. During each lull the enemy crept closer. With ammo running low, they caught glimpses of figures scurrying through the underbrush and dropped several.

"Listen up, boys," Green Ghost shouted over the din. "If they come through, chew the glass. Do not let them take you alive!" His eyes met Vapor's and they both nodded. They'd swallow their suicide pills. The time had come to die.

The firing stopped and the jungle grew quiet, as if both sides paused to catch their breath before the final fight. Then, in the distance, came the *cra-a-ack* of a gun being fired, but not an M16 or an AK-47. Instead, it sounded like a very large-caliber pistol, one he thought sounded familiar. Seconds later, a rocket arched into the sky no more than three hundred yards from their position.

"Ghost, what the fuck was that?" Vapor said. "Do we unass or what?"

Green Ghost held up his left fist. Beneath his feet the soil vibrated faintly, and the rumble of unknown vehicles became louder with each second. In the distance a heavy machine gun opened fire, a sound he also recognized. Birds and monkeys flitted through the treetops, chattering and squawking. The shooting stopped after a two-second burst and quiet again settled over the jungle.

"Listen up, you high speeds!" Green Ghost said. "Unknown incoming. Ammo up. If they're enemy, it's blaze of glory time. You dicks always wanted a range named after you; now's your chance."

His men smirked. He waited for the flankers to move closer.

"Gunner's circle!" he yelled, loud enough for all to hear. It took less than five seconds for all six men to gather around him, squatting behind the tree. No words were necessary because they had made the gunner's circle under fire before. Using hand gestures, he let them know they were going to make for the Dingos, disable the traps, take all three, and try to go back the way they had come. As one, in perfect coordination, they slid over the huge bole and formed the circle on the other side.

With rifles pointed in six directions and Green Ghost in the center, they were almost to the Dingos when shots came from across the road, hitting one man in the left leg. He went down, but did not scream or roll around, which would have increased blood loss. Instead, grinding his teeth against the pain, he fished his first aid kit from a side pocket. As two of his buddies returned fire, Green Ghost knelt and worked fast to staunch the bleeding. Bullets kicked up dirt around them.

"We can't hold them!" Vapor yelled.

More of the enemy opened fire, and then Vapor yelped as a slug creased his shoulder. Two men in tattered green dungarees jumped into the middle of the road about thirty yards away, aiming right at Ghost. Still kneeling, Ghost rolled left and tried to bring his M16 to bear. The men in the road adjusted their aim, but before they could fire, the unmistakable crack of a Magnum Desert Eagle fifty caliber rocked the jungle.

Five times the pistol fired, one after the other in rapid succession. Ghost watched one man's head explode, while the other fell forward with his entrails spilling out. Only one man used such a mammoth pistol, the same man who would travel hundreds of miles into hostile territory, against orders, to rescue his men. His heart lightening, Ghost shook his head. Generals did not do stuff like that, except for this one.

Without warning the foliage overhanging the road burst apart and an APC appeared, with a man standing in the forward hatch holding a Desert Eagle and searching for a target. Two identical APCs followed, both field-modified to mount the deadly M242 Bushmaster 25mm chain gun in place of the turreted fifty-caliber machine gun the factory had installed. All three were Swiss-made MOWAG Piranha V eight-wheeled APCs, used by military forces around the world, and Green Ghost recognized them at once from the motor pool in Kenya. Bouncing down the rutted road, they poured fire left and right, suppressing the enemy. The Bushmasters in particular shredded both jungle vegetation and terrorists alike. The stout man blasting away with the Desert Eagle might have just walked off of a recruiting poster.

The first APC stopped ten yards short of the gunner's circle.

"Saddle up, Snake Eaters!" Angriff yelled. "Let's down range and home, now!"

Green Ghost's body eased as two squads of riflemen poured from the Piranhas and fanned out, providing cover. Bullets still whizzed by in all directions. Angriff sought a target amid the banana plants, then, satisfied no enemies were within sight, he stepped down and walked over to Green Ghost, changing magazines without breaking stride.

"Good shooting," Ghost said, pointing at the dead terrorists in the road. All three APCs had run over them, leaving only a jelly-like smear in the mud.

"Is this it, seven?" Angriff said, indicating the small knot of men.

Ghost nodded. "We lost five, but we recovered the bodies. They're in the third Dingo."

"How bad are they hit?" Angriff said, pointing at Vapor and the other wounded man. An AK-47 round ricocheted off the APC behind him, but he did not flinch.

"Bad enough."

"All right, we'll load your KIAs. You get your men into the APCs and let's unass the AO. The LZ is hot; we can't hold it forever."

"The Dingos are rigged. We could just blow them."

"No, those men are heroes. They deserve a burial on American soil with full honors."

As a trained killer, Green Ghost did not cry. He had survived nightmares most men could not imagine, horrors his brain could only process by shutting down emotional responses. But Angriff's determination to honor his men caused him to tip back his head and close his eyes. He grabbed the older man's thick forearm and stared straight into the famous gaze. "I thought this was Judgment Day, boss. Thank you."

"I don't leave my people behind."

"It's a six hour flight. You had to have left as soon as the XP was compromised."

"I didn't have anything else planned for today."

"I won't forget this," Ghost said.

"Don't even think about kissing me," Angriff said.

They torched the Dingos and made it to the landing zone in fifteen minutes, a bouncy ride smoothed by the independent suspension of the Piranhas' eight wheels. Two Russian-built Mil MI-26 transport helicopters waited in a clearing with rotors turning. The giant machines were registered to a mining operation in Myanmar, a company protected by layers and layers of dummy corporations, and a company which itself did not exist. The three APCs and all of the men fit into their cargo bays with room to spare.

Once airborne and out of Congolese air space, Angriff settled in for the six-hour flight back to Kenya. They would be over Uganda for most of the trip but, since they had bribed all the right people, there would be no hindrance from the Ugandan military.

Angriff had placed a quart of Tennessee Black whiskey on each helicopter, with a box of his favorite Cuban cigars, Cubano Monte Cristo Number Threes. Once the two birds had lifted off, he cracked the bottle's seal and gave Green Ghost the honor of taking the first hit. The bottle gurgled as he turned it up and drank, swallowed with his eyes closed, and passed it to the next man. After the bottle had gone around for the first time, including a mouthful for the man who'd brought it, Ghost stood and raised his hand for quiet.

"Listen up, boys. I've got a toast. Today Charlie Foxtrot paid us a visit. We volunteered for it, which probably says something about how smart we are, but the fact is we were royally fucked. I don't know any other man who would have done what Saint Nick did for us. He put his ass on the line because that's what he does for his men. So let's drink to the health of General Nicholas Angriff. May his wife give him the best blowjob he's ever had!"

Everybody laughed, including Angriff. In no other setting would he let someone mention his wife in those terms, but there had always been a special bond between men in combat, and he loved every one of them. They all drank deep, and when the bottle came back to Angriff, he got the last swallow. He stood and swished that last little bit.

"You're the finest combat soldiers in the world," he said. "Very few men have the privilege to command such heroes. I salute you all." Turning up the bottle, he finished it.

By the time they landed, the buzz from the whiskey had worn off. Fatigue sapped their energy as adrenaline levels dropped. Angriff felt it more than his younger subordinates, but he held himself to a higher standard than he did everyone else and bounced off the helicopter first to help the others dismount. He laughed and slapped them on the back, ignoring his own aching muscles and painful joints. Nick Angriff felt happiest when among soldiers. He loved his family, of course, but outsiders could never understand a kinship with men like Green Ghost, a bond of steel forged in combat.

A long rectangle scraped from the jungle served as the base landing zone. The mammoth helicopters threw up giant clouds of fine mustard-colored dust that infiltrated and settled on everything. When at last he headed over to the command building, little more than a huge shack made from coconut logs, Angriff's sweaty green uniform had turned pale yellow.

His closest friend, Norm Fleming, stood in the doorway with arms folded, looking grim. For himself, Angriff could not stop smiling.

"What's wrong with you?" he said. "Mission accomplished and losses were less than expected, but you look like we took out an orphanage. I lost the optic sight for one of my Eagles; is that what's got you all broken up?"

Fleming shook his head. "No, the op exceeded expectations by an order of magnitude. The early intel is that half the leadership attending the meeting were killed outright. The groups are already blaming each other. I doubt we'll see African terror groups cooperating in the foreseeable future. Reuters has it and it's big news in Europe. Speculation is that Mossad was behind it."

"The Israelis will love that. So why do you look like your dog died?"

"CentCom isn't happy."

Angriff shrugged. "By tomorrow they'll be tripping over each other to take credit."

"You ignored an abort order," Fleming said.

"We were dark. Responding would have endangered the mission." But Angriff sensed something else bothered Fleming besides a pissed-off Pentagon. "And we both know they won't do a damned thing about it. What's really going on here, Norm? What don't I know?"

"Sit down, Nick." Fleming stared down at his hands. His normal low baritone dipped into a deep, mournful bass. Angriff knew that tone from the previous year, when Fleming broke the news that Angriff's oldest daughter, Morgan, had died in action.

Acid filled his throat. "I'm fine standing," Angriff said, keeping his voice even.

"No," Fleming said. "You need to sit down."

In all the long years they had known each other and all the battlefield reverses they had suffered together, Fleming had never spoken to him that way except that one time. Chest muscles tightened and dizziness drove Angriff onto a chair near the doorway.

"Who is it?" Angriff said.

Fleming gave it to him straight. "There was a terrorist attack on a tour boat at Lake Tahoe, like the one in California. The terrorists are believed to have been an ISIS or Al-Queda sleeper cell. They didn't find any survivors. I'm so sorry, Nick... Janine and Cynthia were on that boat."

Chapter 2

O daughter of my people, put on sackcloth
And roll in ashes;
Mourn as for an only son,
A lamentation most bitter.
For suddenly the destroyer
Will come upon us.
    Jeremiah 6:26

One of six Above Top Secret facilities in the world, the Kenyan base demanded extreme security precautions, including forbidding direct flights into Nairobi. As the highest ranking U.S. serviceman in the African theater, Angriff could have overridden his own protocol, yet he did not, even in such an extreme circumstance. Instead, he drove four hours over bad roads to a waiting Learjet 60XR provided by the CIA. The trip to Reno took seventeen hours, with stops in Egypt, Italy, Spain, and Bermuda, before changing planes in North Carolina. The final leg ended at 8:57 a.m. Pacific Standard Time with touchdown at Reno.

Angriff did not sleep during the entire flight. He alternated between drinking coffee and smoking cigars, and convincing himself that somebody had made a colossal error and his family would be waiting for him on the tarmac. He paced the plane's narrow aisle and tried to think of anything except his family being dead. His mind drifted into that semiconscious state of being too stimulated to rest but too tired to think. Counting the long day rescuing his team from the jungle, and the inability to sleep the night before that, sixty hours had passed since he'd last slept. By the time they landed his eyes burned and dehydration gummed up his throat.

The Air Force put a limousine and driver at his disposal, while an Army National Guard colonel met him at the bottom of the aircraft's stairs. After the warmth of the pressurized cabin, Angriff felt the cold breeze like a slap. He expected to get on the road to Incline Village, where he'd been told the FBI had set up their investigation headquarters, but the colonel shifted from foot to foot.

"I'm afraid we can't leave yet, General," he said. "The highway to Incline Village is closed until noon, sir. The president is in town and is also traveling there."

"The president?" Angriff said, surprised. "He's here in person? I'm very glad to hear that. If we have to wait a few hours, that's fine; it's worth it to have him pushing the investigation. Maybe I should try to see him while I'm here? I have some ideas of my own about how we should respond."

"Yes, General... I'm sure he will be very interested to hear the latest on the investigation while he's here."

Angriff never minced words, and so he could always tell when someone else did. "What is it?"

"It's just that...well, the president is here to vacation at the home of a friend, a well-known film director who lives on Lake Tahoe's Nevada shore. The trip has been planned for months, and our Guard unit has been training to help secure the route since July. The timing is just a coincidence, sir."

"I don't believe in coincidences," Angriff said. "So what has the president said about this attack?"

"He said that while it's a tragedy, we should not jump to conclusions about it being terrorism before all of the evidence has been collected."

"Jump to conclusions? What else could it be?"

"General, I'm just repeating what I've seen on the news. Our alert status was raised right after it happened, but we're just a Guard unit. We do not have access to sensitive intel like that."

"I'm sorry, Colonel, it's not your fault," Angriff said. He refused to sigh. "Is there somewhere we can wait that's out of the wind? Maybe have a cup of coffee?"

The colonel led him to the Army National Guard officer's lounge, a small room with tile floors, a stained coffee maker, and an old television. Small talk soon died out and Angriff fidgeted. The program selection on the TV appalled him. Court shows with people suing over unpaid rent, talk shows with women getting DNA tests to see which of multiple men was their child's father, lie detector tests to determine who cheated on whom, infomercials for useless kitchen gadgets, and panels of women talking about the latest shoe fashions.

Scanning and re-scanning the channels for anything that might take his mind off his murdered family, he stopped on a kid's program and smiled.

"This was my girls' favorite show when they were little," he said. "Janine would shower and dress before I left for work, and I'd make their favorite breakfast of Cheerios, grapes, and bacon. I'll never forget it... Morgan always ate her bacon first, while Cynthia preferred the grapes. Their eyes never left the screen, and mine never left them."

The colonel nodded.

"Damn, I can't believe this show has degenerated into such crap. Why do three-year-olds need to hear puppets talking about refugees coming into America? It paints them all as harmless women and children, and most of them are. Who wouldn't want to escape the chaos in the Middle East? They're terrified and I don't blame them. But let me tell you, Colonel, there are others infiltrating the country along with them, trained terrorists—murderers and madmen who think it's an honor to die as long as they kill Americans in the process, like kamikazes. This show makes me sick now; it's nothing but propaganda."

Out of desperation, he changed to the news.

"My God," he whispered after fifteen minutes. "What's happened to my country?"

Angriff tried to decipher hard information from the various broadcasts, but the news stations paid less attention to actual news than to apportioning blame for anything and everything that had gone wrong, anywhere in the world, including what they referred to as 'the Lake Tahoe incident.' Coverage of the war against ISIS and other Muslim terror groups, his personal area of expertise, bore no relation to the reality he knew.

Some of the channels seemed to understand the dire threat facing the civilized world, but the majority downplayed the danger. Some went so far as to insinuate threats did not exist at all. Illegal immigration tended to be a companion story to the war against terror, with a parade of talking heads droning what were obviously rehearsed points about open borders and unlimited immigration without background checks.

On both of those issues, the president sided with the radicals. Angriff despised him for it, which in turn had created pressure to force him out of the Army. His command of the battlefield had saved him so far, but it left him depressed and angry. While he risked his life overseas, at home the very things he fought against found welcoming arms.

Finally the colonel spoke. "General, we can leave now. The Mount Rose Highway is open again all the way to Incline."

Leaving the airport, they passed a group of protesters sequestered well away from the exit roads. Angriff tried to read their signs but couldn't.

"What's their beef?"

"Illegal immigration," the colonel said. "The president signed an executive order the other day for the INS to stand down from deporting anyone for the next year, for any reason, or even rounding up suspected illegals. Those people don't like it."

"But that's not legal. There are laws on the books."

The colonel shrugged. "Not my call, sir."

"You can't even read their signs from here."

"I think that was the point. The governor is a big supporter of the president and didn't want to upset him."

Angriff said nothing more on the ride up the mountain, but his expression spoke for him.

The FBI had set up headquarters in a luxury hotel on the lakeshore, with space provided for every other conceivable federal agency, from Homeland Security to the BATF. Angriff found himself taken to a conference room filled with agents using computers and talking on phones. After a brief wait an older man with hair graying at the temples approached. Angriff stood and they shook hands.

"General Angriff, I'm Special Agent in Charge Terry Bettison. I'm very sorry for your loss. Please sit down."

Angriff sat back down. "Who did this, Special Agent Bettison?"

"We don't know yet, sir. It's an ongoing investigation."

"Don't bullshit me. You know who did this, even if you don't have all the proof yet. I've been told it was probably Queda, by people who don't make shit up and don't lie to me. Is that true or not?"

"I'd say it's possible, General Angriff. Maybe even probable, although the group that has claimed responsibility is new. Nobody's ever heard of them before, which is highly unusual in cases like this. They claim to be part of Queda, that's true, but there's no chatter verifying it. We can't even be sure Muslims are behind this."

"Who are they?"

"They call themselves The Sword of the New Prophet."

"Sounds Islamic to me," Angriff said. Bettison shrugged. "When can I see my wife and daughter?"

"The... remains... have not yet been identified. It may be several days."

"Don't you need me to identify them?"

"That won't be necessary in this case."

"Out with it, Bettison. You don't have to spare me." Angriff cocked his head and studied the FBI agent for signs of deflection or deception.

Bettison flicked his eyes left, a brief but telltale movement. "General, the... killers..."

"Terrorists," Angriff said. "Call them what they are."

Bettison continued as if he had not been interrupted. "The killers used machine guns, probably Uzis, Russian hand grenades, and thermite grenades. The boat was loaded with fuel and the explosion left very little to identify."

Red flags ran up Angriff's spine. "Thermite grenades? Why would they use those?"

"We don't know that, but our pyrotechnic people assure me the burn patterns were definitely caused by thermite. The boat was only half sunk and the first thing we did was tow the wreck to shallow water."

Despite not having slept in two and a half days, Angriff's tactician's mind pictured the scene and the weapons used. He rubbed the bridge of his nose, the way he always did when thinking through a problem.

"You use thermite to completely destroy things, including human beings, but why use them on a tour boat? It's unnecessary if your intention is simply to kill people. You don't need hand grenades at all for that. It's overkill. Terrorists want to leave visible carnage behind. It's like a calling card, horrifying images that get sent around the world, but thermite prevents that from happening. Something doesn't add up, Bettison."

"I'm not sure what else I can tell you, General. I can't read their minds."

"But what you are trying not to say is that my family can't be identified because there's nothing left to identify."

Bettison looked at the floor. "As of yet. We're hoping for DNA recovery, but there's not much to work with."

Angriff stood, clasped hands behind his back, and stared off into space. "There were children on that boat, weren't there? Little kids and their mothers?"

"Yes, there were."

"I'm off in a foreign land fighting to keep my family safe, while at home my own country is letting terrorists run loose to murder at will."

"That's not fair. I know you're grieving, I know how you feel..."

Angriff turned and glared down Bettison. He trembled with suppressed rage.

"Unless this has happened to you," Angriff said, struggling to control his voice, "don't you ever say you know how I feel. I never said that to the parents of those killed under my command, not until it happened to me. Before that it would have been arrogant and condescending. Only after Morgan was killed did I understand their pain. And don't ever correct me again, either, do you hear me? Somebody here at home doped off and my family is dead because of it. That's a fact."

The general's personal aura might have overwhelmed someone less experienced. Bettison said nothing, but his hands curled into fists and his jaw clenched. Like successful operatives in every government since the first Pharaoh united Egypt, however, doubtless Bettison knew how to hold a grudge and how to get even. At the moment, Angriff did not care.

"I'm going to get a room. Find the killers, Bettison. Do your job."

Standing at the end of the hotel's pier, Bettison felt safe enough to make the call. He punched the number from memory, heard a click, and began speaking without waiting for a greeting.

"He's a piece of work, all right. What a prick. He's suspicious of the terrorist angle. Says thermite is counter-productive to a terrorist's objectives, and he's right. That was stupid. This guy's sharp and knows his shit. I can see why he wins battles, even if he is a turd. Nobody's going to manipulate this guy, and anybody who thinks they can is going to wind up getting fucked."

He hit the off button, crushed the phone under his heel, and kicked the ruined metal far out into the lake.

Angriff kicked the sheets off the bed as he tossed for hours. His mind kept replaying a short video Janine had sent him just before she and Cynthia boarded the tour boat. In the one-minute video, they laughed on the Lake Tahoe shoreline, eating ice cream cones and telling him how much they wished he could have joined them. That part tortured him most because he told himself he could have done something to save them. Never mind that the terrorists had had Uzis; his mind made up fantastic scenarios of how he could have stopped the massacre. His brain played the video over and over again, and he cried until tears and sweat made his pillow soggy.

He awoke at sunrise, groggy and drained, and ignored the flood of texts, emails, and phone calls from Army buddies offering condolences. With nothing to do and nowhere to be, he watched TV and smoked cigars, living on room service. The hotel did not allow smoking, and after the third courteous but insistent visit from the hotel manager, Angriff went down to the lakeshore to smoke. Staring over the water, he visualized the attack, trying to understand everything that bothered him about Bettison's version of events.

The attack, which news outlets still called the *incident* on Lake Tahoe, led the national news for several days, but as horrible as it had been, after those days it slipped further and further into the background. When on the third day the lead story became some anorexic boy singer getting arrested for punching a cop who'd stopped him for doing 120 in a school zone, Angriff threw his shoe at the screen.

Later on day three he drew the curtains, turned the lights off, and only left his room to smoke.

On day four Bettison displayed purported photos of his family's remains, but to Angriff they appeared as nothing more than black chunks, like giant pieces of coal. He felt no kinship seeing them, no connection, but it would at least give him something to bury. He called the funeral home in Charlottesville, the Angriff family's ancestral home and the burial place of his parents and grandparents, his sister, and his beautiful daughter Morgan. There had been nothing left of her except ashes, too. Bouts of tears and vows of revenge came without warning.

"Please, God, tell me what I've done wrong for my family to suffer so much," he prayed, kneeling beside the bed. "Forgive my transgressions so that one day I may see them again in Paradise. And if it be your will, lead me to their killers, so that I may send them to Hell."

The FBI released the bodies on day six. Angriff stood in the hotel lobby on the morning of day seven, checking out, drained and dispirited. Special Agent Bettison called him aside.

"General, we have some real miracle workers in Quantico. They were able to salvage a few snippets from the tour boat's onboard security cameras. It's not much, but if you've got a minute, I think you'll want to see it. It's for your eyes only. We're not releasing this to the public, not now, and probably not ever."

"About the other day, Bettison," Angriff said. "I was out of line. I'm sorry."

"It's a difficult time, General," Bettison said. "It's hard for everybody." Opening a laptop, he checked to make sure nobody stood close by and then opened a file. "There's two short bits of video. The first is very graphic, the second... well, you'll see."

Bettison expanded the image to full screen. Without warning, from stark blackness came the screams of women and children as bullets ripped into them and blood swirled, like from a giant blender. One drop ran down the lens. A woman shielding a little red-haired girl took at least ten rounds before she fell, and despite having witnessed almost every cruelty that man can inflict upon his fellow man, Angriff turned away for a moment. But he refused to weep in public, regardless of the circumstances.

The first video lasted for nine seconds and then stopped, with the people all motionless on the deck. In the background a man kept repeating *Allayhu akbar*. The terrorist spoke with a clear and distinct voice, and a harsh Boston accent.

The second video started right after the first and lasted for five seconds, long enough for Janine and Cynthia Angriff to pass from the right side of the picture to the left. The hand of someone unseen pulled at them and terror showed in their faces. After they'd passed by, a short burst of gunfire rang out and blood again spattered the camera lens.

"I'm very sorry, General Angriff, but I thought you would want to see for yourself."

"I knew it in my heart and this forces me to admit it with my mind. Thank you. Again, I'm sorry about the other day. Please keep me in the loop."

"That's a promise," Bettison said.

Angriff wanted nothing more than to go home to Virginia and the Army limousine pulled onto the road at 0900 hours. The president would leave at noon, thereby closing the highway again, after the commander-in-chief had spent the previous week playing golf and fly-fishing. Angriff had waited for a visit to the investigation, or even just a phone call, but nothing had come.

Chapter 3

Dim my warrior spirit,
Lead me to Death's door;
What's the point of living
When there's nothing to live for?
    Sergio Velazquez

December 2nd, seven weeks later
Outside Charlottesville, Virginia

At 0814 the doorbell rang. Angriff had fallen asleep sometime after 0400 and stuck his head under the pillow, trying to ignore the buzzing. For weeks he had avoided the parade of journalists, TV reporters, and conspiracy bloggers, and he waited for that one to leave too, but the buzzer kept buzzing. Fifteen minutes later he rolled off the bed and shuffled out to yell at the intruder.

He opened the door and quit thinking about yelling. Air rushed out of the house like breaking a vacuum seal. "I was in bed."

"I can see that," Norm Fleming said. He turned his head away from the reek. A peek past Angriff's shoulder revealed an armchair piled with clothes. "I've been worried about you, Nick, and it looks like I had good reason to be."

"I appreciate the concern, but I'm fine. Now go away." Angriff squinted and raised his arm, blocking the morning sunshine.

"You don't look fine."

Red veins webbed Angriff's eyes, over purple half-moons that appeared black against his pallor. He had not shaved in at least a week. "Who asked you? I don't need a babysitter; get out of here."

Instead, Fleming pushed past him into the dark house. Closed blinds and heavy drapes kept most daylight from entering. He had been a frequent guest over the years and knew the house's layout, but Janine had kept things tidy and neat. Fleming covered his mouth and nose with a dish towel he found on the floor.

Angriff flushed. "You can leave any time now," he said before disappearing down the hallway.

"What I'm seeing scares me, Nick," Fleming called after him. In a lower voice, he added, "Good God. I should have gotten here sooner."

Dishes tottered in the sink and clothes lay heaped on chairs, tables, and in the laundry room. Liquor and wine bottles sat on every flat surface and the house reeked of rotten food and unwashed human. But the tools of battle—the rifles, shotguns, and handguns on the den table—gleamed from recent cleaning, with boxes of ammo stacked and organized on the floor. Fleming felt some hope seeing that.

But Angriff's appearance shocked him the most. Unlike his role model, Patton, Angriff never worried overmuch about his uniform. He described himself as a rifleman with stars on his collar, a soldier like any other. His personal hygiene, on the other hand, bordered on obsession, and so it worried Fleming to see his friends' dirty and unkempt hair and beard.

Without asking, Fleming found some coffee, cleared space on the kitchen counter, and brewed a pot. He scrubbed two mugs, poured the fresh coffee, and went looking for Angriff. He found him reclining in his office, in the leather chair he'd inherited from his father and with a half-smoked cigar in his jaw.

"You're still here?" Angriff said. "I thought you might take the hint."

Fleming set the steaming mug in a bare space on the desk, between two open laptops. A third laptop was on the table to the left of the desk, and two large monitors were on each corner. Stacks of paper spilled over the sides and onto the floor. A couch and end table backed up to the far wall. Fleming sat there, after first pulling up the blinds on the large picture window. Dust particles floated in the light that flooded the room. Angriff put on a pair of sunglasses.

"If you really want me to leave, I'll leave, but don't give me this *I'm fine* crap." Fleming's resonant voice echoed like the voice of God in the paneled room. "You don't look fine, and you sure as hell don't smell fine. I came all the way from Africa because you haven't returned my calls, but if you want me out of here, then say the word and I'm gone."

Angriff lit the cigar stump and stared back. "You know I don't want you to go," he finally said. "Hell, Norm, you're all I've got left. I don't even have a dog any more. Thank you for coming."

"I've been worried sick about you, Nick. A lot of us have. So talk to me."

Angriff sipped the coffee, took the sunglasses off again, and then rubbed his eyes with the heels of his hands.

"No," he said. "I'm not okay. I don't even know where to start. I can't sleep. I'm not hungry. All I do is think about Janine and Cynthia on that damned boat, dying because I wasn't there to protect them. I should have been, but I wasn't."

"You know better than that. You were in Africa doing your duty. It's not your fault that somebody here at home didn't do theirs."

"Sure," Angriff said. "Objectively, I know you're right, but when the nightmares come that doesn't help. I keep running this movie in my head over and over again, ways I could have saved them, things I could have done... I'm telling you, if I don't get this figured out, they'll be cleaning my brains off the wall."

"It can't help that they haven't found the bastards yet."

"That FBI prick, Bettison, won't even return my calls. Now his voice mail's full. Incompetent son of bitch... it's like he doesn't want to solve it."

"From the look of things, you've been hunting them, too."

"Night and day. If the Alphabetics can't solve it, I sure as hell will. When I'm not thinking about the boat, I'm thinking about how to find these bastards. I've got to kill them, Norm; I've got to kill them all."

"Any leads?"

"No," Angriff said. "Nothing. I don't get it. It's like they sank into the ground."

"But you're not in the loop, right?"

"No, I'm on official leave. Nobody's saying it to my face, but I'm persona non grata. A lot of people getting payback, I guess. They must think I'll go off half cocked and screw up the investigation. Everything I get is back channel, at least second hand, and usually stale, but I do know they haven't got any good idea who did it. They covered their tracks like pros."

"What about the group that claimed credit?"

"Just bullshit. Nobody's ever heard of them, before or after. No chatter, no affiliations, nothing. Nobody has any good idea who they are, why they did it, or if they even exist. They're not even a hundred percent sure they were Muslims. I'm sure, but the Alphabetics aren't. If they were a sleeper cell, they were colder than cold."

"I saw the guns and thought maybe you'd gotten a lead," Fleming said.

"Busy work." Angriff shrugged. "Cleaning them, checking the ammo to make sure it's still good. It was something to do with my hands that I didn't have to think about. I can still field strip an M1 blindfolded in the dark."

"You and your Garands." Fleming smiled. "You've always had a thing for big guns."

"Are we having the Desert Eagle discussion again?" Angriff said.

"We can if it distracts you."

"Well, I'm not giving them up, and I'm not gonna stop loading my own ammo, either."

"Have you stopped overloading the rounds?" Fleming said.

"I never overloaded them. I pressure test my ammo and I've never had a problem."

"Look, I'm sorry, Nick. I really am. I wish I could do something to help you track these guys down, but I don't have your juice with anybody in Homeland, and things in Africa have been pretty hot. Obviously, if you get a line on them and need backup, I'm your man."

Angriff smiled a little and drank more coffee. "You have your job and I have mine. Besides, where I'm going you can't follow."

Fleming snorted. "You act like you can stop me... but is that the best idea?"

"To kill the bastards? Are you really asking me that?"

"I—" Fleming stopped. "What if that was their intent all along? To hurt you, get you off the front lines. Nobody is better at beating these guys than you are, and they know it."

Angriff leaned forward, resting arms on his knees. "I don't give a damn why they did it." He gestured with the cigar for emphasis. "If they were trying to get my attention, then it worked. They took everything from me. Everything. There's nothing left for me except making sure they never do this to anyone else, ever again."

"Every time there's a terror attack, it leaves behind people like you. Some can't get over it. Some can. You have to. Your country needs you. We're at war, and you're the best general we've got."

"Good luck finding somebody who agrees with you. Those ass-kissing idiots in the Pentagon were glad to see me go."

"See you go?" Fleming said. "What do you mean? What did you do?"

"Turned in my papers. January fifth, I'm a civilian."

"You can't be serious."

"Maybe not, but I am."

"This isn't the Nick Angriff I've known for thirty years. I think those terrorists killed you, too."

"Hey," Angriff said, rising from his chair and pointing. "You're my best friend, but you can't talk to me like that, and especially not in my home. My family is dead. Everywhere I turn I see their faces, in my mirror, in my pillow, hell, even when I've got my eyes closed, all I can see is Janine and Cynthia screaming my name as the bullets tear them apart and the thermite grenades burn that boat to cinders. Do you know the only shred of hope I've got left? Thinking they were already dead before the fires started. It's driving me nuts and I can't make it stop. I don't care if they kill me as long as I get to kill them, too. And I can't do it as long as I'm in the Army. There's no way they would let me."

"Who are *they*?"

"You know damned good and well who I'm talking about… Tom Steeple and his crew of barking sheep in Washington. They're terrified I might personally kill a terrorist. God forbid I do that. If you can't do it with a drone, it's a no-go. Too messy for the new Army. It might look bad on TV."

"That's not fair," Fleming said. "And you know it. Drones save lives."

"Yeah, I know, but you get my point."

Quiet settled over them as the outburst faded.

Angriff slumped backwards, exhausted. "There's one more thing. I think sometimes this bothers me more than anything else. Something's not right, somewhere. I don't even know what I'm trying to say, but something doesn't add up."

"What doesn't?"

"That's just it—I don't know. My mind keeps telling me I'm missing something, that something is wrong, but I can't think what it is. It's constantly there, this voice that keeps whispering words I can't quite hear. I think I'm going crazy, Norm."

"Is it about the terrorists? The FBI, the style of the attack—can you pinpoint anything?"

"No, nothing. I've stared at the ceiling for hours trying, but I just draw a blank."

Fleming paused. "If you're really going to resign from the Army and go after these guys, then will you listen to a suggestion?"

Angriff shrugged.

"You constantly preach that in combat, emotions are your worst enemy," Fleming said. "That they cloud your thinking and cause mistakes. Didn't you tell me that Patton was at his best when surrounded with the beauty and harmony of his surroundings? That discord of the mind caused more mistakes in battle than anything else? Have I remembered that correctly?"

"Yeah," Angriff said. "Patton thought best when there was order around him. What are you getting at?"

"I'm saying get out of this house, go somewhere where you can think. There's nothing here but ghosts, Nick. If you really want to find these guys, then take your own advice, go put your mind in order first, then you can start outthinking them."

"Go where? There's nothing for me anywhere else."

"I don't know... what about Austria? You always loved it before."

"Austria? Janine loved it, that's true, and I liked it well enough."

"Perfect. Christmas in Salzburg. Why not? Sitting around here hasn't gotten you any closer to finding them, so go try something new. Refresh your mind; quit dwelling on it. Maybe then you'll figure out what detail you've missed."

"Austria..." Angriff said. "Snow and Mozart balls. That's actually not a bad idea. I'll think about it. And I'm sorry about how I treated you earlier, Are you hungry? You want some breakfast?"

"Sure, but not here. This place needs a hazmat team. Clean up and let's go get some pancakes. I'm buying."

"I guess I could use a shower."

"I guess you could. Use a lot of soap. And shave, too, while you're at it."

Chapter 4

Target me at your own peril.
  Nick Angriff, responding to reports he was on a terrorist hit list

December 2nd, 1037 hours

Hot water and close shaving proved powerful anti-depressants. Angriff stayed under the spray longer than intended and emerged energized and hungry. By rummaging in a seldom opened drawer, he found a clean change of clothes. Jeans, a flannel shirt, and a stout pair of boots were topped by a black baseball cap with the Army logo.

"You almost remind me of a human being," Fleming said when Angriff returned to the den. "Instead of a feral pig."

Fleming sat at the table stacked with guns. He cradled an M1 Garand and looked down the sight. The Garand had a twin, next to two Colt M4s and couple of shotguns. On the floor sat the crates of ammo and cleaning supplies.

"I even brushed my tusks... let's go eat," Angriff said.

"You're buying."

"Then you're driving."

Fleming had parked his car near the front door. Angriff turned the dead bolt and moved aside to let his friend go first.

His peripheral vision caught a flash in the distance. He reacted by pure reflex, pushed Fleming down, and dove on top of him as a bullet struck the door. The loud *crack* of a high-powered rifle echoed.

Two more shots followed. One struck the door frame and the second shattered a lamp. Angriff kicked the door closed and three more shots punched holes in the wood.

"Did you see him?" Fleming said.

"Middle of the yard, big oak tree a hundred yards out. One shooter. Assume there's an assault team flanking. Wait here."

Angriff belly-crawled toward the table with the guns while Fleming crouched against the outside wall and called 911 on his cell phone. Two more shots left neat holes in the window glass, although neither man offered a target. From the report, the sniper used something large caliber, like a hunting rifle.

He reached up and grabbed an M4 from the table, shoved in a full magazine from the stacked ammo, and slid it to Fleming, then tossed two more magazines as reloads. While Fleming gave the 911 dispatcher the situation, Angriff slid an M1 off the table and carefully lowered the heavy gun to the ground, not wanting to jar the sights. A drop of sweat rolled into his left eye, but he blinked it away. Unloaded, the M1 weighed two pounds more than the M4. With the rifle in his hands, he pulled back the bolt and shoved in a clip holding eight thirty-caliber rounds.

Angriff flashed thumbs-up and Fleming nodded. After scores of firefights over the years, their shared experience made speech unnecessary. Using hand signals, Angriff told Fleming to rise up, squeeze off enough rounds to draw counter-fire, and give him a chance to ID the shooter's exact location. An experienced sniper would not be fooled by such a basic tactic, but Angriff doubted these guys were pros. Paid assassins did not miss clean shots like that first one, when the intended victim stood oblivious to danger and presented a perfect target.

He counted with his fingers where Fleming could see… one… two… three, and then pointed. In the corner of a window Fleming rose to one knee, smashed the glass, spent one second finding the right tree and the dark shadow peering around the side. On full automatic he emptied the clip. The rounds tore into the wood with the desired effect; no sooner had Fleming dropped back out of sight than bullets shattered the window above him.

Amateurs, Angriff thought. He rose and did not break the window. Instead, he sighted on his target through the glass. He knew the heavy thirty-caliber slug would be thrown off by the impact with the pane, but the second round would not. Even after he'd shot every weapon in the U.S. arsenal, including most of the artillery, Angriff still felt a kinship with the heavy, deadly Garand. When he squeezed off the first round, the recoil felt like the friendly prod of an old friend.

Spent shell casings clattered on the floor as he emptied the clip at the dark figure huddled under the towering pin oak. From the left side of the house a second figure took off running for the street. Angriff thumbed in a reload in time to get off two rounds before the man disappeared behind the long hedge running the length of his home's frontage. Fleming had re-loaded and both men tracked for more targets. Tires squealed on the road, speeding away.

"You hit one of 'em, General," Sheriff Stanton Laughlin said. "There's blood under that oak. Looks like you got him pretty good. Should get some DNA, anyway."

Angriff leaned against a column on his front porch, smoking a cigar. Fleming spoke to two Sheriff's Department detectives a few yards away.

"I usually hit what I shoot at."

"One of 'em's gonna need medical attention, that's for damned sure. We've alerted every hospital, doctor's office, and vet clinic from the Potomac to the Carolina border to be on the lookout. APBs up and down the state. They're gonna get found, General."

"These guys were amateurs. If we assume they were actually trying to kill me, they did everything wrong. They couldn't even flank a stationary target that didn't know they were coming, so either they weren't serious, or they were CVs."

"CVs?" Laughlin said.

"Combat virgins."

"What do you mean, assuming they were actually trying to kill you?"

"Nothing, really, except that level of incompetence makes you wonder. Stan, I have the utmost confidence in you." Using his cigar, Angriff pointed down the driveway at several black SUVs approaching the house. "These guys, not so much."

"Shit," Laughlin said. "The Alphabet Squad, right? I guess I should have known, you being a general and all. They probably smell a headline. Any idea which one?"

"I don't think Army CID would get here that quick, so it's probably the FBI. If I'm right, don't let those arrogant pricks push you around. As far as I'm concerned, you're in charge of this investigation and they're background noise."

"Tell them that."

"I'm going to."

The SUVs were mirror bright. For a moment he wondered what low-level agent got stuck with the job of waxing night-black vehicles to that level of polish. When the cars stopped, three squads of men and women in dark business suits dispersed in a disciplined tactical formation ringing the vehicles. Once they'd deployed, a final man emerged from the middle SUV. He took his time walking to the porch, like a monarch surveying a new acquisition.

"Sheriff Stan Laughlin," Angriff said when the man drew close, "meet Special Agent Terry Bettison."

The two men shook hands. Bettison turned and started to speak, but Angriff cut him off.

"Since you haven't returned my phone calls for more than a month," he said, "I assume you're here to fill me in on the latest progress in your investigation of my family's murder. And I want you to know how much I appreciate the personal attention, Agent Bettison."

Flanked by two stone-faced women in navy business suits, Bettison smiled, although it looked more like a grimace. The lines in his face tightened around his eyes and Angriff could see the self-control it took for the FBI man not to snap at him. "I wish that were the case, General Angriff, but unfortunately there are no new leads in the tragic *incident* in Nevada. No, as soon as I heard about the attempt on your life I came down to assist in the investigation."

"Great to hear," Angriff said. "Stan's people have got some blood they need you to run for DNA, and I assume Quantico can do it faster than the state lab."

Bettison turned to Laughlin. "Sheriff, tell your people to stand down until my CS team gets here. I want them to process the scene. No offense—it's just that I know them and I don't know your people."

"No offense taken, Agent Bettison, but it doesn't matter if you know my people or not, because it's not your crime scene; it's mine. Your assistance is much appreciated, though. I'll get you those blood slides before you leave today."

"I can't allow that, Sheriff. This is a federal matter now. Tell your people to stand down."

"Whoa, boys," Angriff said, raising his hands. "No need to get up on your hind legs about it. We all know whose crime scene it is… it's mine. It's my house and I say who investigates this crime. And if you don't like it, that's too bad."

"Sorry, General," Bettison said. "I can't allow that, either."

Fleming stood several feet away, still speaking with the detectives, but at that he stopped in mid-sentence.

"Who asked you to allow anything, Bettison? Let me make this very clear to you. Sheriff Laughlin is going to conduct this investigation. You and your team are going to assist him in every way possible. If you do not, I will get the FBI director on the phone—his son fought under my command in Iraq—and I will start asking embarrassing questions about why the lead investigator of my family's murder has the time to drive to Virginia to muscle his way into a situation where he was not asked to intervene. Especially when there has apparently been no progress made in the highest profile terror attack in this country since Nine Eleven. I will plant the seed that maybe you're a loose cannon who's in over his head and needs re-assignment... I hear North Dakota is nice in the winter. It's your choice; do I make that call?"

Special Agent Bettison stepped back, scowling. "As you wish, General. I will instruct my people to give whatever assistance is needed."

"Thank you, Bettison. I knew we could come to an agreement."

Fleming shook his head and stifled a laugh.

"Norm?" Angriff turned to his friend. "You ready to eat? I'm starving."

"Whenever you are, Nick."

"I strongly advise against that, General," Bettison said. "They could still be out there."

Angriff ducked back inside and came out wearing his trademark criss-crossed shoulder holsters, with his twin Desert Eagles tucked into them.

"That's what I'm hoping for," he said. "Stan, we'll be at Netty's if you need us. You've got free rein of the place, but make sure these people don't go anywhere except the front. And if you hear shooting, give us time to finish the bastards before you show up."

"Got it, General."

"If you get hungry, Bettison," Angriff said, "Netty's is down that way about a mile. It looks like a bombed-out building, but Netty serves up a mean bacon pancake. Oh, and a word of advice: if somebody shoots at you, shoot back."

Sheriff's Department technicians crawled over the house, porch, and front yard, like ants sniffing out every crumb of food left over from a picnic. Bettison did not get in the way. Instead, he wandered over the crime scene and pretended to inspect the evidence for himself. When no one was openly watching, he slipped into the backyard, dappled in shadows from the dense woods that backed up almost to the swimming pool deck.

The burner phone picked up a weak signal and it took three tries for the call to go through. When the line clicked on, nobody spoke. The FBI agent put a voice scrambler over the microphone.

"It's a clusterfuck," Bettison said. "I told you to use pros; they almost hit him. Fleming showed up out of nowhere and they panicked, barely missing Angriff. The idiots tried to flank the house for some damned reason. Angriff returned fire and one of them was hit, so they've got DNA. We got here in plenty of time to process the scene, but Angriff demanded the locals handle the investigation or he would call the director. The shooters need to disappear, permanently. As for Angriff, you know my opinion. He's the wrong man for the job, and if you give it to him anyway, the day's going to come when you regret it. I'm gone."

Slipping the phone into his pocket, he waited until he re-crossed the Potomac before throwing it out the window.

Chapter 5

If you do not know yourself, and you do not know your enemy, then you must fear everything.
  Attributed to Hannibal Barca, circa 216 B.C.

January 1st, 1215 hours

Norm Fleming had been right. Angriff knew it the instant he stepped onto Austrian soil.

Salzburg preened in the crystalline sunlight, as dazzling as a daughter of royalty draped in diamonds at a Viennese ball. He felt calmness in Old Salzburg he could not explain. Rage never left him for long—he almost smashed the bathroom mirror in his hotel room on the first morning—but as he had been trained to know, and as Fleming had pointed out, anger had to be suppressed for the mind to function at its peak. Any strong emotion affected the decision-making process, and none more so than anger.

At first it seemed obscene, his family erased from the face of the Earth but Salzburg as enchanting as always. When he shielded his eyes from the glare, the red roofs standing above the white streets and fields seemed artificial, like the magical city of some children's movie. Under the surface, however, he knew all too well how many refugees from the wars in the Middle East and Africa choked Austria, with no regard for Austrian customs, traditions, or laws.

After the assassination attempt, and with the mass of refugees, his personal protection was no longer something he took for granted, especially in Europe. An old friend in the Austrian Army arranged a special permit for him to carry a forty-caliber Glock.

The human flotsam of war threatened to forever change the core of what made Austria so enchanting, and yet Salzburg remained glorious, a last reminder of European culture. Angriff thought the schnitzel superb, and found something curative about a late-night treat of Salzburger Nockerl. He drank a lot of Austrian beer and, in deference to his beloved wife, tried to like the local wines. Drafts of Jägertee warmed him after long hikes over snowy trails in the surrounding hills, where during one outing he glimpsed a wild hare hopping through deep drifts.

Early one morning late in December, he made the short drive to Werfen and wandered for hours in the giant ice caves, then lunched in Krimml and spent most of the afternoon marveling at the thousand-foot waterfalls, which seemed too magnificent to be real. Without him even realizing it, Austria began to drain away the stress and calm his mind, and that brought the clarity he craved. Sleep became deeper. He looked in the mirror to shave one morning and realized the skin along his jaw had tightened.

The serenity of Christmas and the following week gave him time to reflect. Heavy snows lasted all of New Year's Eve day but slackened as midnight neared, and the first day of the new year dawned bright and clear, emptying the city as tourists and locals alike streamed to the ski slopes near Kitzbühel to take advantage of the new powder. The sheer ice-covered slopes of the Austrian Alps never lost their ability to inspire jaw-dropping awe. Shops in the Old Town saw few visitors during the normal slow post-Christmas season. Mozart balls were a Yuletide favorite, after all, and *Sound of Music* tours would not start up until spring. Little traffic crossed the bridges over the Salzbach River.

On New Year's Day, Angriff stood alone atop the Hohensalzburg, bundled against the cold and leaning on the battlement as he looked down on the birthplace of Mozart. The pastel green tops of Salzburg Cathedral contrasted with the new snow. He could feel his muscles letting go. The knots of tension mirrored the knots in his mind, and as he stood motionless, despair gave way to tranquility. The freezing air carried with it the scent of better times, and in his mind's eye he formed images of Janine standing on that very spot. He closed his eyes and tipped back his head.

Most winter days dawned hazy and gray, obscuring the rooftops below. But that day, with skiers away, Angriff basked in sunlight off snow and he reveled in solitude on top of the mountain. As the wind picked up he felt the icy stings with something akin to pleasure, turning his face for the full effect.

Standing at the far end of the platform, he stuck a cigar in his mouth and cupped his hands to shield the flaring matches. On his third match the wind died down and the tobacco began its slow, luxuriant burn. He preferred matches to lighters: something about the sulfuric smell of a match added to the pleasure of fine tobacco. Soon enough a security guard would show up to make him put it out; they always did. Janine hated cigars and hated him smoking them even more. He knew the dangers; he always told those who reminded him about the health hazards that if Churchill had not smoked he would not have died so young, at 90.

Angriff had never felt a man of his time. Vices and enjoyments were frowned upon in the modern world, unless they involved some form of sex or drug. His recent trip home had made it obvious that his sense of morality no longer synched with that of modern America. Like some Orwellian nightmare, the media celebrated deviance while condemning virtue. Patriotism headed the list of mortal sins. For decades, on battlefields across the globe, he'd risked his life to protect the American way of life, yet he now wondered if that way of life deserved the price soldiers had paid for it.

The windswept stone atop the Hohensalzburg and its view of the historic city had been Janine's favorite place on Earth. She had said there was some magic that pervaded the city and made men transcend their limitations. Angriff had never felt that.

For a long while he smoked his cigar in silence, staring over the rooftops below into the cobbled streets of Old Salzburg. A few people ducked from shop to shop while others strolled along the narrow streets, but he did not move. His ears turned red and started to hurt. For the first time in a long time he felt something like contentment. Or if not contentment, than at least a resigned peace to all that had happened; in the end that might be all he could hope for.

"General Angriff, sir?"

He did not move, did not react, merely squinted and drew deep on his cigar. Smoke trickled from his nostrils and the sides of his mouth, and then his left eyebrow twitched. He could not decide if the intrusion angered him more than not having heard the newcomer approach.

"Whoever you are, whatever you want, I'm on leave," he said without turning. He did not mask his irritation. "If you don't know what that means, it means I'm on vacation. So go away. And if you're in the American military, that's an order."

"With all due respect, I'm afraid I can't do that, sir. I've been ordered to bring you with me."

Angriff still did not turn around; he drew deep on the cigar and ash flew away in the breeze. "So you are military. Since you know who I am, you also know that I have three stars on my collar. So unless you want me for an enemy, making your life miserable in ways you cannot imagine, go away and leave me alone."

"No can do, sir. My orders are to bring you along regardless of circumstance, by whatever means necessary."

Angriff noted the newcomer's accent. "You're a Southern man?"

"Yes, sir. Guntersville, Alabama."

Drawing on the cigar again, Angriff watched a delivery van park in front of a small shop below. "Our ancestors may have fought together, son, at Chancellorsville, or Gettysburg. You should know better than to do this."

"Sir, I am sworn to carry out legal orders from a superior officer, regardless of my personal feelings. The only thing I am allowed to tell you is that someone wants to see you. Please come with us."

At last Angriff turned. "What's your name and rank, soldier?"

"Tompkins, sir. Lieutenant Dennis D."

Tompkins towered at least six feet, four inches tall, cheeks reddened by the wind and cold. Despite being bundled in jeans and a heavy jacket, Angriff could tell his clothes fit tight because of the heavy muscles beneath. Three other, similar men stood behind him.

When Angriff spoke he leaned forward to be heard over the wind and looked up at Tompkins, not something he often had to do. The cigar moved to the side of his mouth and flared, but he did not remove it.

"Well, Lieutenant Tompkins, since you've got the balls to tell me to my face that you're prepared to hog-tie me and throw me in the trunk of a car, I suggest you tell whoever sent you that I don't want to meet him. Or her. I don't want to meet anybody, even if they did send a goon squad to fetch me." Angriff tapped his left wrist, though he wore no watch. "I'm off the clock now, on leave. I've put in for retirement and then I'm gone for good. Discharged, retired, free to do whatever the hell I want. And what I want right this minute is to stay here and be left alone."

Tompkins sighed. "Please, General, don't make me use force."

"I wouldn't try it, Lieutenant. I'm armed."

"Yes, sir. I know. But I've been given a lawful assignment, and I will carry it out in a timely manner. Orders are orders."

The three other men inched closer and fanned out into a semicircle.

Angriff squinted and realized, much to his surprise, that Tompkins meant what he said. In that same instant, he knew that he had no choice, either. Leave or not, pending retirement or not, the United States Army still ruled his life and he had to obey orders just like Lieutenant Tompkins, whether he liked them or not.

One thing stood out. If Nick Angriff could not frighten a lieutenant, the orders came from way, way up the chain of command. The order had to have been issued by someone who could protect Tompkins from the wrath of an angry three-star general. And that intrigued him; very few officers held superior rank to Nicholas T. Angriff.

He had pushed it as far as he could. "All right, Lieutenant, have it your way. But if I find you had discretion in this matter, you'd better find the deepest cave in Pakistan and never come out again." He took one last long, delicious pull from the Cuban cigar and tossed it over the parapet. The red glow of its burning tip swirled away in the wind.

"What a waste," he said.

Chapter 6

*Something tapped me on the shoulder
Something whispered, "Come with me,
Leave the world of men behind you,
Come where care may never find you.
Come and follow, let me bind you
Where, in that dark, silent sea,
Tempest of the world n'er rages;
There to dream away the ages,
Heedless of Time's turning pages,
Only, come with me."*
    Robert E. Howard, 'The Tempter'

January 1st, 1339 hours

They drove for hours. The twisting alpine roads led through deep ravines flanked by rivers of foamy green water and rocky outcroppings, then up sharp slopes covered in dense stands of English yews and Austrian pines. The sun began to set early and dappled the road with night-black shadows followed by dazzling unfiltered sunshine. Angriff could not be sure what country they drove through. Not all roads had barriers between national borders, or even signs that you had left one country and entered another. Germany, Austria and Switzerland had long been friends, after all, and in the era of all-watching satellites few things could move unseen, anyway.

Nearing nightfall, with the sun hanging low over the Alps, the car broke out of a dark stretch between two sheer walls into a long, broad valley, with a small river on one side and deep snow covering the fields.

Sunlight had cleared the road and what appeared to be a short landing strip several hundred yards ahead. No buildings stood near the airfield, not even a shack, just the tarmac itself and a small, sleek jet parked at the far end.

Angriff's curiosity rose. He was no aircraft expert, but the angular fuselage, swept wings and canted elevators meant stealth technology. The matte black finish meant radar absorbing materials. The plane bore no markings. If that plane belonged to the American military it was a well-kept secret, and a secret plane on a secret airfield in an unknown country made him wary. Covert operations he understood, but not the shadow world of politics and espionage.

The cars stopped next to the plane and Angriff got out before the driver could open his door. Stairs lowered from the aircraft's side, For a moment he felt the surreal disorientation of being in a dream. Sucking a cold breath that burned his lungs revived him. He scraped ice from his boot soles and climbed into the aircraft's warm interior.

At the far end of a small, well-appointed cabin, one man sat holding an unlit cigar. He stood as Angriff entered and extended his right hand. He was short and slight, wearing jeans and a black turtleneck. Angriff recognized him as General of the Army Francis Thomas Steeple, head of the Joint Chiefs of Staff, adviser to the President, the highest-ranking officer in the United States military, and the architect of its ruin.

Angriff drew up to attention and saluted, even though both men wore civvies. Steeple waved that off and took Angriff's hand, forcing a shake. He then handed Angriff the cigar.

"Happy New Year, Nick. Cubana, Especiales Number Three, right?" Steeple said.

Angriff nodded. "Yes, sir, that's right."

"I've got good intel. Sit down."

Steeple indicated one of the leather chairs bolted to the floor on either side of the cabin. Angriff chose the closest and sat, still wary, eyeing the cigar, the plane, the chair, General Steeple, everything. Head cocked to one side, his eyes cut to the door as it retracted into the fuselage.

"Don't be angry with poor Lieutenant Tompkins," Steeple said. "He's terrified of you. Especially when he found out you had a sidearm."

"I'll keep that in mind, General Steeple."

Angriff despised Steeple, had never tried to hide it, and didn't now. Angriff blamed him, more than any other, for wiping out centuries of tradition and training to curry political favor with those he believed hated America, namely, the commander-in-chief and his circle of cronies. The promotion of politically reliable but incompetent officers in the Army, as well as every major U.S. agency charged with protecting the country, and the overt coddling of terrorists and their sympathizers, had led to the murder of his wife and daughter. He could never forgive anyone who put self above country. Angriff saw Steeple as a traitor to his oath to defend the Constitution.

"First, let me apologize for all the cloak and dagger stuff," Steeple said, "but time was of the essence. You've put in for retirement, and once you were retired I couldn't compel you to meet me. You're not exactly president of my fan club, now, are you?" He paused.

Angriff crossed his arms and stared.

"Right. So much for small talk, eh? Nick, I first want to tell you how very sorry I am for your loss. My Regina has been gone five years now, and there's not a day goes by that I don't think about her."

"Thank you, General Steeple," Angriff said, leaning away from his host. The whole setup felt off.

"When she died, I was lost. I didn't know what to do with myself. We never had kids, so all of a sudden it was just me. I wasn't Chief yet, but I was a mover and shaker, and it didn't seem to matter because the only woman I ever loved was dead. I almost quit the Army then, because I'd lost my whole purpose in living. So I hope that when I tell you that I know how you feel, you realize that I really do."

Angriff nodded. He recalled vague memories of Steeple's wife dying some years before, but not what killed her. Cancer?

Steeple looked out the window as if gathering his thoughts. "My career has been guided by the dictum that a battle is won or lost before it's ever fought. I have stuck to that over the years and found it to be mostly true."

"Sun Tzu usually is," Angriff said. "So this is a battle?"

"In a manner of speaking, yes, but before we get ahead of ourselves, I'm going to tell you what I believe to be true and I want you to tell me if I'm correct."

"Yes, sir," Angriff said.

After a muffled clang the plane vibrated, followed by the rising whine of turbines being started.

"Try to have an open mind, Nick," Steeple said. "That's all I ask. And there are some things you should know right off the bat. First, you won't need that Glock. There are no recording devices on this plane of any sort. No bugs, cameras, or lasers outside recording our conversation. This is strictly off the record, and it has to remain that way. Even this aircraft is off the record. Its design is unique and it's the only one in the world. Much like your operations in the Congo, it does not officially exist. If you were to dismantle it, not one part has a serial number or manufacturer's mark; there is nothing to indicate who made it or where. And you and I are completely alone here. The pilot is in the cockpit. Your luggage is already on board and we'll be taking off soon. For four hours, it's just you and me."

Angriff uncrossed his arms and leaned forward, never taking his eyes off of Steeple's face. "Where are we going?"

Steeple ignored the question. "Second, I want you to forget anything you think you know about me, about what I've done or what I stand for. Everything you know is wrong, and that's on purpose. Last but not least, this meeting and conversation never happened. Got it? National security. You can never, ever disclose that we even met today. Clear?"

Angriff nodded.

"Good, then let's get started." Steeple paused again. "Correct me if I'm wrong, but you believe that the United States military has been betrayed, not only by a narcissistic, incompetent president who hates the American ideal as much as or more than many of our enemies, but also by the officers who serve in the highest echelons of our armed services and pander to his whims, furthering their careers at the expense of their country. Correct so far?"

Shocked by the directness, and correctness, of Steeple's statement, Angriff also knew dangerous ground when he trod it, and he paused. Although true, if he agreed, he committed a court-martial offense, and the assurances of a man he did not trust counted for nothing in that situation.

"Fine, you don't trust me," Steeple said. "I can't say I blame you, so let me put it to you this way: if you agree with that statement, then know that I do, too. The only difference is that I know things you don't, which means I know it's a lot worse than you think."

Angriff scratched the back of his neck. What the hell? Was it some kind of setup?

"Aside from all those domestic programs bankrupting the country—intentionally, I might add—our military is being re-designed from protector *of* the nation to protector *from* the nation. Homeland Security hasn't bought billions of rounds of ammo for nothing. Did you know that they also possess the equivalent of an armored brigade, complete with an artillery regiment? It's true. Nobody knows it, but this president is tailoring our security forces to put down a national revolt. But not *just* our security forces. What good would it do to have a Homeland Security armored brigade if the military could field armored divisions against it, complete with air support? So the military also had to be co-opted, along with all of the watchdog agencies like the FBI, NSA and CIA. That has taken a long, long time, but the process is nearly complete."

"Zero defect," Angriff said.

"Not originally," Steeple answered. "The original idea was flawed, but innocent enough. It was only later that it was co-opted to weed out politically unreliable officers. And now we've become sort of a European co-op, a corporation with something for everybody, as long as we don't actually have to fight a war. Everybody's walking on eggshells their whole career."

"Not everybody."

"No, Nick, not you, just everybody else. It's why you only have three stars, but I admire you for it. You were one of the few warriors left, only now you're leaving, too. And we can't replace men like you. Presumably you've seen the latest resiliency assessment reports?"

"No, General Steeple, I've been otherwise occupied."

"So you have. I'm sorry, that was inconsiderate of me." Steeple took a sheet of paper from a folder on the small table next to his chair. "The latest numbers continue the trend that started in 2009. Let me see... here it is: 'Twelve months of data through early 2015 show that 403,564 soldiers, or 52%, scored badly in the area of optimism, agreeing with statements such as "I rarely count on good things happening to me." Forty-eight percent have little satisfaction in or commitment to their jobs.' Half the Army doesn't give a shit about its job, and doesn't expect things to get any better. We're fighting a global war for our very lives, and the biggest force we have to fight that war is demoralized and pessimistic."

Steeple leaned over and lifted the lid of a cooler crafted into the polished woodwork and made to double as a table. He withdrew a bottle of water and offered one to Angriff. The plane had taken off without them even noticing and Nick wondered if it were VTOL. How could he not notice a light plane lifting off?

"No, thank you, sir."

"Please call me Tom. It's just water, Nick. We aren't toasting my health."

Well, he *was* thirsty. "Thank you, sir."

Steeple tossed him the bottle and he drank half at one time. Steeple then pulled a bottle of Tennessee Black from a cabinet and cracked the seal. With a tilt of his head he offered some to his guest, who declined. Angriff narrowed his eyes. Steeple not only knew his favorite cigar, but his favorite whiskey, too. This had to be leading somewhere, but where?

Drinking three fingers of the water, Steeple refilled it with whiskey, swirled the bottle and sat down.

"Light your cigar; it won't blow up. My doctor won't let me smoke them any more but I can sure as hell smell them. Second hand smoke is as close as I can get to having one myself."

"I'm good."

Steeple shrugged.

"Save it for later, then. Where was I? Oh, yes. The situation is both simple and extremely complex. The simple part is that the guy in the White House is intentionally trying to drive the country into bankruptcy to provoke riots and insurrection. Then he will declare martial law and suspend elections until such time as they can be held safely. Just as Lincoln did during the Civil War, he will suspend habeas corpus and the Constitution itself. Congress may or may not protest, they're more spineless than you can imagine, but the projections are that as long as he protects their privileges and treats them as if they still have power, most of both parties will go along with anything. Some will fight back, it's true, but they will be arrested and charged with supporting the insurrectionists. Any station which broadcasts the truth will be shut down immediately, and secret camps already exist to house everyone who opposes the administration. So what about the primary guarantor of our personal freedoms, the men and women we lead in the U.S. Army? That report tells you what the rank and file think about it; they don't much give a damn what happens."

Angriff swallowed. Every paranoid conspiracy theory had sprung to life and been certified as true. He had imagined all of those things *could* happen, but now one of the most powerful men in America stated, in no uncertain terms, that a conspiracy to take over the country had already begun. He held out his hands, palms up, aghast. "And you're helping them do this?"

Steeple rubbed a jowl. "Whether I help or not doesn't matter. If this happens, it will happen with or without me."

"You could at least try to stop them!"

"As long as I do my duty, the rest will take care of itself?" Steeple said.

"Something like that," Angriff answered, surprised that Steeple paraphrased George Patton. In return, he quoted Patton against Patton. "'Moral courage is the most valuable and usually the most absent characteristic in men.'"

Steeple smiled back. "You overestimate my importance," he said. "I have more enemies than just you, Nick, I have a lot of them. And some of them don't hate me because they believe I've ruined the Army; they hate me because I haven't done it fast enough. There's a small but very dangerous group called RSVS—don't ask what it stands for because we don't know—and they would like to see me dead, and you, too, apparently."

"They're the ones who shot at Norm and me in Virginia?"

"We think so."

"Who are they? Were they involved in Tahoe?"

"We don't know too much about them, except they're old-style Stalinists right out of 1952 and they want to install a dictatorship. We do know they were not behind the attack on your family, however."

"Then why shoot at me?"

"You're asking the wrong guy. I can guess, though. You're a powerful leader within the Army, you're well respected, and people believe what you say. You hate communists and, what's worse, you can't be bought and you won't keep your mouth shut. You're their nightmare."

"If they had anything to do with Tahoe, I'll be theirs," Angriff said.

"They didn't. Do you know the exact chain of events that led to the death of your wife and daughter, Nick?"

Angriff sucked in a breath, the air whistling in his nose. His hands clenched and he leaned forward again, from the waist. "I don't know, General Steeple, do I? The latest I've got is that a traitor infiltrated Homeland Security and gave the bad guys intel about a boatload of American tourists on Lake Tahoe that just so happened to include my wife and daughter. They attacked the boat and mowed down women and little children along with the men, using thermite to make sure nobody had a body to bury. The FBI still cannot identify the Muslim terrorists responsible, and the White House insists that it could have been white supremacists, not Islamic radicals, despite the intel that led them back to the leak at Homeland Security. Oh, and the identity of the leaker has not been discovered. That's the version I've been told. Now tell me what I don't know."

Despite what Steeple had said earlier, Angriff expected an argument. But Steeple nodded. "You're right about everything, except that the identity of the leaker is known. He is an ISIS sympathizer and may have been trained at one of their schools. What's more, this was known when he was hired."

Angriff leaned back in shock, his mouth open, and tried to digest the magnitude of the horror he had just been told.

"But... why?"

"Because the president is a terrorist sympathizer and he absolutely hates America." Steeple let that sink in before continuing. "The president knows he can trust such people to kill as many American citizens as necessary to keep his poll numbers up—you know that after a terrorist attack people rally to their elected officials, right? He wants a third term by declaring martial law, although it's pretty late in his second term now. Oh, and just so you know, the terrorist who fingered your family still has his job."

"Are you telling me the president of the United States authorized the murder of my family?" Angriff said.

"I didn't say that," Steeple said. "In fact, I doubt that he knew about it personally. But whether he did or didn't, it suited his purpose, and he has materially hindered the investigation. That much is a fact."

He would never rest until everyone responsible lay dead at his feet. But when the initial wave of rage tapered off, his instincts told him the moment of battle had not arrived. Steeple had not yet come to his point; everything so far had been just a prologue. The discussion of his family had changed his outlook on the conversation, however.

"What's to stop me from going to the media with this? You're fucking with me. You know I want to kill the sons of bitches, you know I want the name of the leak, so why tell me this? See, I haven't forgotten that whoever hired that terrorist bastard is just as guilty as he is. Shit flows downhill, but it can also flow back up. If everything you say is true then it flows all the way to the top, and maybe that means it has to go through you."

Steeple rose and went over to the humidor near the small bar fitted to the bulkhead. He withdrew a cigar, snipped the end and picked up a box of matches. Striking one, he toasted the foot of his smoke and sucked it to life. Gesturing with it, he said: "Screw my doctor. I'm gonna die of something; might as well be a fine cigar." He sat back down and tossed Angriff the box of matches. He caught them but did not light one.

"Maybe you're right. Maybe it does all go through me. But you won't go to the media, because first, nobody would believe you, and second, you swore a few minutes ago never to divulge that this meeting took place, and you're not the kind of man who goes back on his word." Steeple paused for a long pull from the water bottle. "So now comes the tricky part—explaining why you're here."

"That would help, all right," Angriff said. "So far none of this makes sense."

"Have you ever heard of *Generalmajor* Henning von Treskow?" Steeple pronounced the name and rank in the German manner, with the G like the hard g in *gun*, the j as a y and the w as a v.

The question caught Angriff off guard but he answered without having to think about it. "Architect and prime mover behind Operation Valkyrie. Stauffenberg gets all the credit, but Treskow was the heart and soul of the opposition."

"Correct. For many years he opposed Hitler. Yet he continued his work in the German Army nonetheless, helping the regime he opposed by doing a thoroughly competent job. He simultaneously worked for German victory while leading a resistance clique within the Army and personally trying several times to kill his commander-in-chief. He didn't mind Germany winning the war, he just didn't want Hitler running the country. So, was he a hero for trying, but failing, to kill Hitler, thereby giving the regime even more power than it already possessed and ensuring that Germany would fight to the finish? Or was he a villain for helping Germany conquer Europe and slaughter millions of people? Less than a month before Stauffenberg planted that bomb near Hitler's feet, von Treskow signed an order that deported between forty and fifty thousand Polish children to Germany to work as slave laborers. That's evil incarnate, or so you would think. But by trying to kill Hitler, he's remembered to history as a martyr."

"What's your point?" Angriff asked.

"My point is that von Treskow could, at any time, have resigned his commission on grounds of honor and nobody would have blamed him, although the Nazis probably would have thrown him and his family into a concentration camp. But he could have done it. Hell, it might even have been the 'right' thing to do. There might be statues of him in little parks all over Germany for the pigeons to shit on. But if he had, if he had chosen the high road, then he would never have been in a position to orchestrate Operation Valkyrie."

"So what are you saying? That you're the American von Treskow?" The surreal situation exceeded anything Angriff could have dreamed. Had the most powerful American military leader alive just suggested the assassination of his commander-in-chief?

"To a point, maybe I am, but only to a point," Steeple replied. "I have no intention of initiating or participating in any attempt to kill the president, not that I've heard of any that were legit. It's not that I'm squeamish, the son of a bitch has virtually destroyed the country, but it wouldn't do any good. We are too far gone for the death of any one man to make a difference now. In historical terms, we are Rome in 470 a.d., or Germany in 1945. The barbarians have breached the gate and are about to overrun the empire and there's not a damned thing we can do to stop it. If this president is eliminated there are others in his party far worse than him.

"But I will take action to save my country. I took the first steps a long time ago, I've taken a lot since, and today I'm taking another one. I'm talking to you."

And just like that, they reached the real reason why Angriff had been kidnapped for a private meeting with a superior officer he barely knew, on board an airplane that did not exist.

"You obviously expect me to ask 'What are you talking about? Why me?'"

Steeple rubbed his face with both hands. "What I'm about to tell you, very few people in the world know. Not the president, not the Secretary of Defense, Army High Command. You cannot tell anyone what I'm about to tell you. Nobody. I've been working on this project for more than twenty years. Now it's nearly finished and the fate of our country, hell, the whole damned world may rest on the answer you give me right now. Do you agree to complete silence concerning what I'm about to tell you?"

Angriff hesitated; none of this made sense, and he did not want to trust Steeple. The fate of the world at stake? Did he really say that? "If I say yes, if I agree to keep silent about whatever it is you want to tell me, there's a price."

"What's that?"

"I want everything you've got on my family's murder, including the name of the informant."

"I can't do that, Nick. For security reasons you're not cleared for, I can't do that. Especially if you're retired, the potential blowback is off the charts."

"Then count me out."

Steeple held us his hands in a placating manner. "Maybe we can compromise. What if I promise to use the full force of my position to wipe these bastards off the face of the Earth? If you agree to silence, I will personally guarantee the death of the terrorists who killed your family."

Angriff leaned forward with elbows on knees, considering the offer. Steeple had the power to carry through on his promise, he did not doubt that. "I still want the name of the fingerman."

"And if I give it to you?"

"I'm going to kill him."

"You can't involve the Army. If you get caught, you're on your own."

"It'll just be me and these hands," Angriff said.

"So you agree to keep absolute operational security?" Steeple said.

The two men locked eyes. Angriff then did something he never thought he would, he offered Steeple a handshake, which Steeple accepted.

"I agree."

"Be certain. There's no going back once you are in the loop."

"I said I agree," Angriff said.

"Then it's a deal." Steeple paused again. "What do you know about cryogenics?"

"Cryogenics?" What the... "You mean like freezing Ted Williams' head?"

Steeple guffawed. "No, that's cryonics. Different thing altogether. The cryonics people think they can freeze something dead, like Ted Williams' head or a body riddled by cancer, and somehow bring it back to life later. Utter bullshit. Cryogenics, on the other hand, is proven science."

"All right..."

"Cryogenics studies the performance of materials at very low temperatures," Steeple continued. "For our purposes, it is the effect of very low temperatures on the living human body. I don't pretend to understand how it works, that's for the Mensa people to know. I'm sure you've seen movies or read books where people have been put into cryogenic storage, or, as it if often called, 'suspended animation.' Most people think it's crap but it's not, the science is quite real..."

Steeple rose and began to pace, passing Angriff in the narrow space and bracing himself against the bulkhead whenever the plane jolted in turbulence.

"The United States is not going to last much longer. It's going to implode, explode, be overrun, or wiped out. Unfortunately, that's a truth that can't be denied or wished away. Islamic terrorism, bioterrorism, catastrophic economic collapse, volcanic eruption, plague, nuclear strikes, EMPs, our own government, or getting smacked by some asteroid we don't see until three days before it wipes out most life on Earth, or some combination of all of them or some threat we don't even know about yet.

"NASA wrote a paper back in 2001 and put the damned thing on their website, predicting future war and collapse. Go check out Youtube if you don't believe me, it's still there, and then read what the crackpots have to say about it. But when you do, remember one thing: a lot of them are right. Most of them are using government reports as the basis for their predictions and theories, but the American public writes them all off as nuts. Some are, of course, I don't think aliens really had anything to do with the Civil War, but who knows, could be they're right about that, too.

"At some point in the not too distant future our country will no longer exist, every simulation we've run for the past five years gives the same results, and there is nothing we can realistically do to stop it. We have grown weak and soft and we no longer have the national character to save ourselves, and there are just too many potential threats. We are dangerously dependent on energy for everything... shut off the power and we all starve. When the collapse happens it will take whatever is left of the Western World with it. Europe is already compromised by the Islamists, they have a unifying belief and when the collapse comes they will simply wipe out the Europeans."

Steeple braced himself as they hit an air pocket. "That's why Project Overtime was green-lighted, because in the future our country is going to need to be rebuilt. For decades, ghost money has been diverted into this project, lots and lots of ghost money. And it works, Nick, by damn it works. We can freeze people then wake them without them having aged at all.

"Project Overtime is our insurance policy against disaster. A battalion of hand-picked soldiers will be put into cryogenic storage to be awakened at a future time when an activation code is signaled. That might be ten years in the future, or twenty or two hundred, there is no way to predict. And if we're wrong, and things stabilize, then we can wake everybody up and they will not have aged a day.

"The idea is that when no more coherent military forces are left, we will have one extremely well-trained and well-armed battalion with which to restart the country. It may not seem like much, 1,000 or so soldiers, but they will have everything necessary to sustain them once they are awakened, including weapons and plenty of ammo. It's an all-volunteer force of men and women with no family to keep them here now, no strings, people who can walk away and never be missed. It will have everything it needs to succeed, but it still needs one key component... a commander. That commander has to be one hell of an aggressive and motivated leader, capable of inspiring his soldiers to achieve the impossible. That's where you come in."

Section C, page 7 of the *Washington Times* gave a paragraph to the disappearance of Lt. General Nicholas T. Angriff (Ret.), who vanished while skiing in the Austrian Alps. Despite massive searches, rescuers found no trace of his body. Angriff had just retired from the Army after the tragic loss of his wife and only surviving child in the tragic *incident* at Lake Tahoe while they were on vacation. Angriff was said to have been writing a book critical of his former commander-in-chief and, when asked, the president declined to comment. Angriff had no known living family, a childless sister having pre-deceased him. A memorial service was planned but arrangements were incomplete at the time the paper went to print.

Several days later, a small article on page 12 reported that a Homeland Security technician had gone missing. Mustafa Mohammad left work around 8 pm, three days before, but never arrived at the home he shared with his brother in Arlington. Authorities asked anyone with information on Mohammad's whereabouts to please call the Sheriff's office.

Chapter 7

*I lost my friend forevermore,
My friend has passed beyond the shore;
Beyond the mist, beyond the moor,
My friend has passed through Heaven's Door*
   Roman funerary inscription for Centurion Septus Sulpius Vita on Hadrian's Wall

January 16th

From 30,000 feet Diego Garcia appeared as a smudge of white paint spilled in the empty blue of the Indian Ocean. The Gulfstream G650 had lifted off from Nairobi less than five hours before and headed southeast. The sleek aircraft's sole passenger knew his destination without being told. There was nothing else out there besides water.

Norm Fleming stared out the window. What the hell was up? Since returning from Virginia in early December, he had been de facto commander of Operation Wipeout, the secret Kenyan initiative begun by Nick Angriff before the death of his family. Along with that went command of Task Group Zombie, aka the Nameless. Fleming had always assumed Angriff would return someday, despite his assertions otherwise, until the fabled warrior went missing in the Alps. With search crews coming up empty and a fresh obituary in the *Washington Times*, the reality could not be dismissed. His best friend was gone.

And now, with several critical ops in countdown to launch, Fleming found himself ordered away from the scene of action to the middle of nowhere. There could only be two possible reasons. Either he would get his third star and command of Wipeout, or he would be transferred elsewhere, with the clear implication that with Nick Angriff gone, his enemies would take out their hatred on Fleming.

Just over one thousand miles south of India, Diego Garcia was less of an island than a thin horseshoe of coral atoll bent around a lagoon. Although it was a British protectorate with a grisly history of human rights abuses, the United States maintained a naval base there with landing strips capable of handling the largest aircraft in the U.S. inventory. The British zone contained a variety of installations.

The unmarked Gulfstream touched down at 1541 hours local time and rolled to a stop near an enormous hangar. Hot winds blew over the tarmac. Fleming found a white Lexus sedan waiting at the bottom of the stairs, AC on high and an Army corporal holding open the rear passenger door. He snapped to a sharp attention as Fleming ducked inside.

"Where are we headed, Corporal?" he said when the driver slipped behind the wheel.

"British zone, sir. It's about a fifteen minute drive. We'll never be more than a few hundred yards from water."

Fleming was dying to ask the man if he knew what awaited him on the other end of their drive, but a general did not ask a corporal such questions.

They drove south, away from the airfield at Point Marianne. The neat signs, trimmed flora, and immaculate roads all testified to an American military presence. Palm trees lined the road and provided a shady canopy. They passed a power plant, then a sign announcing the pistol range, before a long curve in the road bent north. Soon they came to a manned gate and a sign that read BRITISH ZONE. Showing his credentials, the corporal exchanged a casual salute with the gate guard and drove on. That area was far less developed.

They had gone half a mile when the driver slowed and turned into a circular driveway in front of a two-story beach house facing the lagoon. The corporal grabbed Fleming's bag and led the way inside. He set the bags down in a small, neat kitchen.

"I believe you're wanted on the beach, General. There's a stone path just outside that screen door and there's beer in the refrigerator."

"Who's out there?"

"I have my orders, General. Will there be anything else?"

"No, thank you, Corporal. You're dismissed."

Although tired from the flight and sweating in his heavy uniform, Fleming headed outside and down the path. He caught a faint whiff of smoke. Across the bay a plane took off, turbines screaming over the water. Fleming stalked down the crushed coral path and emerged from the tree line. Ahead in the sand, someone lay in a beach chair folded most of the way back. An empty chair waited beside it. He did not recognize the figure until he towered over him.

"I should have known," Fleming said.

"Did you get a beer?" Nick Angriff used his right hand to block the westering sun. "I brought Newcastle, your favorite."

"That's it?" Fleming said, visibly upset. "You let me believe you're dead and think a beer makes everything right?"

Angriff rose and adjusted his chair back to the sitting position. "Since when do you take military necessities personally? I let you know as soon as I could."

"There's a dozen ways you could have let me know before this."

"Damn, I'm glad to see you, too. Go change out of the monkey suit, grab a beer, and let's talk. We've got two hours until dinner and it's make-your-own-pizza night at the O Club. I've got a lot to fill you in on."

Fleming wanted to be angry. But aside from his abiding weakness for Angriff's boyish streak, it was hard to be mad when your best friend turned out not to be dead after all. Without another word he turned back to the house.

"Don't drink the water," Angriff called after him.

When his best friend settled into the chair beside Angriff, Fleming had changed into shorts and a T-shirt. The chair creaked under the weight of his muscled body. He drained a beer in one gulp, tossed the bottle aside, and rolled a second one over his forehead. The sun had sunk low enough for the trees across the bay to block it.

Fleming closed his eyes and took several deep breaths. "For the record, I'm glad you didn't fall into some Alpine crevasse."

"Thanks for that heartfelt sentiment."

A comfortable silence fell. Angriff wanted to light another cigar, but he knew how much Fleming hated the smell and refrained.

"Tell me about Austria," Fleming said. "There's obviously a story in this."

Angriff let out a loud breath, the way Fleming had heard him do many times before. "I'll say a long one. Let's see. You were right and Salzburg was perfect. I did everything you advised, ate all the stuff Nini wouldn't let me eat, drank a lot of beer, smoked cigars..."

"I didn't say anything about cigars."

"Don't interrupt a good story with facts. I even liked the weather. It snowed a lot but for some reason I found it refreshing. Anyway, I spent the week after Christmas seeing all the sites. I made it to Kitzbühel. On New Year's Day I went up to the Hohensalzburg to look down at the Old Town. My God, it was beautiful. I was up there on the battlement, minding my own business, when four MPs showed up to drag me to a meeting."

"What kind of meeting?"

"Stop interrupting and you'll find out. First, they drove me all over western Austria into Bavaria, and after three hours we came to a stop in a valley surrounded by steep mountains. Turns out it was in Switzerland. The only thing in the whole valley was an airstrip with a single unmarked black airplane."

"Somebody has a flair for drama."

"Huh. Wait'll you hear who. I was invited to climb into the plane or walk home. There was one passenger waiting for me. Care to guess who it was?"

"The president?"

"Shit, no. I was carrying a Glock. I might have shot him. But think of somebody almost as bad, somebody who's got the juice to requisition an unknown aircraft, order it flown into Switzerland, then have a three-star general hauled to a meeting against his will?"

"Tom Steeple."

"Bingo. Our illustrious leader wanted a man-to-man chat with me. Before I tell you what he said, I want you to know that if I didn't believe everything he told me, now that I've had a chance to verify most of it, we wouldn't be having this talk. I didn't think anything could dissuade me from chasing my family's killers to ground..." His voice dropped and Angriff turned away so Fleming wouldn't see the tears in his eyes. He wiped them with the back of his hand.

"It's okay, Nick."

"I tried to let it go, Norm, I swear to God I did, but it was still eating me up. I... I had to be honest with myself. No matter how hard I tried, no matter how long I chased them, I could never get all the bastards who wiped out my family. It was burning a hole in my gut. I wanted to kill them all so bad but I knew I never would. Steeple gave me an option I didn't know existed, and in return he promised to kill the killers for me, to use the full power of the Army to exterminate them. And he gave me one of them, a guy who worked at Homeland and fingered my family. Him I took care of personally. So in a way, Steeple did me a favor."

"You killed him?"

"With my bare hands." Angriff looked him straight in the eye and there were no tears.

"I can't blame you for that, if you're sure he was in on it."

"Steeple said he was, even showed me his jacket. He trained in Yemen. I'm sure."

Fleming held up a hand. "Look, I'm the last guy to talk you out of dropping the vengeance crusade. My only question is, can you really do that? You got one of them. Is that enough? Do you trust Steeple enough to let it go?"

"If I go through with it, I won't have a choice. And that's probably for the best."

"You lost me."

"Hang on, this is gonna get weird. What do you know about cryogenics?"

Angriff told the story as Steeple had told it to him, leaving out most of their conflict.

"I was skeptical when he offered me command," Angriff said. "I asked him, command of what? If I believed him, which at that moment I didn't, somewhere they had stored a bunch of frozen bodies accumulated over two decades. From what I could tell, most of those people never met each other before going under what they call Long Sleep, so at best you had a bunch of strangers packed away with some equipment. It certainly was not a functioning battalion. Steeple assured me I could see the whole thing, and he kept his word.

"He showed me the whole process of freezing people, down to the tiniest details. I saw the security protocols. Hell, you even have to supply a middle name or the computer won't accept you. I got a look at the equipment, all first rate stuff. We probably won't have the latest toys, no Joint Light Tactical Vehicles. We'll have to make do with Humvees, but that's actually better. Plenty of surplus on those. I was impressed. This is a first rate operation."

Fleming didn't speak for a minute or so. "What's it called?"

"Operation Overtime."

"Assuming this is all true, there has to be a base somewhere, some fortified position to store all of... well, the people."

"Steeple said there's a site out west in Arizona, but there was no way for two such senior Army officers to pay a visit there. Too many eyes in the sky. He's right. Satellite facial recognition has gotten too sensitive, and too many people know his whereabouts. He can disappear for short periods, but no more than ten or twelve hours."

"You're putting an awful lot of faith in a man you once despised for betraying his country."

"I don't think so. The op is real enough. I saw the frozen bodies, lots of them. I saw the equipment storage, the security protocols, everything. None of that was faked for my benefit, if that's what you're getting at. And I read the classified reports on what the computers think will take us down and when. It's not a pretty picture. We're already seeing escalation in the terrorist war, all the attacks in France, Orlando, California, Tahoe... and the American people are no closer to being motivated to win this war than they were ten years ago."

"So you're really going through with this?" Fleming said.

"I am. There's nothing left for me here, Norm. I hope you can understand that. Everything just seems so... temporary, so transient. Except for you, everything and everybody I've ever cared about is gone. Nothing I do here seems to matter any more, but maybe I can make a difference in the future. Maybe there will be a time when we can start over again."

"There're plenty of fights left in the here and now. And I can't believe you're letting those snipers get away with taking shots at you."

"That's a neo-Stalinist group Steeple knew about, said they've targeted me for a while, but none of them have combat experience." Angriff shook his head. "That's why it was such a botch. They needed a high-profile action but couldn't pull it off. As for the rest of it, those fights are for other people now. There's too much sadness for me here, too much anger. I'd spend the rest of my life killing scumbags during the day and drinking myself to sleep at night. I'd be fighting for a country that has lost the will to win."

Fleming drained the bottle and wished he'd brought a third. He couldn't argue with his friend's last point. "So why tell me? You were already dead as far as I knew. Why fly me all this way just to explain yourself? Hell, from my standpoint, the other way was cleaner. I was already into stage four."

"Eh?"

"Bargaining. I promised God all kinds of stuff if they could find you alive somehow."

"Like what?"

"I'd go to church more and drag you with me, try to get you to quit cussing so much... hell, I don't know."

"Sounds like you owe him a few promises."

But Fleming had known Angriff too long. After two beers in the warmth of the waning day, with water lapping at the shore a few feet away, he had almost forgotten his friend's modus operandi.

Almost.

"You haven't answered my question yet."

"Which one? You ask a lot of questions, Norm. It's what you do best."

"Why tell me about this? Why not just let me keep thinking you're dead?"

"Yeah, about that. I am the sum total of my friends and family. Without them in my life I'm nothing. So it's pretty simple. I have no more family, and you're my closest friend. I want you to come with me."

Section 2

Chapter 8

I walked the road of glory
And I strode that road alone,
None will know my story,
And the sun will bleach my bones.
    Found carved into a stone in the Superstition Mountains

June 17th, 59 years later, 1311 hours

    The broken ground of the Sonoran desert soaked up the heat of the midday sun. As the desert floor warmed it began to heat the air close to the surface, which then caused that air to expand and grow lighter. The lighter air rose in bubbles of warmth called atmospheric convection, better known as thermals, rising higher until the temperatures of the air surrounding the bubbles became cooler, causing them to sink again and create updrafts. On that blazing hot day the cooling effect did not occur until the warm air had risen high into the atmosphere.
    Wheeling high on those thermals, a prairie falcon sensed the subtle changes in air temperatures and stayed in the updrafts, using the energy of the warm air to provide the lift under its great wings and keeping it where it could see for miles in every direction. After a fruitless search it banked off south in search of better hunting.
    The humans below knew nothing of convection, except for the heat they felt rising from the dry soil, like standing over an open fire. Twenty-three people worked the rows where tiny green shoots pushed into daylight, eight women riding herd on fifteen children. For them, life began and ended in patches of hard-scrabble dirt never meant to sustain crops. Escape existed in dreams, not real life. They lived daily with no shade, no

rest, and very little food. Crops had first priority for water, guards came second, and slaves tilling the soil were allowed just enough to keep them working during the day's two breaks. And for one of the women, not even then; most of her water she gave to her children, keeping a bare minimum for herself.

Her dark skin had burned darker than the soil she scraped with a hoe, and the summer sun burnt through more layers of skin, almost roasting her alive, but if her masters did not care, neither did she. Her personal condition had no relevance. No matter how much she bled from cuts and cracked skin, no matter if her vision blurred from too much heat and too little water, her thoughts never left her children working the soil beside her. She had to protect them any way she could, and that meant staying on her feet no matter what happened. If she fainted or collapsed she risked being declared unfit to work, and those unfit to work were dead weight on the Caliphate. Precious resources would not be spent on unproductive infidels, and so she kept working when others would have dropped.

"Mama, I'm thirsty," said Elena, her eight year old.

"I know, sweetie," she said, trying to moisten her lips without success. "But you've got to be a big girl and keep working. They will give us water soon."

"How long?"

"Soon."

Her eldest daughters, twins with fair skin burned red, had grown old enough to understand the situation. They kept working and said nothing, but sometimes glanced at the guards who watched them as they bent over to work. The older they grew, the nearer they came to being snatched like their older sister had been one morning, and taken to the city, where female infidels served the Caliphate as slaves to satisfy the urges of the faithful. She would never know what become of her daughter.The girl's name had been Mary, a name the Sevens hated, and she had just turned thirteen when they took her.

The twins would be twelve on their next birthday.

She spent most of each day silently praying to God to save her family, pleading with Him to at least let her know why He had abandoned them. So far she had resisted all pressures and remained true to the religion of her birth, yet her loyalty had brought only more pain and misery. Then, realizing she questioned the will of God, she would spend more time apologizing for doubting His wisdom. God's kingdom existed elsewhere, not in this world, so if she and her daughters needed to suffer on Earth to achieve salvation, then so be it.

The sun climbed high and at length the slaves got a rest. They gulped their meager water ration and then curled up in balls to hide from the omnipresent sun. The mother huddled her three girls beside her and attempted to shield them from the sun with her wilted body, giving them blessed relief, even if only for a moment. The guards watched every move, making jokes when someone stumbled, or leering at a torn blouse. They could not touch the children, but nobody cared what they did with the older women, as long as they kept working.

The balls of hot air floating skyward distorted vision and gave the desert floor a shimmering effect. High overhead, a falcon glided in slow figure eights, making its way west. Adjusting his binoculars, Major Dennis Tompkins watched the four guards kick at the women and children crumpled in the dust, as they had done the previous five days. Break time was over. He watched, grinding his teeth, as one of the guards hauled a woman to her feet and stuck his hand down her skirt.

Tompkins knew the scenario. He and his men lay behind a low ridge five hundred yards from the corn fields. A narrow road skirted the ridge on his right and ran past the field and into the distance, its surface pitted and holed but still navigable. They had one working truck and he knew they could never fit twenty-odd women and girls, plus him and his men, into that one truck.

But the guards had two trucks parked under the lee of the ridgeline on the other side of the valley, and if he and his men could seize those that would change everything.

The women had once been part of a larger settlement a hundred miles to the north, a place dubbed Roundup by its inhabitants. Over the years Tompkins and his men had often stopped there for news. It provided a safe haven for free men and their families, survivors of the old United States who still flew a ragged American flag over their compound. They kept alive the dream of a nation where liberty allowed them to say what they felt and worship as they pleased.

Roundup had kept a wary eye on the growing threat to the south, the Caliphate of the Seven Prayers of the New Prophet, and through them Tompkins had also been aware, but he could do little to stop the caliphate's spread. At its most numerous, Tompkins' command had numbered just over one hundred men, remnants of this or that American military unit covering all five branches of the armed forces, including one from the Coast Guard. Most had had no training as combat infantry and learned from brutal experience

Now, his surviving command consisted of himself and five others, four of whom had been with him since The Collapse. Six old men, they'd sought out Roundup because they had grown too old to wander the western United States looking for any more survivors. But they found only the devastation left behind by the dreaded Sevens, the Caliphate's raiders. Not one building had been left intact and anything worth looting had been taken. The tattered American flag they found in the mud.

The noonday sun scorched the desert. Tompkins waved for his company sergeant, John Thibodeaux. The small Cajun scrambled up the ridge, minimizing loose gravel and dirt in his wake. With caution tempered by long years of hiding from enemies, he took the binoculars from Tompkins and eased his head until he could see over the crest of the hill.

"Tell me what you see," Tompkins said.

Thibodeaux inspected the tableau spread before him. Minutes dragged by and Thibodeaux wiped sweat from his eyes several times before he lowered his head and slid down a few feet from the crest.

"It ain't good, Skip. If we's goin' in, we'd best be doin' it."

Tompkins grimaced. They were old men now, all of them, old and slow. Their truck had even more years on its chassis than any of them did. Almost five hundred yards separated them from the women, and if the guards suspected a rescue they would start shooting, and that would be that.

Tompkins put his hand on Thibodeaux's shoulder. "Tell the boys to pack up and get ready."

"We goin' need them trucks." Thibodeaux indicated the vehicles parked so the guards could sit in their shadows. "Cain't get ever'body in this one ole truck."

"I know."

The six men moved in silence, their movements precise and efficient. Everything had a place: the tents, cooking gear, and other necessities had their own nooks in, under, and on top of their World War Two era truck. They checked their weapons and took their battle stations on board, with Tompkins in the cab and Thibodeaux driving. Wilson, Zuckerman, Hausser, and Tandy sat in the back, ready to jump out and start firing.

Clumps of weeds grew through long cracks in the road's pavement, and the old M35 deuce and a half truck bounced and slid as Thibodeaux avoided pot holes. His grip on the wheel tightened. Sweat rolled into Tompkins' eyes. The salt burned and he used a dirty rag to wipe his and Thibodeaux's foreheads. Hopefully the guards would think them friends returning from a mission, but the slow pace gave the guards a lot of time to examine them. If they opened fire before Tompkins' men could deploy, none of them would survive.

"Speed it up," Tompkins said.

"I don't know, Skip," Thibodeaux said. "We hit a big ole hole and we might break an axle."

"We've gotta take that chance." Tompkins shifted the M16 in his lap.

Less than two hundred yards separated them before the one of the guards looked their way. Thibodeaux stuck his left hand out the driver's window. The guard waved back. The other three did not react, as if the heat had sucked the life out of them.

Thibodeaux stopped between the guard on duty and the three guards lounging in the trucks' shade. The one on duty slung his rifle and walked into the dust cloud around the cab. When he stopped beside the truck, Thibodeaux put the barrel of his .45 between the man's eyes and pulled the trigger. The back of his head exploded, spattering blood and brains on the ground.

Tompkins shot another guard. His men jumped from the back and finished off the other two. None made it to his feet.

The girls and women began to scream and ran, scattering.

"No!" yelled Thibodeaux, stepping down and waving his arms. "We're friends! Friends!"

"Monty, you and Sig collect anything of value, especially guns and ammo," Tompkins said, rifling the pockets of the man he'd killed. Finding a small bag of corn biscuits, he stuffed them in his pants pocket. "Paul, Derek, you guys help John get those girls in the trucks. I'm going to see if I can get them started." With the caliphate's poor maintenance, it wasn't a given.

They scrambled through the dust clouds. Voices, wheedling, angry, placating, drifted to him, drowned by the cough of the first truck starting up. Tompkins left it idling and climbed into the second one; it started, too, thankfully. When he climbed down, the women and girls were half loaded. A lean, haggard woman, her arms sheltering a pair of adolescent twins and a younger girl, stared at him from beside the first truck's rear bumper.

"Skip!" Thibodeaux yelled, cupping his hands to be heard over the rough engines. "We got company!"

Tompkins turned and Thibodeaux pointed down the road. Perhaps a mile away a dust cloud boiled along the ridge. "Damn," he said. "Ma'am, I need you to get these children into the truck and do it now. Please."

She nodded. "You were sent by God," she said. Her tone was not questioning; it was a definitive statement. "I asked Him to save my girls and he sent you." Then she turned and lifted the younger child into the back.

Two vehicles approached, not one, and it took time to turn the three trucks around. Before they got on the road that led to the highway, the newcomers came in rifle range. Tompkins waited for them to open fire, or pursue, but instead they pulled over to check on the guards.

It gave them a chance. The Sevens feared darkness as if the demons of Hell lurked in the shadows, waiting to drag them to Satan's court. If they could elude pursuit until sunset, they had a good chance of getting away altogether. And even in darkness they could drive on.

"All right," he said to Thibodeaux. "We caught a break. Now get us the hell out of here."

Chapter 9

The sky above me sparkled red as I sped down a broken road,
The sky behind me faded to black as I hauled my precious load;
In the fading light and dust of my wake, came men who wanted me dead.
But I let them see they don't scare me, and they will die instead.
   "The Ballad of the Last Six Men," Anonymous

two hours later

The walkie talkie crackled to life. By that alone Tompkins knew it wasn't good news; batteries could not be replaced, and even rechargeable ones could only be used so many times. Only emergencies justified draining them by using the walkie-talkies.

"Bad news, Skip," Hausser said from the rearmost truck. "We've got company, maybe two miles back. A lot of company. It looks like a dust storm back there."

"Thanks, Paul. Out."

He and Thibodeaux exchanged glances.

"We can outruns them til it gets dark."

"If they catch us on this road, we're dead." Tompkins rubbed his face, remembering. "But maybe..."

"Gots to decide soon, Skip. The road of life is paved with flat squirrels."

"Keep us ahead while I think."

Less than an hour later, when a rocket exploded one hundred yards to their right, Tompkins knew they had run out of time. The truck slammed into a pothole and veered left, toward an arroyo, before Thibodeaux jerked it back onto the highway. Sweat rolled down his face and dripped from the white stubble on his chin. Screams came from the back, where the women and children had nothing to hold onto except each other. In the passenger seat Tompkins tried to blink away the shimmer in his vision caused when his head struck the dash.

Ahead, the broken road stretched due west into the setting sun. Behind, dozens of vehicles closed in on them, each filled with angry men who wanted to kill them. To either side, empty desert between distant ridges. A prairie falcon flapped out of the path of the speeding truck, abandoning a wounded rabbit on the pavement.

Hot air poured into the cabin from the searing heat outside. Tompkins leaned out the passenger's window, peering around, and banged his head on the window frame when they hit another hole. Somewhere out there he remembered an old Army training ground that might be defensible, a place where they might at least make a stand, but the swirling dust made it impossible to see.

Craning his neck back out the window while shielding his eyes with his left hand, he sought the landmarks to indicate they were close, blinking against the dust and dirt whipping into his eyes. Before The Collapse, Tompkins had been executive officer of a rifle company that participated in war games in that part of Arizona. Somewhere in the area, the Army had flattened a small plateau to act as a combined observation point, brigade headquarters, and field hospital. It was several hundred feet above the desert floor, where flies, mosquitoes, dust, and other pests could be better controlled. A dirt ramp had been constructed leading up to the plateau, wide enough and strong enough to handle large military vehicles. He remembered because he drove the CO's Humvee up that ramp with an injured man in the back. He recalled the plateau walls being jagged and vertical.

Leading to this ramp the Army engineers built a road through the desert, complete with several bridges over shallow arroyos, with a crushed rock bed. His memories pictured the bridges being metal, or metal-reinforced wood, either one of which meant they could still be standing. If they could somehow find that road, and if the bridges had not collapsed, and if they could get to the plateau, it would at least give them a place to defend.

So many ifs... but in his own quiet way Tompkins had always been a religious man who believed that if you had breath in your body and faith in God, then He could make the impossible possible. Miracles could happen; he had seen them.

And that woman's words kept haunting him. Could it be true? Could all the long years of tribulation and hardship have been leading to this day, this moment? God did move in mysterious ways.

"Paul, Sig, listen," he said into the walkie-talkie. "We've still got a chance. Somewhere around here there's an old road built during maneuvers a long time ago. The turnoff should be up ahead on the right."

"How far ahead, Skip?" Paul said. "They're sniffing our butts like coyotes hunting rabbits, and we're not far out of rifle range."

"I don't know how far it is, and I can't guarantee I can give you a head's up. Just be ready to turn off suddenly, find the road, and pray the bridges are standing."

"Bridges?"

"Yeah, bridges. Stop talking and pray."

Ten minutes later, without warning, something in his brain connected and a flash of memory shot into focus. There, in the distance, a small plateau jutted from the ridgeline on the right.

"That's it!" he shouted, pointing. He picked up the W-T. "The road, look for the turnoff, it's got to be close. Paul, Sig, get ready!"

As the sun sank lower and the shadows lengthened, Tompkins strained to see anything that looked like a road. The terrain had no significant features aside from arroyos and small ditches; no definitive landmarks.

Where was it? he kept asking himself. *Where?*

"Skip, they've opened fire!" Hausser shouted.

"There!" Tompkins yelled, pointing. "See it, John? Over there! Paul, Sig, we're turning off. Floor it and pray like hell!"

One after another the three trucks screeched off the old highway and onto a barely visible track never meant to last more than a week. Bouncing, jostling—items flew around inside the trucks. The terrified children in back screamed.

"Are they following, Paul?" Tompkins said into the W-T.

"No, Skip, not yet. They must think we're about to circle the wagons and fight."

"Don't slow down."

The truck slid, slammed into deep holes, and got caught in ruts, almost toppled twice, but somehow Thibodeaux kept it upright and moving forward. He coughed as dust clouded in the cabin. "Skip, I cain't breathe."

Tompkins held the old rag up to Thibodeaux's mouth, several times hitting his nose when the truck smacked into a hole. The gritty dust was getting into their eyes, too, but he could not do anything about it.

"There's a bridge, and it's still up. Don't slow down. Gun it, gun it."

"It might be all rotted!"

"It doesn't matter. If we can't get across that arroyo we're all dead anyway."

The bridge's weathered gray wood and rusted metal supports did not give them confidence. They hit it doing forty. The timbers groaned, but the structure held. The other two trucks followed close behind.

The road straightened and had fewer holes, and the second bridge rattled by under their tires, before their pursuers began coming into the desert after them. After that a long straightaway led to the ramp, giving them a chance to gain momentum for the long climb. The afternoon had darkened toward night and shadows covered their route, making it difficult to see where they were going. Nevertheless, Thibodeaux floored it and the ancient truck hit the ramp and rocketed upward, with the others close behind. All three bounced over the top edge, rocking on their springs.

"Park at the far end, as far from the ramp as you can."

Before the truck had stopped moving, Tompkins was out and running for the others. "Everybody out! Hurry! Paul, take Derek and see if you can hold them off until we can set up a defense! Ladies, gather every rock you can and start building a wall right here—something we can hide behind! There should be some over there by the ridge wall. Monty, John, Sig, help the women. Let's move!"

Tompkins grabbed his rifle and trotted back to the ramp. Paul and Derek knelt on the edge, staring through gathering darkness at the more than two dozen vehicles surrounding their plateau. Scores of men dismounted from the trucks.

"That's a lot of Sevens, Skip," Hausser said. "We sure pissed somebody off."

"Why ain't they comin' up?" Tandy said. "They're just standing around."

Tompkins adjusted his binoculars, focusing to pick out details in the twilight. Despite the dim lighting he could see figures standing and talking, and a few more gathering wood. "They're not coming today or tonight. They're going to wait for dawn."

"That don't make sense," Tandy said.

"They're afraid of the dark," Tompkins said, "remember? None of these guys like fighting at night. Derek, your eyes are better than mine or Paul's, stay here and keep watch. Holler if something changes. Paul, let's give them a hand with those rocks."

A prairie falcon glided into its nest overlooking the platform.

In desperate haste they worked until sweat drenched their skin and clothes, even the children, and within half an hour a stone wall seventy-five feet long and two to three feet high stretched across the plateau. Although not much of a defensive position, it would at least turn small arms fire. Tompkins then allowed a short water break. They found two five-gallon cans in one of their stolen trucks, both full, and a third can a little less than half full. The men shared what little food they had, stale corn biscuits and jerked jackrabbit, and everyone ate in exhausted silence. Some of the children fell asleep. As they leaned against the wall chewing the tough strips of meat, the oldest woman found Tompkins and slumped down next to him.

"Remember me, general? Mama Powell, from Roundup. You stayed with us once, what, ten years back?" She peered at the wall. "Not lookin' too good, is it, general?"

Now that he saw her up close, he did remember. "I'm a major, ma'am. No, I'm not gonna lie to you, I've been in better spots before. But we're not dead yet. Me and the boys don't look like much, I know, but we got a lot of fight left in us."

"We appreciate what you tried to do for us, whatever happens next." She smiled. "You're a good man, Major. It's not your fault it didn't work out."

"Thank you, Mama Powell, but don't give up yet. I just don't think God is gonna let us die out here like this."

She laughed, but it came out as *ha!* "God," she said. "Maybe he listens to you, Major, 'cause he sure as hell ain't been listening to me. Do you have any idea what those... those animals do to young girls? The God I grew up knowing doesn't let that happen."

"Yes, ma'am, I know. I don't pretend to understand how He goes about things, and I sure can't see much godly about the last fifty years... I can't say why I feel this way, I just do. He hasn't forgotten us."

She reached over and stroked his cheek. No woman had touched him in... how many years? Fifty? And while the brush of her fingers held no sexual connotations, even simple kindness had become an alien experience.

"You're a dear man, Major. You remind me of my Charles. He always put himself before others. I thank you for what you tried to do for us."

With that, she pushed herself to her feet and walked off into the night.

Chapter 10

Men will volunteer to die before they will endure the pain of patience.
   Julius Caesar

June 17th, 2344 hours

The boredom was crushing. Howard Wilson Dupree felt like someone had strapped an anvil between his shoulder blades.

Twelve hour shifts. Two and a half days off every seven days for one year, then back to Long Sleep.

In theory, Dupree monitored communications, except there were no communications, none whatsoever, and had not been for more than fifty years. The workload did not drive him close to madness, but the lack of a workload did. He could not even tinker with computers, or run audits, both his specialties. He spent his time fidgeting and praying for time to pass faster.

Dupree sat for his entire shift in front of one small workstation, backed up by a communications complex so vast three of its sides and the ceiling were all lost in darkness. Ninety-nine percent of the base's massive computer power lay silent, with only enough powered up to run essential machinery. His station had three monitors, with six-foot high banks of processors and scanners flanking him, and they spent twenty-four hours per day, seven days a week, scanning every possible frequency, listening for signs that humans still lived somewhere above.

In the first years there had been television, radio, and even cell phone traffic, but as time passed it all died away, dwindling into sporadic broadcasts, until one day the airwaves went silent, a silence unbroken now for half a century.

Twelve hours per day.

Had they survived the extinction of humanity? Did other human beings still walk the Earth, or did they comprise the last people alive? The skeleton crew of the huge base debated those questions with the same fervor people once held for politics or sports, neither of which seemed to matter any more.

A surprising percentage of the twenty-one currently-conscious crew members for that year thought mankind had, in fact, committed mass suicide. But Dupree found that idea ludicrous. Eight billion people could not all be dead, not even after so much time had passed; some would have survived, somewhere. But if he was right, those survivors avoided using the radio, phone, television, or any other device more sophisticated than two cans tied together with string.

For Dupree, dwelling on their isolation seemed counter-productive. If mankind as a species no longer existed, then they all might as well wake up and go topside, because the whole purpose for the base would be gone. America could not be resurrected without first having Americans to resurrect it for. To do his job, he needed to believe that it still had a purpose, and so Dupree stood his long watches and played poker against the computer and tried to watch old movies about people and subjects that had long since vanished, but mostly he drank coffee and tried to stay awake until his shift ended. Every few days one of the standby helicopter pilots might wander in to chat, or the Officer of the Watch might drop in during his rounds to shoot the shit, but most of his watches Dupree stood alone.

Not for much longer, though. One more week and his replacement would wake up, then a week of training him or her, and then a return to the blank bliss of deep sleep. Once a year twenty-one crew members would awaken to watch over operations and maintain the base for when, or if, the receivers ever picked up the activation code. The twenty-one on duty would then renew their own personal wait, knowing in deep sleep aging stopped. Somebody else could do their duty and endure the boredom for a year.

For two more weeks, however, night and day did not matter. Under the mountain no cycle of dark and light differentiated time and no seasons passed. Circadian rhythms no longer regulated rest patterns and most of the crew depended on drugs to sleep.

Standing and stretching, Dupree poured yet another cup of coffee and selected an energy bar from the food shelf stuck in the corner near the latrine. Maybe somebody would come by to kill some time. Maybe Captain Randall; Dupree had not seen him for a few days. But nobody did.

The clock moved past 2359 hours. A new day began, same as the old day, same as every day.

Chapter 11

I have not seen the face of Pan, nor mocked the Dryad's haste,
But I have trailed a dark-eyed Man across a windy waste.
I have not died as men may die, nor sin as men have sinned,
But I have reached a misty sky upon a granite wind.
    Robert E. Howard, from 'Recompense'

June 18th, 0015 hours

    Natalie Merchant's haunting voice echoed through the cavernous hangar deep below the surface as she slipped into the chorus for *Because the Night*. The music pumped through the powerful P.A. speakers and the bass rattled a system built for voice, not music. Echoes reverberated from the labyrinth of steel girders unseen overhead, but the poor acoustics did not bother the sole man present in the gigantic space. Captain Joe Randall remembered the video of Merchant fronting 10,000 Maniacs, backed by an entire string section, on Youtube in the Old Days, before The Collapse and his Long Sleep. Listening to it reminded him of a time gone and a world lost.
    Oblivion had long since swallowed every video artist and digested them in the bowels of history, as dead as the United States of America. Randall stood in a pool of light, one man in a huge black void, and keenly felt the loneliness of his job. As Merchant's voiced faded the next song in the queue came to life as Neil Young scratched out the opening lines of *My, My, Hey, Hey (Into the Black)*. Randall started singing along without looking up from his work. He sang more off key than Young, but that did not matter.
    The helicopter crews maintained their own aircraft, but aside from starting the engines periodically they never flew and hadn't for half a

century. Sometimes Randall's co-pilot, Bunny Carlos, hung around for companionship, and sometimes either the pilot or co-pilot of the other ready chopper worked in their revetment, but not that day. The two Boeing AH-72 Comanche attack helicopters stood as the base's Ready Response Team, and while the four air crewmen acted as their own ground crews, keeping them combat ready at all times, they did not work regular shifts, which let Randall indulge his passion for loud music. His fellow pilots did not share his taste for classic rock, or maximum volume, and he made fun of them for the music they preferred. Bunny was a jazz fanatic, for cripe's sake.

The AH-72 would forever be the final helicopter gunship developed by the United States Army. A direct successor to the AH-64 Apache, the nickname Comanche had been previously used for a cancelled project. Re-used on the AH-72, there had been P.C. controversy about the name and the Army officially changed it to the unpopular but safe Golden Eagle. Unofficially, however, it stayed the Comanche, and only official publications ever referred to it in any other way.

And like all military aircraft since the first fragile monoplane appeared over the trenches of France in 1914, Randall's AH-72 had a name. On either side of the fuselage, behind the cockpit doors, the image of a semi-topless blonde with improbably large breasts sat holding a long, phallic-shaped sword in both hands, with her naked legs wrapped around a missile. In bright yellow letters a foot high, the caption read *Tank Girl*.

The Apache design reached its zenith with the AH-64G-1a, when the prototype designs for the AH-72 were well advanced. The Comanche was designed to have capabilities the Apache did not. Larger and faster, in fact the largest helicopter gunship ever built, with an anti-personnel ordnance package centered on the new fifty caliber Gatling-style miniguns, each Comanche could carry two pods with 2,000 rounds of ammunition. If they mounted the thirty millimeter gun pods instead, the Comanche could still carry two, with 1,400 rounds each, instead of one pod on the Apache. Up to 96 Dragonfire missiles could be mounted, depending on the gun package selected and whether it transported troops.

In the bay eight fully armed soldiers could be carried. Various other ordnance packages were available, including air-to-air missiles, side-firing fifty caliber machine guns mounted on stands for manual use, and a variety of specific purpose packages, such as grenade throwers and anti-missile defenses. Substantial power plant upgrades pushed top speed for the Comanche to over two hundred knots.

Randall cleaned and field stripped the fifty caliber gun pods for the second time that shift, despite the hangar environment being virtually dust free. Powerful filters purified the air to minimize accumulation of dirt on critical parts. Randall took no chances, however, that when the time came and he squeezed the firing trigger his guns would fail to spew two thousand rounds per minute onto the target. Tomorrow he would work on the thirty millimeters, although he doubted they would find many targets that justified expending the massive cannon rounds. Then he would inspect the Dragonfire missiles, the engine, cockpit panels, fuel stability, rotors, and anything else he could think to check.

Randall knew they would be called into action soon. He could not explain how he knew it; he just did. He even had the music picked out for his first attack run on the enemy. A lot of the base thought the activation signal would never come in, but Randall felt sure that it would, and soon. In the meantime nothing would keep him from getting his massive killing machine ready.

If Operation Overtime received the activation signal during Captain Benjamin Franklin Walling's tour of duty, he would become Officer Commanding until the base CO could wake up and take over. He felt overwhelmed knowing that, if it happened, on his shoulders and his alone would rest sole responsibility for activation of every aspect of the titanic base, from powering up the unused hydroponic farms deep beneath ground level, to ensuring the ready weapons systems could go into action on a moment's notice.

More than 700 miles of tunnels, halls, high-speed rail passages, walkways, and footpaths, not to mention the huge hangar decks, crew quarters, Long Sleep caverns, nooks, crannies, and assorted unknown spaces, and everything in them, were all his personal cross to bear. No matter what problems cropped up, if anything went wrong, anywhere, solving the issue depended on him and no one else.

If they were ever activated. Walling kicked back in his chair, scowling. He'd finished his dinner but hung around the mess hall hoping someone would come in. The days never varied. Neither did the food. Every meal involved Long Shelf Life Meals Ready to Eat, nasty mixes of alleged foods sold to the Army under the guise of being safe. Nobody had ever guaranteed they'd be particularly digestible.

Nobody came in. Grumpy, he rose and shoved back his chair. He'd be talking to himself again. And loneliness made for a long year.

Chapter 12

Dreams of Glory Are Lost in the Ages,
Bare Feet Fail On A Broken Trail—
Let My Name Fade From the Printed Pages,
Dreams And Visions Are Growing Pale.
   Robert E. Howard, from "Lines Written In The Realization That I Must Die"

June 18th, 0122 hours

He saw the clear night as one final gift from God, a panoramic view of the universe spread overhead in a spray of stars and a full moon. Dennis Tompkins studied the constellations as he had so many times before, hoping they might cheer him up. They reminded him God still ruled in Heaven and the travails of men crumbled to dust in His overall plan, and the reward for faith came not in this life, but the next.

Yet try as he might, the wonder of the spectacle depressed him. In the countless wars through the ages, how many times had those stars watched over sleepless soldiers on the eve of battle, warriors who stared at them while contemplating their own imminent fate and praying to their gods? Thousands of times, or tens of thousands, so that one more such requiem might pass unnoticed. Men condemned to death had been mesmerized by the grandeur of creation since humans first walked the Earth.

With the sun gone the night turned cold and the chill deepened his gloom. Tompkins tried to think of some way out of the trap. The ridge rose sheer from the platform and climbing up would be slow, laborious, requiring rappelling gear and strong legs and upper bodies. The drop to the desert floor would require scaling hundreds of feet down jagged granite. No, even if they had still been young it would have been impossible.

He'd forbidden a fire but his men watched him from the shadows. He'd told them they had survived fifty years wandering the wasteland of the dead United States, using only their wits and their brains and maybe a little luck, to go on living after they should have died. He'd told them that, of the entire American military machine, they were the last survivors. They'd continued fighting to protect the weak. They could count their lives well lived. All of those things he'd told them, but he did not tell them they were going to survive the next day.

Tompkins stared into the darkness. He didn't hear Sergeant Thibodeaux walk softly across the plateau and sit beside him.

"Whatcha thinking 'bout, Skipper?" he said.

"Just remembering. What it was like, you know, before. Really, I was *trying* to remember. There's a lot of things I know we had, but I'll be damned if I can see them any more, or remember what they smelled like, or how they tasted. Football, television, cold beer, cheeseburgers, ice cream... they're just words now. I know I liked them, but now they don't even bring a picture to mind. They're just... just words."

"I know whatcha mean. I was growing up eating boudin and crawfish, a hot gumbo with shrimp—" His voice cracked.

"There's one thing I do remember," Tompkins said. "One time when I was a kid, my dad took me to this place way down south, right on the beach. There was this big, long wooden building; I think it was a bar but it could've been a restaurant. It might have been painted green, I'm not sure. Half was in Alabama, half Florida. I remember it was really hot and crowded and my dad made me hold his hand, even though I didn't want to. After a while, somebody handed him a pail with some dead fish in it. Not big fish, little ones..."

"You mean like a cigar minnow?"

"Yeah, that's right, cigar minnows. Mullet, I think. They handed my dad this bucket and he hands me a fish. Then we stood there, I guess we were over the line in Florida, and threw the fish as far as we could over into Alabama. I don't know why we did it, but everybody else did so we did, too. I smelled like fish for days, but of course I went fishing all the time so I was used to it. I don't know why I remember that so well, but I do."

He smiled at the bittersweet memory and fell silent again. In his soul Tompkins felt every one of his years.

"For me," Thibodeaux said. "I wish I could've tasted pecan pie one more time... and a Coke. My daddy used to take a cooler of Cokes, all filled up with ice and running with cold, every time we fished in the back bayou. I loved them Cokes, me. Daddy drank Jax."

"What did you fish for?"

"Sac a lait, mostly. My daddy had a recipe for sac a lait croquet so good it made you wanna slap yer mama. He cooked them with hush puppies and greens. That was good eating. And when them crawfish was in season, everybody wanted to be Cajun then.... We're gonna die out here, ain't we, Skip?"

"We're going to die somewhere, that's for sure. Never give up, John. We've been in some bad spots before and we're still here."

"C'mon, Skip, don't feed me no shit. Them boys down there ain't hanging around because they like sleeping in no desert. They're hanging around because they ain't leaving 'til they get the women back. And you, me, and the boys ain't gonna let them just walk up here and take them, now, are we? Only this time, I don't see a way out. Six of us, couple hundred of them—that don't add up to us getting out of here alive."

Tompkins could think of nothing to say.

"Guess you answered my question," Thibodeaux said. "Damned shame I should die so young, before my prime and all."

Tompkins could not help but chuckle, even with a tight throat. "Yeah, you're not seventy-five yet. You're just a kid."

"Cajuns don't reach their sexual peak 'til at least a hundred. So like I said, not even in my prime." Thibodeaux squatted in the darkness. "Hey, Skip, whatever happened to them codes you used to read into the radio? You ain't done that for a long time."

"Codes? Oh, right, the activation codes. John, I must have read those damned things every night for ten years, but I got sick of getting nothing in return. Do you know what I mean? It was a reminder that there was nobody out there, that the country I loved and bled for was gone and wasn't coming back, and that millions and millions of people were dead. Every night that I read those codes all I could think of was everything we had lost. I knew what was gone and I didn't need to be reminded of it."

"So, you still got them?" Thibodeaux said. "Them codes, I mean."

"Yeah, they're in the big trunk somewhere. Why?"

Thibodeaux shrugged. "Cain't see where there's much to lose trying it one more time."

Tompkins shook his head. "The cavalry isn't riding to the rescue. Besides, I'm not even sure those projects were real. There was a lot of bullshit back in those days."

"Gotta be straight with you, Skip. Right now me and the boys need any kinda hope we can get. False hope ain't so bad if it's all you got."

Tompkins knew it was futile. But if Thibodeaux wanted him to read the codes one more time, why not? Half a century wandering desolate North America together had earned him at least that much.

"All right. Why the hell not? Go find the radio and start cranking; the battery is probably shot. Then go find the codes. They should be in that brown leather case inside the trunk. I'm going to need the flashlight, so charge that, too. Then I'll read them and we'll see what happens. It's not like we've got anything to lose."

Chapter 13

Yesterday upon the stair
I met a man who wasn't there.
He wasn't there again today;
I wish, I wish he'd go away.
    From *"Antigonish,"* William Hughes Mearns

June 18th, 0117 hours

Less than three hours remained in the interminable shift. Nobody had shown up to distract him. Soon enough his replacement would wake up, then a week to train him and Dupree could sleep... yeah. Sleep.

In college he'd had a job as a night desk manager in the Tulane dorm, where his main job responsibilities had involved staying awake and not letting anybody feed the aquarium full of piranhas. At least then he could watch the fish swimming.

He could watch a movie, listen to music. Without enthusiasm he perused the selections from Beethoven and Mozart. Nothing appealed to him. Finally Dupree settled on Beethoven's Eighth symphony and turned up the volume. He was about to click the PLAY icon when the speaker did something it had not done for more than five decades.

It came to life.

"To any United States military forces within sound of this transmission, this is an Overtime activation warning. I repeat, this is an activation warning for Operation Overtime. Prepare to receive codes; activation sequence to begin in ten seconds. Nine, eight, seven..." The voice crackled as if traveling a long distance or riding a weak signal, shaky but loud, with the volume turned up for Beethoven.

Dupree froze in his seat, staring at the speaker as if a live snake coiled on his desk and hissed. Adrenaline flooded his body. He quit breathing without knowing he did so.

"...two, one... Begin Overtime activation sequence..."

The voice rattled off a long series of numbers and letters, sixty-seven in all, then said, "Repeating activation sequence," and did so. Once finished, it said, "Activation sequence ended."

Then the unknown voice dropped lower, almost to a whisper. "If anybody is out there, if anybody can hear me, for God's sake hurry. We don't have much time." The transmission terminated with a loud *click* as someone keyed the microphone off.

Stunned, Dupree followed his training and waited. The computer had to first verify the activation code. Only then would he have duties to perform. On the computer screen, the list of Beethoven's symphonies had given way to numbers and symbols flashing by so fast he could not follow them. Some program had been triggered, but he hadn't seen anything like before.

For more than a minute silence filled the cavernous space. Dupree began to wonder if he had dozed off and dreamed the whole thing. Then a new voice came through the speakers, a pleasant female voice he had not heard before. "Activation code accepted and verified. Operation Overtime is now active. All personnel should follow Activation and Deployment Protocol A."

The mountain shuddered. Far below the surface, massive machines came to life, including the twin nuclear reactors. Electric energy flowed through tens of thousands of miles of cables, and in the seven hundred miles of tunnels burrowed through the rock, lights flickered on and dark corners became visible, shadows receded and ominous shapes were revealed as more machinery. At the heart of the mountain enormous pumps dipped into the wide, swift river that ran deep underground, sucking up hundreds of gallons of water per second and sending it under high pressure throughout the huge base to bathrooms, kitchens, purification tanks, hydroponic farms, storage silos, and drinking fountains.

Outside, on the high meadows near the mountain, a herd of pronghorn antelope stopped grazing and sniffed the air. Sensing the seismic event beneath their hooves, their instincts warned them not to wait and they ran. Birds scattered, lizards sought the cover of rocks, and mice scurried back and forth. A prairie hawk shadowing its favorite prey did not swoop down for an easy meal, because under the desert something rumbled to life, something powerful and dangerous, and the animals knew better than to stick around.

The bank of computer stations to Dupree's left booted up, sending electronic commands throughout the base via thousands of miles of fiber optic cables. Lights flashed on and he saw the true vastness of the chamber he'd worked in for the past year. Dull noises came from below and the ground shook again. In vast caverns, a precise mixture of chemicals started pumping into thousands of individual chambers where the base's crew lay in Long Sleep, injecting it into the pods to bring them back to consciousness.

Shaking himself free, Dupree managed to key the comm. switch connected directly with the quarters of the Officer of the Watch, who had just been promoted to Officer Commanding.

0125 hours

Captain Walling pulled the pillow over his head and wondered what the hell that noise was. It took a full minute before his sleeping brain registered that it was the base alarm. He sat upright and only then noticed the alert button on the phone beside his bed flashing red, which had never happened before. His mind sharpened in an instant. The readout on the phone stated the call came from the command center.

Picking up the handset, he said, "Walling here. What's going on, Hudson? Do we have a fire?" That fear haunted him most, a fire in one of the ammunition chambers, or maybe a hangar or, God forbid, in a sleep chamber.

"Not Hudson, sir, this is Dupree. No fire, but... Captain, we've been activated."

"What are you talking about?"

"The code, sir, the activation code. It came in about four minutes ago, and whoever sent it seems to be in big trouble."

Adrenaline or not, Walling's mind was slow in processing the information. "The code? Who sent it? How do we know it's authentic?"

"They didn't identify themselves, Captain, but they repeated the code and the computer accepted it and everything is happening automatically according to Deployment Plan A. I haven't touched anything, not one thing, but if this is real then I need your permission to begin the checklist."

"I'm headed your way. Don't do anything until I get there."

0158 hours

Nothing existed. Time did not flow because time did not exist. Thoughts did not register because thoughts did not exist. No dreams, no reality. No darkness, either, because darkness implied the absence of light and light did not exist.

Nothing existed, until something did.

Exactly when sentience returned he could never say, but the first sensation did not involve sight or touch, or even sound, but smell. No conscious thought registered that he smelled something familiar, or connected the appropriate memories with the smell, since as yet he had no conscious thought. But the scent did trigger the firing paths among synapses that had lain dormant for a long, long time. Eventually his sluggish brain interpreted it as the smell of warm bread filling a favorite café in Vienna, although the chemicals flooding his chamber smelled nothing like bread. Images began to reinforce the memory, colors, sounds, people... none of which made sense. Self-awareness had not yet returned, but part of him knew enough to mistrust the memory.

At length sounds registered, loud sounds... voices? Yes, a voice! It seemed to be yelling. A pathway in his brain cleared enough to know the voice spoke words, and the words began to make sense.

A crust over his eyes made them hard to open. When he did, he turned away, unused to the light. After half a century of disuse, even the dim lighting in the chamber assaulted his optic nerves.

A young man hovered over him, speaking. "I'm Captain Walling. General Angriff, can you hear me, sir?"

He formed two dry words. "How many?"

The man leaning over his pod came into focus. He wore a uniform, an Army uniform, with the insignia of a captain.

As his body warmed, Angriff's skin broke out with chill bumps. "Clothes," he whispered, and then sat up, stiff. "Uniform."

He blinked and rubbed the crust from his eyes. The captain handed him a plastic glass with a straw. He sucked on it and felt the indescribable pleasure of water moistening his throat for the first time in fifty years.

"How many?" Although cracked and harsh, this time his voice carried.

"How many what, sir?"

"The battalion. How many in the battalion?"

Walling drew back, his eyes uncertain. "Which battalion do you mean, sir?"

Angriff paused. Frozen muscles had warmed close to their normal temperature, but tightness made his skin feel three sizes too small. Concentrating, he marshaled his thoughts and they came easier. "What do you mean, which battalion? How many do we have?"

"Eight combat, twelve total, counting logistics and communications, and not counting smaller attached units. But sir, there's an unknown American military unit in trouble. As temporary officer commanding I've proceeded with Deployment Plan A and the Comanches have the standard anti-personnel package, but we need to get rolling on follow-ups."

Angriff's eyebrows creased into a V. "What the hell is Deployment Plan A? Or a Comanche?"

Walling rocked back and forth as if impatient. "A Comanche is an attack helicopter, the AH-72. It replaced the Apache."

"And we have those?"

"Yes sir, two on standby, armed and ready, and ten more in storage."

"Captain," Angriff said. His voice had grown stronger. "If Americans need help, sortie those gunships."

Walling took Angriff's uniform from its storage drawer in the pod. He looped the General's left arm around his neck and helped him out, then helped him dress. Once clothed, he supported Angriff as they made for the hallway. Throughout the immense space the CHILSS, Cryogenic Human Life Support Structures, opened as their inhabitants came back to consciousness.

As overhead lights brightened to their full illumination, Walling noticed scratches on the lock panel for General Angriff's CHILSS. Had someone tried to tamper with the machine? Video cameras recorded every person who entered the massive bay, and he made a mental note to look into it when time permitted.

0301 hours

Lita Ford begged Joe Randall to kiss her deadly and Randall would have obliged if he could. Tank Girl or no—and he didn't mean the helicopter—he had seen pictures of Ford with her first band, the Runaways, a punkish jailbait blonde in tight pants and a fuck-me smirk. Even as she'd aged, she'd remained a gorgeous woman. But as he bobbed his head in time with the music, Tank Girl's image replaced Ford's and that made him glad, because that way he forgot Ford had been dead for half a century.

As the song ended and the last echoes faded in the immensity of the hangar, running footsteps approached along the tunnel from the central complex. Looking up from close inspection of an intake valve, he saw the shadow of someone entering the hangar. The next song started, but the grinding guitar opening of Mott the Hoople's *Violence* got cut short as someone shut down the computer Randall had plugged into the P.A. system.

"Hey, what the hell?" Randall's words echoed in the vast space.

Randall's co-pilot, Lieutenant George "Bunny" Carlos, stood on the catwalk ten feet above him, near the tunnel opening into the hangar. Panting, the large ears that earned him his nickname waggled as he gulped air. "Hey, Joe, what are you doing? Time to kick the tires and light the fires! Haven't you heard the alarms? We're active, 50 caliber pods and mixed delivery on the Dragonfires, no riders, max ammo. Skids up in thirty."

"What are you talking about?"

"Active! Signal just came in, open season on burps!"

"Is this some kind of drill?"

"No, man, turn and burn! This is the real shit! You couldn't hear the alarm because of your fucking music."

As if to underscore Bunny's words, the irritating buzz of the alarm replaced Mott on the P.A. Lights began to glow far overhead, where there had been only darkness for more than fifty years. At first the long tubes shone with a vague dimness, but they warmed to gray and then white. Long unseen details began to emerge. Randall stood motionless, absorbing the life-changing news, before he began to move, fast and with practiced precision.

Between them, Carlos and Randall wrestled the massive gun pods into their dollies, wheeled them to the cradles, then man-handled belt after belt of ammunition into the feeds. The Dragonfires got loaded next and could have been the trickiest part, but Randall and Carlos had practiced the procedure over and over again, and it only took five minutes to load and wire them into the firing system. Fuel came last, then the preflight checklist. The gleaming aircraft had been maintained in pristine mechanical condition and was takeoff ready with ten minutes to spare.

With *Tank Girl* combat ready, they got into their flight suits and tucked in maps, sidearms and a dozen other things they might need. Settling into the cockpit, both men performed a visual inspection and test of the instruments. Carlos powered up and all systems registered normal. With five minutes left, they turned on the comm. system.

"Test, test, test." Randall looked at his co-pilot.

"Read you fine," Carlos said.

"Command, this is Ripsaw Real, do you copy?"

A third voice broke into their practiced takeoff routine, not the voice of Sergeant Avery, acting base ATC, but a voice both men recognized as Captain Walling's. "Ripsaw, this is Officer Commanding Walling. Listen up for the CO."

"Ripsaw Real and Ripsaw Two, do you read me?" A new, unfamiliar voice came through their headsets. Randall thought it vaguely familiar, but the slur and hoarseness from Long Sleep made it hard to tell for sure.

In their frantic haste to prepare for the mission, Randall and Carlos had forgotten to radio check with the second Comanche, Ripsaw Two, their wingman, crewed by 2nd Lt. Alisha Plotz and her co-pilot, Sergeant Andy Arnold. Outranking Plotz, as mission commander Randall should have coordinated with her, something they had practiced over and over but still forgot. He smacked his flight helmet three times with the heels of his hands.

"Read you loud and clear," Plotz said. Randall added his clearance, as well.

"Good. I'm not sure what you're flying into, but whatever it is the safety of you and your aircraft comes first. You are irreplaceable. Your first mission objective is to come back safely. Don't get involved in a fight you can't win. Having said that, once you have assessed the situation, if you determine that a United States military unit is under attack by hostiles, then you are authorized to use all force necessary and at your disposal to shoot the shit out of whoever thinks they can attack Americans in America. Is that clear?"

"Yes, sir!" Randall and Plotz said at the same time. "Kilo tango alpha!"

Angriff covered the mouthpiece and turned to Captain Walling. "Kilo tango alpha?" he whispered. "What does that mean?"

"Yes, sir, KTA. Kill them all. You're supposed to respond—"

"I got this one," Angriff said, holding up his hand. He uncovered the mike. "Kill them all, Captain. Let God sort 'em out."

Randall turned to Carlos and tapped on his helmet. Carlos shoved it up so they could speak without using the comm.

"Did the CO give his name?"

"Not that I heard," Carlos said.

"I thought he sounded familiar."

"Shit, Joe, he sounded drunk. We've got more important things to worry about."

The hangar's massive steel doors slid upward for the first time in half a century, revealing the panorama of the high desert spread far below, and Randall punched the ignition. Huge rotors began to turn and soon the deadly gunship lifted off and eased toward the now-open rectangle in the mountain's face.

"Wanna bet the bastards thought we were all dead?" he said into the com. "That the party was over?"

Carlos knew Randall as well as Randall knew Carlos, maybe better. They had flown together in the old days and joined Operation Overtime together. "You're not starting that shit again, are you?"

"Bro, it's my trademark."

"So what's the song, Joe?"

Randall turned so Carlos could see him smiling inside his helmet. He touched the large musical note on the onboard computer screen, the one he'd created to store thousands of songs picked from the base archives, and within seconds found the one he wanted. The opening guitar riff filled his earphones, followed by a fast tempo. He smiled at the lyrics and sang along with Status Quo's *The Party Ain't Over Yet*.

Chapter 14

*Time and tides have blurred my mind,
And the gods have forgotten my deeds;
But once I was a warrior feared,
Who rode a mighty steed.
My sword is dull, my shield is rent,
I've seen too many snows;
My body is scarred, my spirit spent,
But I vanquished all my foes.
So after I'm dead, let it be said
That evil men marked the day;
When the Gods were finished, forever more,
Writing the Legend of Nick the A.*
    "The Legend of Nick the A," by Green Ghost

June 18th, 0339 hours

Angriff keyed off the microphone, swiveled in his seat, and nodded. "All right, Captain—?" He squinted at the captain's uniform.

"Walling, sir."

"Right, Walling. Bring me up to speed. When I went cold there were four hundred fifty men and women in the one battalion I thought I'd command. Now you tell me I've got, what was it, eight battalions?"

"Not counting four support battalions and smaller specialized units, yes, sir. Eight combat battalions. And a sizable civilian contingent, too."

"So instead of a reconnaissance battalion, I command, what, a division?"

Walling wagged his head. "We're technically not a division, General, although ration strength is almost that large. You command the Seventh United States Cavalry Brigade."

"The Seventh Cavalry? As in George Custer? That was an active regiment when I went cold; what happened?"

Walling shrugged. "Custer's old regiment, sir, but upgraded to a brigade. I have no idea who assigned us our unit designation."

"Custer." Angriff shook his head. "Glory-hound bastard got himself killed and damned near got his entire command wiped out. If he'd lived, they should have shot him."

"But he is a legend, sir. And, if I may say, so are you." He paused and pursed his lips. "It can't hurt morale to have a commanding officer who's considered a legend. And General Angriff, people know what you did in Kuwait, Iraq, and Afghanistan, and especially in Africa. Every recruit had to learn your ode by heart."

"My ode?" Angriff said. "What ode? What are you talking about?"

"After you went missing, somebody put on ode to you on the internet and it went viral. It was called... you might not like the title, sir."

"I'm a big boy."

"It was called *The Legend of Nick the A*. All we know about the guy who did the video is that you were his commander at some point and you must have really done something to impress him. In the video he was dressed all in dark green camo, non-reg, with a pullover mask. Oh, and he went by the name Ghost."

"Green Ghost?"

"Yes, sir, that's it. You knew him?"

"Yeah, I did. Finest black ops guy I ever met. Do you remember how it went?"

"Not off hand, General, sorry. But that's why I'm glad to have a legend as our CO. If there's anybody around to remember we ever existed, then I imagine we will be a legend too. So we might as well act like one."

Angriff paused and admitted Walling had a point.

"Maybe we should head for the Central Command Center and start there, sir. It's your headquarters."

Angriff swiveled and spread his arms at the small room around him. "I thought this was the command center."

"Oh, no, sir, this is Secondary Dispatch and Emergency Control Center Two. You said you wanted to talk to the helicopter pilots ASAP and this was the closest comm. center. Until the internal network is up and running we'll have to use control centers, of which there's eight. Central Command is quite a bit larger than this."

"Then get me there."

They took one of the ubiquitous Emvees used for getting around the base and Walling floored it, maxing out the aluminum vehicle at its top speed of seventeen mph.

"The main elevators aren't far, sir."

"How many elevators does this place have?"

"Six locations with four to eight shafts each, plus four much larger service lifts."

Angriff inspected everything they passed, from stretches of bare rock walls to the periodic drains on each side of the wide tunnel, illuminated along its length by countless LEDs overhead. As he looked over his right shoulder at a yellow rectangular box fastened to the wall and labeled EMERGENCY USE ONLY, he asked, "Why do we need elevators? When I went cold there was just going to be one main floor, with ramped drives leading in and out through one main set of doors."

"Sir, may I suggest we wait to go into all of that until you can see the holograms? I think that will make the scope of this place a lot easier to grasp."

"But it's bigger than that," Angriff said, making it a statement, not a question.

"Much bigger, General. There's over seven hundred miles of tunnels and hallways, not counting hangars, Long Sleep chambers, and assembly areas. Overtime is huge."

"How long had I been asleep when whatever happened happened?"

"The Collapse? I don't know, General, but it couldn't have been too long."

"This place couldn't have been built in just the few years after I was recruited."

"I'm no construction engineer, but I'd say this place took decades. You should see the nuclear reactors and hydros. God only knows how they got those so far underground."

Angriff could not help being impressed as they sped along the corridor, but along with the wonder came a queasy doubt. Overtime had been far more advanced than Steeple told him, but why lie? What difference did the size of the unit make? Lying made no sense.

The tunnel widened into an octagon, with more tunnels leading off in four directions and with four banks of elevators in between. Two PFCs stood at the closest elevators, dressed in fatigues, men Angriff had never seen before. Like everyone who came out of Long Sleep they had beards and long, ragged hair at least four inches past regulation. At the sight of the two officers, both snapped to attention and saluted. Angriff returned their salutes.

"Where are you men headed?" he said.

"Central Command, sir. Except we aren't exactly sure where that is."

"Fifteenth level," Walling said. "Follow us."

The nearest elevator opened and the two men started to get on, then realized their mistake and moved aside to allow the officers on board first. Walling drove into the large elevator and the two men got in after. They stood as far away from their commanding general as possible, looking at the floor, each other, and their fingernails, anything to avoid eye contact.

Angriff smiled to himself. "How's the wake-up going, boys?"

The taller of the two looked up. "I wouldn't know, sir. We were up before most of the others, and a Lieutenant Noshimura told us to gear up and find Central Command." His pained expression clearly showed his hope the three-star general would accept his answer and leave him alone. "She also told us to shave and get a haircut, but we don't even know where the latrine is, sir."

"That's fine, son," Angriff said. "I need one, too. We'll get all that straightened out. Thank you both for volunteering for this mission."

"It... it's an honor, sir. When we heard you were the CO, we were down for whatever happened."

Angriff cocked his head in surprise. "Why is that?"

"Excuse me saying so, but you're a legend. Sir."

Angriff looked over his shoulder at Walling, while the captain stared at the ceiling.

They exited the elevator into an octagon exactly like the one seven flights below. The fifteenth level hallway was fifty feet wide. Unlike the other passages Angriff had seen, with walls of either bare concrete or shaped stone, cream-colored sound deadening panels lined the tunnel walls leading to Central Command. The floor, inlaid with polished white marble tiles, was designed for durability, not aesthetics. When they rounded a gentle curve in the tunnel, Angriff had his first awe-inspiring glimpse of Central Command.

A wall of clear glass two hundred feet long and twenty feet high, stretched down the east side of the hallway. In the center two massive sliding doors, also glass, had slid to either side to create a doorway thirty feet in width, and beyond the glass a huge room with terraced levels lay flooded with moonlight.

Walling parked the Emvee—it couldn't possibly be in the way in that wide corridor—and Angriff slid out, still staring. Retractable titanium blast doors had opened and, spread gloriously before them, the high desert outside glowed pale white under a cloudless sky, with the faintest trace of an orange dawn in the east.

General Angriff found himself speechless for one of the rare times in his life. "What drunken son a bitch designed this?"

A sergeant directing several dozen milling personnel to their duty stations turned and met Angriff's eyes. "Ten-hut!"

Angriff waved at them. "As you were."

Central Command formed a semi-circle of five terraces, with chairs facing long, curved wooden tops holding computers and monitors. The terraces ended at the bottom of the room twenty-five feet below in a sort of stage, backed by huge video panels. Beyond those were more electronics. Much like ancient Greek amphitheaters, the design of the room made the person at the bottom the focal point. By far the more striking feature, however, rose on pillars from the floor and soared high overhead.

"What in the nine circles of hell is that?" Angriff pointed.

Starting almost at the doorway, a ramp sloped up to a circular steel platform ninety feet across and supported by slender titanium columns, as well as braces coming down from the ceiling overhead. Side supports ran to either wall. A guard station stood at the top of the ramp. Steel grates made up the platform's floor with a double rail circling the perimeter. In the dead center of the platofrm stood the most impressive part of the elegant structure, a large, circular glass enclosure. It reminded Angriff of a science fiction movie.

"Sir, it's the office of the commanding general," Walling said. "Your office. That's electrochromic glass; push a button and it turns opaque, push it again and it's clear. From up there you have a three-sixty degree view of Central Comm, as well as a line of sight outside. There's four outer stations for your aides, a private bathroom inside your office, and a small kitchen for coffee and the like. Oh, and a meeting room, although it's tiny. There's a larger one on this level."

"It reminds me of Saddam Hussein's latrine, without the gold. I was expecting something simple, a room with some map boards and a desk, maybe with some folding chairs. Instead I get a futuristic whorehouse."

"Yes, sir. Umm—"

"Speak freely, Captain."

"Sir, I've been looking at this headquarters every day for the past eleven months, and I kept wondering why they needed such a... such a unique office for a military headquarters. It didn't make sense to me. I thought about it for months, and then it hit me. It has to be impressive, because if this brigade is really going to lay the groundwork for a rebirth of the United States, then that's where all the planning will be done. It's where anybody you want to impress will be brought. You are the supreme authority now, General, and you need surroundings that are commensurate with your stature."

Angriff had never thought of it in those terms before. "Are you're saying I'm president now?"

"No, maybe not president, sir. More like supreme military commander."

"So I'm a warlord. Whatever I am, Captain, as you said I'm the supreme power now, although of what is the question."

"Isn't that our mission, General, to define who and what we are now?"

"It is," Angriff said. "It's why we all chose to vacation in this lovely place and time. Now this command has to fulfill that mission, so the sooner this base is ready, the sooner we can get to work. By the way, does this place have a name?"

"Base Prime, sir. Or simply Prime."

"That sounds like a surgical ward. We've got to come up with something better. Who's in charge of getting this place up and running, Walling?"

"The commanding officer, sir. That is, you. Before you woke up, it was me."

"Me? I don't even know where the latrine is. Which I need to find soon, by the way. How long is this Deployment Plan A supposed to take to implement?"

"Estimates are a week, sir."

"Walling, as of this moment you're Officer in Charge of Deployment Plan A, and you have three days, not a week, to get me a detailed order of battle. I need a briefing in two hours, what it is, what you've done, what remains to be done, and when I can expect it done. You have my authority to do whatever is necessary to complete this deployment, and if anybody gives you any crap, have them see me. You report to me and only to me. Whatever your previous assignment was, make sure it's filled. Tell all officers at colonel and above that I want a staff meeting in three days at 1800 hours. If I have to order us into battle in three days, I want to be ready. Clear?"

Captain Walling's wonder showed on his face. "Clear, sir. Thank you for your trust."

"Don't make me regret it. Oh, and Captain? As of this moment you're a bird colonel. Are there any other officers who you need to help you get this show on the road?"

"Th-thank you, sir! Ummm... Lieutenants Noshimura and Jackson have been standing watch with me. Both are superb officers who know every detail of the base as well as I do."

"Fine. Make one a major and the other a captain. Handle it with personnel later. Do whatever it takes to get this thing going, Colonel, and I'll see you in two hours. Oh, and one more thing. As soon as General Fleming is squared away, bring him here immediately. Understand? Wake him up, give him some clothes, and get him up here."

Dazed, Walling saluted and turned, almost running into a corporal. Angriff smiled as he watched Walling head for the elevators. Then he surveyed his new kingdom. "Sergeant!"

The sergeant who had called for attention earlier looked up, then dropped some paperwork and came at a run. Over six feet tall, he looked Angriff in the eye. "Yes, sir!"

"What's your name, Sergeant?"

"Schiller, sir, John C."

"Sergeant Schiller, are you assigned to my headquarters?"

"Yes, sir. I've been awake for eleven months, sir."

"Good. Show me around this crystal palace. Let's start with my office. Oh, and we've got a strike mission out. I want an update. Better yet, loop me into the comm. network. And get me some coffee."

Chapter 15

There is no stone to mark my place,
Weep not for me, though there is no trace
Of the works I did upon this Earth,
I am with the One who knows my worth.
　　　From a 5th century sarcophagus found near Capua, Italy

June 18th, 0355 hours

Lying on the rocky soil looking at the sky, Tompkins was grateful that the stars overhead kept vigil with him, old friends on this last night of his life—so bright and clear in the cold sky that not even the luminescent moon could wash them out. Unlike his native Alabama, when the sun set in the high desert the temperature plummeted and the chill seeped into his body. His feet went numb, hunger pains gnawed his stomach, and exhaustion made him feel every bit the old man his age said he was. But staring at the familiar constellations reminded him of his long-ago boyhood.

Growing up had been different for Dennis Tompkins than for his classmates. His parents had not let him play with the video games his friends grew up playing. He did not own a computer until enrolling at Kennesaw State, and Johnny Tompkins never bought his son a cell phone. Tompkins' father had not liked the modern world, said twenty-first century civilization had a foundation of sand, and that some day it would all crash when the power went off. He insisted that young Dennis learn the ways of the woods, how to shoot a gun and how to survive in the wilderness without one, how to fish without a rod and build a fire without flint or matches, all against the day when civilization would end.

He made Dennis learn astronomy, where the stars and planets were in the night sky in each season and how to navigate by them. And how to enjoy them, too, lying in a field of cool green grass under a bright summer moon while fireflies floated under the trees, marveling at the silver beauty of the glittering universe overhead.

Dennis' friends all made fun of his father, however, they called him Dr. Nutjob and Bigfoot and other cruel names, the way only preteen boys can. One day, Dennis became so embarrassed he skipped school. When the school called to ask where he was, his father found him huddled on his bed, knees pulled close to his chest. He'd worried he'd get a whipping. Instead his father and mother pulled him out of school and began home-schooling him.

In the end, Johnny Tompkins had been right. Civilization did crash and all of Dennis' friends who'd spent so much time playing with their electronics were long since dead. He'd outlasted all of them.

Every one of the skills Johnny Tompkins taught young Dennis had been necessary to keep him alive for fifty years after The Collapse, but no skill would save him now.

Most of his men and the rescued women and girls had drifted off to sleep, but on the last night of his life Dennis Tompkins could not have slept if he'd wanted to. Tense and alert, with senses keyed to his environment, he listened for signs of infiltrators. The distant flutter of bats startled him as they entered the small cave in the cliff face as sunrise drew near. Night sounds quieted in the chill of pre-dawn. Sniffing, he smelled sage, dust, and the faint, sour scent of unwashed men, both his and those on the canyon floor below. And his vision was much sharper than he expected... the imminence of death could do that.

The sleepers were lumps in the moonlight, huddled together behind the stone wall. The trucks were ghostly outlines near the cliff's edge. The radio lay by his feet, but his rifle he never let go.

He jumped at a loud *click*. It sounded like a stick cracking, or maybe a rock giving way underfoot. He spun around and aimed where the ramp emptied onto the plateau. Sighting down his rifle, he wished for a night scope. Were they sneaking up during the night after all? Despite the moonlight, he couldn't see anything. He tried to control his breathing but found himself panting instead.

The screech of a prairie falcon startled him. And then a voice came from behind, a voice he had never heard before.

"Will the unidentified United States military unit who broadcast the activation code earlier tonight please identify yourself? I repeat, to the unknown United States military unit who made an earlier broadcast, please identify yourself."

Tompkins trembled, raising goose bumps on his arms and legs. He stared in disbelief at the voice's source—the radio, which hadn't spoken for more than forty years.

Gingerly, as if the battered metal rectangle housed a rattlesnake, Tompkins reached down and picked it up. The loud voice had awakened his men. In silence they crawled nearer, keeping their heads below the lip of the wall. Was it some sort of trick?

Tompkins keyed the mike, not sure what to say. "Hello?" His hands shook.

"Is this the American unit who broadcast the overtime activation code?"

"Yes."

"Skip, is that real?" said Hausser.

"Ssh!" he said, with the mike key off. Depressing it, he said, "Yes, I broadcast the code. Who is this?"

"Please identify your unit," the voice said, through a lot of static.

"Unit? What unit? What are you talking about?"

"If you are a United States military unit, please identify branch of service, call sign, situation, and unit strength."

"We're not a unit. We're just a few survivors, and when the sun comes up we won't even be that."

"You used highly classified United States Army codes. Where did you get them?"

"From the U.S. Army, where do you think? Look, whoever you are, we're just a bunch of guys who were in the army and got together when it all went to shit. And right now we're surrounded by Sevens who want to splatter our brains all over the rocks when sunrise gets here, unless you're the Sevens, in which case come and get us. We haven't heard from anybody in more than forty years and suddenly you're on the radio demanding to know all about us, but I've got a better question—who the hell are you?"

"Stand by, please." There was a short pause. "Please define Sevens."

"Sevens are the Caliph's men, the ones trying to kill us. Enemies."

By this time most of the women and some of the children were awake and within earshot, while his men huddled as close as possible. Thibodeaux forgot the danger, stood, and walked in circles, holding his pursed lips and listening. No telling how much longer the battery would last.

The disembodied voice clicked back to life. "We have a radio fix. Help is on the way to your location, ETA forty minutes. What is your exact situation?"

The thought again crossed Tompkins' mind that this could be some sort of trick, but then, their situation could not get any worse. With nothing to lose, he explained who he was and how they'd found themselves trapped on a flat plateau left over from the Old Days, and why two hundred heavily armed terrorists would storm up the ramp in less than half an hour. The voice promised to hurry the help as much as it could, but they would have to fight off their attackers until it got there.

The radio's battery began to fail and the voice faded. Tompkins turned up the volume to maximum hoping to get one final answer.

"Our battery's shot but you still haven't told me who you are. Who the hell am I talking to?"

"This is Overtime Prime."

"That doesn't tell me a damned thing. What or who is Overtime Prime?"

With the volume all the way up, the reply burst from the little speaker despite the weak battery. This time, it was a new voice, deep, gruff, and commanding, the voice of somebody in charge, and some part of Tompkins' brain recognized it. He had heard that voice before, a long, long time ago.

"Who are we? Hell, son, we're riding to your rescue; who do you think we are? We're the United States Cavalry!"

Tompkins shouldered his M16 and glanced down the sight. The edge of the plateau appeared as a jagged line a hundred yards from the low rock wall they'd built. Sharp stones dug into his knees, but he dared not rise to relieve the pressure. In the lightening sky he would make an easy target.

"Cavalry better hurry up, Skip," Thibodeaux said. "Else they'll be rescuing dead men."

"They'll be here when they're here. If they're really coming. For all we know they're riding horses. In the meantime, we get to have some fun." He forced a smile, but in truth Tompkins had decided it had been a trick, a ruse of war. Hell, it had to be! But if by some miracle they had found a long-lost United States Cavalry unit...

A head poked over the lip of the plateau and squeezed off a shot, which missed. It was time to fight.

"Mama Powell, everybody, no matter what happens, keep your heads down. All right, boys, they're coming. Time to earn your pay!"

With the sky getting brighter by the minute, details became visible. Fingers rested on triggers and eyes scanned the rocks for targets, and despite lack of sleep the six old men crouched behind the wall, ready to fight and die.

Without warning more than a dozen men rose at the plateau's far end and opened fire with automatic weapons. It was suppressing fire, designed to spray the low barricade so nobody could shoot back. Tompkins and his men returned fire anyway, but aiming was hard as bullets splattered against stone, sending rock chips flying as shrapnel.

During a brief lull Tompkins risked raising his head and saw two men stand up and start running toward him. Taking aim, he squeezed off two short bursts. His rounds hit both men, who fell backward as if swatted by a giant fist. He slid back behind cover and heard bullets whiz overhead.

As enemy fire increased, he stuck his M 16 over the barricade and fired blindly until the magazine was empty. When he pulled the gun back his hands were bloody and torn where splinters had cut them.

"Can't hold 'em, Skip!" Thibodeaux yelled. "There's too many!"

Tompkins slipped in a full magazine. "You first, John!"

Their eyes met, and Tompkins pointed at him. Instead of firing blindly above the rocks, Thidodeaux rose and squeezed off aimed shots, drawing return fire from dozens of Sevens as they poured onto the plateau. A bullet struck his left shoulder and knocked him back, but he kept firing with one hand.

"John!" Infuriated, Tompkins rose and found no shortage of targets. Fire discipline was overcome by events and he held the trigger down, spraying the mass of men running right at them. Several went down, screaming. When his gun ran dry he slipped behind the rocks and glanced down at Thibodeaux, who, while in obvious pain, otherwise looked all right. His faded green shirt had turned red.

"Flesh wound," he said. "I'm okay, Skip."

Panting and sweating in the chill of early morning, Tompkins slipped in his third to last magazine. Through a small hole in the rock barricade he checked how close the enemy had gotten and, like a wave, twenty men charged the wall at fifty yards distance. Swallowing, preparing to rise up and shoot until either he died or they did, he took one last look through the tiny opening.

The running Sevens disappeared in a tornado of dust, like a vortex had descended from Heaven and spun off body parts and blood. Shocked, without thinking he stood and stared as men were tossed and jerked around, and chunks of flesh and bone flew as if a giant piñata filled with meat had burst overhead. Slabs landed all over the plateau.

Only then did his mind register the heavy thump of a helicopter's rotors and the long-forgotten zipping sound of Gatling guns. A massive machine hovered in mid-air like a giant prehistoric insect, and through the canopy glass he could just make out the helmets of the two pilots. Painted on the helicopter's side was a large white star. The pilot stuck his hand out the side window and turned his thumb up, and the old man felt tears welling in his eyes.

"Well, butter my butt and call me a biscuit," he said.

Chapter 16

When you shoot, shoot to kill. When you attack, attack to destroy.
   Nick Angriff

June 18th, 0427 hours

Dawn painted the tops of the mineral-rich peaks flanking the valley in shades of orange and pink. Where the shadows of night held sway the slopes drained of color, from the bright hues near the top, to brown and then black. The last javelinas and packrats sniffed the desert floor for scraps left behind by the owls and bobcats.

Without warning, a strange vibration put every creature on alert. The animals made for safety in treetops and underground warrens. A storm bore down on them, coming fast, unlike anything they had ever known.

Racing down the valley at one hundred feet, the two AH-72 Comanches ripped through the dawn air as the huge rotors propelled them north at more than two hundred knots, spraying dust and rocks in their wake. The rumble of the massive engines echoed from the ridgelines and the air itself pulsed with energy. The Comanches stayed in the valley between the two ridgelines because the cold and heavy night air close to the ground offered a more stable flying platform. No thermals rose from the prairie yet, as they would by midday when the sun scorched the arid soil, and the two helicopters were steady in their pilots' grip. Plotz and Arnold flew in the wingman's position, thirty feet to Randall's right and fifty behind.

"Ripsaw Two, this is Ripsaw Real. You take the ridge and see what you can do to keep the shitheads off our people. They could be breathing heavy, so watch your aim. I've got the valley. You heard the CO. No mercy. Vaporize the fuckers."

"With extreme prejudice," Plotz said.

The Forward Looking Infrared (FLIR) picked up multiple signatures on the valley floor ahead, but the dawn washed out most of the screen. It did not matter; within seconds they made visual contact.

Smoke funneled upward near an outcropping of the ridge and Randall knew they had found their target. They could not tell if the trapped Americans had been overrun or not, but things appeared desperate. Randall firewalled the throttle, turned the FIRE switch to ARMED and flipped the gun-sight screen down over his helmet's faceplate. The valley came into sharp focus. Vehicles of all shapes and sizes clustered around the rocky outcropping. Dozens of men milled around the vehicles.

"Ripsaw Real, I've got Ali Babas on the plateau and closing on some sort of barricade. Time to second wife." Alisha Plotz veered left in a long arc, closing on the ledge at two hundred miles per hour.

"Roger that, R2. Prime, this is Ripsaw Real. Have visual on multiple vehicles in the valley, many burps. Am commencing attack run."

"Roger that, Ripsaw Real."

Randall focused on his target. "All right, Bunny, let's ruin somebody's morning."

Randall pushed the music note on his control computer screen and selected song number twelve. He had dreamed about this moment, this song, the very rightness of the whole fantasy, pictured it over and over in his mind, and now it had come to life. A thousand times he'd imagined the Forward Targeting Sight centered on a cluster of burps while he depressed the trigger, and now it was happening. Then the music started. Two hard drum notes, two more with a kick drum and repeated three more times, followed by a grinding guitar, and the singer's voice asking if Randall knew his enemy.

Bobbing his head as the vocals screamed through his headphones, Randall squinted into the gunsight and sang along. He had no damned idea who his enemy was and he did not care. He intended turning them into jelly using a storm of fifty-caliber American get-fucked.

Paco Mohammed paused with a mouthful of goat jerky. In the distance was a weird *whop-whop-whop*, fast and unlike anything he'd heard before. It was like the wind, but also not like the wind. Electric fingers jolted his spine with a primitive fear he could not explain.

Everyone in the valley stopped whatever they were doing and peered around. Paco squinted. Nothing moved in the deep shadows that lingered in the valley, but the sound grew louder, echoing from the canyon walls and making it hard to tell which direction it came from.

Someone shouted and pointed to the south.

"¿Donde?" Paco asked. "Ernesto, what are they pointing at?"

"There, in the air, see the sun reflecting off of something?" Ernesto's eyes bulged.

"Mi Dios," Paco said. "¡Esos son los helicópteros!"

Two dark shapes headed straight for him, and Paco realized what the metallic blurs were. His aunts and mother had told him of flying monsters the Mexican Federales had used to patrol the empty lands around their village, fire breathing demons named helicopteros. Paco assumed El Emir had sent them, but why? If the Emir controlled giant flying monsters, why send them to re-capture some runaway girls and kill a few old men? The Emir knew Paco would not fail him, so it made no sense. And if the Emir had not sent them, who else could have?

One of the helicopteros split away from the other and headed for the ridge. The other kept coming, and Paco heard the faint sound of music over the droning *whop-whop-whop*. As the monster neared, Paco felt more fascinated than afraid. He started waving, but as the beast came closer, he could see through its huge eye into its soul, and what he saw looked like two men with bubbles on their heads. Were those the souls of bad men they had eaten? He could not explain it any other way.

Then two bright lights appeared on either side of the monsters' belly, strange lights that flickered. Paco knew those lights well, but a millisecond's delay between his mind processing what it saw and deciding what action to take had a high cost in blood. He had just opened his mouth to scream a warning when dust and debris flew up the canyon floor, speeding straight toward him.

Men disappeared in sprays of red—the men who'd traveled north from Mexico with him a decade ago, seeking loot. His childhood friends, cousins, brothers—the men he'd kept safe for so long.

They weren't safe any longer.

Trucks and cars jumped and flipped around as jagged bits of shrapnel zipped through the air. Men screamed, tires exploded, and trucks ignited. Those not killed in the first firing pass wound up spattered with gore. One second Paco saw Ernesto standing twenty feet in front of him; the next his cousin's upper body vaporized in a storm of bullets. The legs and hips stood for a moment before collapsing. The river of bullets sped his way.

Paco dove under a nearby truck as dozens of fifty caliber slugs tore up the spot where he had stood. Before he stopped rolling, pain lanced through his left hand, left shoulder, and leg. Bullets ripped through the truck and smacked all around him. A splinter struck his left eye and the stream of shells moved on.

It had taken less than four seconds.

Closing his eyes he said a quick prayer. In his mind he made the sign of the cross, careful to show no outward sign of doing so, or to utter the name Jesus. Either would lead to a bullet in the head from his Islamic masters. He could not be sure they cared whether he truly had converted to Islam or not, but they cared a great deal about people who openly had not.

Paco inspected his wounded hand and tried to roll over. The pain felt like something sharp and hot lodged in his shoulder, while his leg had gone numb. The truck sagged low to the ground, so he had a hard time twisting his body. Several times he banged into the metal chassis. A hole in the palm of the wounded hand caused the muscles to spasm into a claw. Skin hung loose from the exit wound and blood ran down his wrist. He could feel his shirt and pants getting sticky and wet, and knew he was bleeding out. He needed to crawl out from under the truck and stop the bleeding, but when he moved the pain caused him to black out.

Seconds later, Paco woke to a smell so dangerous it penetrated the fog in his brain—gasoline. Blinking away tears, he twisted his neck forward, where a stream of gas poured from a ruptured fuel line, pooled, then ran straight toward him. All around him vehicles exploded and burned. One spark and he would burn to death under a truck in the middle of nowhere.

The *whop-whop-whop* faded away.

He yelled for help but none came. Using his good arm and leg, he scooted and slid clear of the truck. His shoulder throbbed; his wounded leg still felt stiff but not painful. His vision blackened at the edges. Half stumbling, dragging his mangled leg, he moved away from the knot of trucks and toward some heaps of rock fifty yards away.

A man without legs reached out to him, mouthing something incomprehensible, and Paco recognized his cousin Jorge. Horrified, he limped faster for the safety of the rocks. When he was close enough to lower himself behind the shield of stone, his vision blackened again from blood loss. The world spun. He blinked and tried to stay on his feet.

Here came the *whop-whop-whop* again, heading back for another attack run. Paco turned as it flashed by. A huge white star was painted on the helicopter's side, and there were letters on its long tail—U.S. ARMY.

Paco could not read Spanish, much less English, but his memory was excellent and the letters burned into his mind. As the blood flowed freely from his torn body, Paco fell unconscious into a clump of stones.

"Ripsaw Real, I've got at least fifty Ali Babas over here in the rocks, I'm going to make another pass." Plotz's voice remained keyed up but professional.

Banking his own Comanche for a second pass, Randall could not help smiling at the mention of Ali Babas. "Ripsaw Two, flashbacks of Iraq?"

"You know it, Double R. Fun times. I'm about to stream live; we can swap war stories after."

"Roger that. Drinks on me."

Flaming vehicles littered the valley as tiny figures scattered, like roaches when light caught them in the open. Many more lay still in the dirt. Two trucks sped off to the east and Randall turned toward them, slowed, and hovered. Carlos armed two Dragonfires. The holographic display in Randall's helmet gave him adjusted real-time flight path and target data, and prompted him to fire when the circle with the crosshairs lit bright green. When it did, Carlos punched the launch button and the first Dragonfire sped from under the helicopter's thick starboard wing. Flight time clocked at less than one second, and the explosion ripped the lead truck's chassis in two, scattering metal and body parts for a hundred yards.

The driver of the second truck, a battered Volvo, swerved hard right to avoid the cart-wheeling wreckage. He cut right in front of Randall's gunsight at a range of three hundred yards. A burst from the miniguns tore through the Volvo. The driver disappeared in a spray of gore and the vehicle jackknifed, rolled over three times, and rested on its side. Flames engulfed the wreck and Randall spotted someone staggering in the fire.

The rest of the burp's panicked and scattered. For fifteen minutes Randall and Carlos hunted the valley without mercy. No vehicle made its escape and no refuge proved safe against the relentless stream of fifty caliber shells. Men vanished in clouds of bloody mist. A few tried to fight back, but Randall stood off and smoked them without ever being in danger himself. By the time he ran out of targets, the valley floor resembled a scrap yard choked with shredded steel, dead bodies, and the reek of burning gasoline.

"Ripsaw Two, this is Ripsaw Real. Burps all smoked. What's your sitrep?"

"Double R, still a few Ali Babas playing hide and seek in the rocks. Could use help if you're free."

"On our way."

Caught between the two Comanches, the remaining men were hunted down one by one and wiped out. A few buried themselves deep in the rocks, but a well-placed Dragonfire solved that problem. The last man climbed onto a large outcropping, knelt, pressed his hands together, and held them up, begging for his life. Plotz got to him first. She held her gunship in a hover fifty feet away and watched the man sobbing. Tears glistened on his cheeks in the morning sun. She watched him a moment longer before pressing the trigger.

Several of the girls rose, peering over the makeshift rock wall, watching the fighting with their eyes opened wide. Tompkins waved and yelled for them to get down, but nobody heard him over the screams of the wounded, the *whump-whump* of helicopter rotors, and the ripping stutter of the Gatling guns. He tried to duck-walk down the line to pull them under cover, but those days had vanished. Having no other choice, he rose and half-stumbled, half-trotted the fifty feet to where the women and girls were pressed hard against the stones. Panting from the exertion, he pulled the standing girls down and out of the line of fire.

"What's going on, Major?" asked Mama Powell.

"I'm not sure," he said. "But I think we're being rescued."

After minutes that seemed like hours, the ruckous died down, with no more zip of the Gatling guns or pops of rifles. Even the wounded stopped screaming. The *whump* of the rotors became the only noise.

Tompkins motioned them all to stay behind cover and rose to his knees, then to his feet. Several hundred feet away, one of the giant helicopters hung in the air, its front pointed to the ridgeline. Shading his eyes, he saw a man kneeling, hands clenched as if begging. There was a quick *zip* and the man vanished in a fountain of red. A glob of meat slid down the stone and fell to the valley floor.

The two helicopters prowled back and forth above the valley without firing. Then one of them drew near the plateau, slowed, and landed in a swirl of dust and pebbles. Tompkins motioned everybody down again. The whine of the huge turboshafts quieted as the pilot idled the engine.

He didn't move as the pilot's door opened and a man in an orange flight suit stepped down and walked toward him, holding a helmet. Although he could not believe it, Tompkins finally recognized the giant aircraft as the last helicopter gunship ever developed by the American military, the fabled Comanche. He had seen a squadron of them once, a lifetime before.

The pilot stopped short of the wall and looked him up and down. Tompkins could not help staring at his shoulder patch, the American flag. For the first time he felt shame over his faded dungarees that might, or might not, have once been a uniform.

"I'm Captain Joseph Randall, United States Army," the pilot said.

Tompkins cocked his head. "The United States Army? How is that possible?"

The wind blew his mutter away and the pilot shook his head. He seemed so young. "Could you repeat that, please? I couldn't hear you."

"I am Major Dennis Tompkins, also United States Army," Tompkins said in a louder voice.

Randall saluted and held it. Nobody had saluted Tompkins for decades and it took him a few seconds to remember protocol and return the salute. Everybody behind the stone wall crowded close, except for two small girls who ran to the helicopter, followed by their mother.

"How is this possible, Captain? How did you get here? Better yet, where have you been all these years?"

"I think we'd better leave the questions for debriefing, Major. We're low on ammo and there could be more burps around."

"Burps?" Tompkins said.

"Slang for butt-ugly raghead pricks. The people we've been killing."

"Oh. We call them Sevens."

"I suppose so, sir. How many people do you have?"

The question snapped Tompkins back to the present and he glanced over his ragtag crew. Other than some cuts from rock splinters, and the flesh wound to John Thibodeaux, he could see no serious wounds and no fatalities.

"Let's see, twenty-three women and children, six of us, so twenty-nine total."

Randall scratched his neck, peering into the distance at nothing. "I don't want to make two trips, Major, but I'm not sure we've got the room or lift capacity to take everybody in one. Hang on a minute; I'm going to see what my co-pilot thinks."

Randall trotted back to his helicopter. Tompkins turned. His men encircled him, with the women and children standing close. They all seemed stunned, anxious, as if this were some kind of fantasy.

Thibodeaux spoke for them all. "Skip, are we saved?"

Tompkins felt tears again and this time he could not stop them. "John, I think we are."

"Overtime Prime, this is Ripsaw Real. We are heading back with Ripsaw Two. Both of us have a full house. Request all available medical teams meet us in the hangar bay to treat civilians. We also have six United States Army personnel on board who may require treatment. Over."

"Read you, Ripsaw Real. What's your ETA?"

"About forty-five minutes."

"You are cleared to land when you arrive; the hangar doors are open. Will have med teams standing by."

Again another voice broke in, and Randall recognized it from earlier that morning. It carried more vigor this time. "Ripsaw Real, this is General Nicholas Angriff. Please verify that you are transporting United States Army personnel."

Joe Randall froze in his seat. That was why the CO's voice had sounded familiar! Nick the A... shit! What was *he* doing there?

Carlos nudged him and Randall came out of his shock.

"I'm sorry, General Angriff. Yes, I have U.S. Army personnel on board, six to be exact."

"To be clear, Ripsaw Real, do you mean six survivors who have not been in Long Sleep?" Angriff said.

"Affirmative, sir. That's what they claim, anyway. And sir, they're all... well, they're not young men."

"Ripsaw Real, if they are survivors of the collapse, they should be at least in their seventies. Does this appear to be true?"

Randall turned in his seat. Tompkins and his men squatted just behind the cockpit, squeezed in tight and ears cocked to one side of the conversation. "Yes, sir, that would appear to be the case."

Someone tapped his shoulder; it was Tompkins. Randall slipped off his right headphone cup and leaned close.

"Captain, did I hear the name General Angriff?" Tompkins shouted. "Or was I imagining it? It's very loud back here."

"Yes, sir," Randall said. "It looks like General Angriff is our CO."

Tompkins could not have looked more shocked. "Nick Angriff? Nick the A?"

"I wouldn't call him that, sir. Do you know him?"

"We've met," Tompkins said.

Randall waited for him to say more, but he did not, so he slipped his headphones back on. "General, this is going to sound pretty weird, but their commanding officer says you two have met."

Chapter 17

*I left behind all of my friends, in the stream of Time that never ends;
But when I saw your face again, I knew that I should make amends.
The wrongs I did were never right, and the rights were never wrong,
Now I have one final chance, to sing one final song.*
  "Lament," Sixtus Calliphus, 3rd century A.D.

June 18th, 0934 hours

Somehow, somebody had found Angriff a cup of coffee and he could not believe how good it tasted.

"Ripsaw Real, say again."

"The commander of the army personnel on board says he has met you, General. He's a major."

"Ripsaw Real, does he mean that he knew me before I went cold, is that what he's trying to say?"

"I believe so, sir."

"Please verify."

While he waited Angriff looked around his new command. Hard to believe enough money had been found to build such a place. He'd expected to wake up to a single battalion with nothing more than the bare necessities of survival, maybe living in tents and hunting food. From the look of it, he got a mountain crammed with enough military gear to win a war against a small country. Or maybe even a big one.

"Overtime Prime, this is Ripsaw Real. Sir, that's affirmative. He says he knew you before the Collapse. His name is Tompkins."

He knew the name, which meant he knew the man. But how? His eyes roamed as he tried to remember. Forgetting radio discipline, he said, "Did he say where we met?"

"Sir, he says you met on top of some castle in Austria."

The terra-cotta landscape raced by as they skimmed south at more than 150 knots. Tompkins caught a glimpse of some animal running for cover, then, straight ahead, the rising silhouette of a mountain range. The peaks rose for thousands of feet but the Comanche flew at barely two hundred feet. When more seconds passed without the helicopter going up, he started to panic. They were getting real close!

After a jolt, airspeed bled away. Winds hugging the mountainside buffeted the helicopter as it approached the wall of bare rock. Below them, the slope began to rise. The aircraft crept forward, suspended in the air like a kite as the pilot fought to hold it steady in the strong air currents.

Inside the helicopter, bodies had shifted and Tompkins could no longer see straight ahead. He shouldered into the packed bodies of his men. Between the pilot's headrest and Thibodeaux's cheek rose the mountain, less than fifty feet away, but instead of rocks and trees, an enormous gate had opened, revealing what appeared to be a hangar. The impossible sight disoriented him and he leaned back, shaking his head.

The overloaded helicopters passed into the rocky slope. Tompkins had a brief moment to inspect the massive sliding doors themselves, and could not believe the how much the texturing matched the surrounding landscape. Inside, the helicopter hovered over a bright landing area and then descended until the wheels touched down with a light bump. The whine of the engine died as the Comanche powered down.

Once the rotors stopped turning, the cargo doors slid back. A crowd poured from tunnels into the hangar and surrounded the aircraft. Gentle hands began helping the women and children down.

Needing a moment, Tompkins deplaned last. His legs ached and he feared the four-foot drop to the hangar deck would cause them to buckle. Strong hands reached up, however, and lifted him down into the group of men and women wearing the uniform of the United States Army. Everybody seemed to be talking at once, patting him on the back and asking him questions, then silence fell like a blanket.

A large man appeared at the tunnel's mouth, a man with three stars on his collar. The soldiers made way for him and he walked straight for Tompkins. A lifetime had passed since Tompkins had met General Nicholas Angriff, but he would never forget Angriff's angry face on that bitter cold day so long before, a face that did not look one day older than it had fifty years ago.

He saluted even though his shoulder ached. Angriff stopped in front of him and returned the salute, examining his face. Tompkins could tell Angriff recognized him, but struggled to put his face with the memory.

If this man has really had been in the wilderness for five decades, Angriff thought, *he looks pretty damned good.* Sure, Tompkins had scratches and dried blood on his left cheek, and he needed to gain some weight, but otherwise he looked better than fine, all things considered.

"Major, you and your men are American heroes," he said. "I want a personal debriefing, just you and me. I can't imagine what you've lived through. But first, the medical staff is going to check you out; we're going to get you some fresh clothes and then some hot chow. When was the last time you and your men had a hot meal?"

"Hot meal, sir?" Tompkins said. "We cooked a snake yesterday, or maybe the day before. A big one."

Gads. "A snake?"

"Yes sir, a green rattlesnake. The Mexicans used to call them Verde Mojave. Not bad tasting when you're hungry. Just don't let it bite you. The venom is nasty."

"A rattlesnake," Angriff repeated, as if he could not believe it. "Damn, Major... Tompkins, was it?"

Dread filled his voice. "Yes, sir. Tompkins, Dennis D."

"And we've met before?"

"Yes, sir." Tompkins' body tensed and his elbows dug into his sides.

"Where and when did we meet?"

"On top of the Hohensalzburg, sir. I escorted you to an airplane that was waiting on you." He said it fast, as if preferring to get the whole thing over with.

Recognition dawned. Angriff laughed. "Oh, yeah, now I remember. *Escorted* isn't the word I would use, Major. Kidnapped, maybe."

"Sir, I was under orders—"

Angriff held up a hand. "I'm not angry, Major. In a very real sense, I'm here because of you. And I'm glad that I'm here, so I'm glad you... *escorted* me to my meeting. Now, go get checked out and cleaned up. Have a cup of coffee; it's pretty good. When you feel human again, I want a full accounting of how and why you wound up on that ridge."

A few steps away, Joe Randall dropped his eyes and took a step back. Nick Angriff stood less than ten feet away. Nick the A, in the flesh.

Shit!

Somebody pointed at Carlos, someone else at Plotz, standing beside him. Before Randall could sink back into the crowd, somebody shouted he was the mission commander. Angriff turned and waved him over.

Shit!

The crowd parted for him. After exchanging salutes, Angriff sized him up and nodded. "You were mission commander, Captain Randall? I spoke with you on the comm."

Randall forced a smile and nodded. "Yes, General. The team responded beautifully. They're true professionals."

"Bravo zulu, Captain. I'm damned proud of you." Angriff shook hands all around and said something to each in turn. He watched a medic bandage Arnold's hand, injured by small arms fire. "That was good work, Sergeant. You need anything?'

Arnold grinned. "My grandmother had a recipe for ambrosia, General. She made it at our family reunions every Christmas. Her name was Ather Lee Dowdy Berry, Dowdy being her maiden name. I can't say why, exactly, but tasting her ambrosia again would be special. I've got the recipe." Arnold tended to be quiet and reserved. Randall was surprised by the long answer.

"I see," Angriff said, amused. "Ambrosia? Well, Sergeant, I don't know what our food situation is yet, but I'll see what I can do. Hell, I like ambrosia as much as any Southern boy."

He moved on, staring at the massive helicopter, and smiled when he came to the image of the semi-naked blonde on the aircraft's side and the name *Tank Girl.*

"Should I pat her ass for good luck?" he asked, and did. Randall smiled back, but it was a sickly smile. After a few more minutes inspecting the massive gunships, the general walked off and vanished in the crowd, heading toward the hangar's exit.

As the crowd dispersed, Carlos turned to Randall. "So?"

"So what?"

"Really, Joe? You're gonna bullshit me? When you saw Angriff, you damned near fainted. What's up with that?"

Randall looked around to make sure nobody could overhear and lowered his voice. "You remember Morgan, don't you?"

Carlos grinned. "Tank Girl! I remember her tits; I see them every day." He nodded at the image painted on their Comanche.

"Well, I wouldn't say anything about her tits around the CO."

"Yeah, why not? He got something against hot blondes?"

"Not unless they're his daughter."

"Are you shitting me? Tank Girl was Nick the A's daughter? Is that why you never used her last name?" Carlos did a double take. "And he just stroked her ass?"

Randall nodded. "It gets worse."

"Worse? Does he know about you two? If he doesn't, you're golden. It's not like she's gonna tell... whoa, I'm sorry, Joe. That was thoughtless of me. I know you really cared for her."

He clapped Carlos on the shoulder. "It's okay. There's a little more to the story than I've told you."

"So give."

"Not now. Maybe later. But trust me, this is really not something you want to know."

Everybody wanted to be near the CO, to get a look at the legend up close, and most were officers. As a PFC, she could not muscle her way through the crowd; the risk of being stopped outweighed the chance of success. However, her lowly rank guaranteed nobody would pay attention to her until she'd sunk the blade deep into Nick Angriff's neck.

Working the edge of the crowd, she spotted a lane opening up thirty feet away, and while she couldn't see for certain, Angriff had to be moving toward the hangar exit. On the crowd's outer edge she slid through to where the people thinned out and she saw the man himself, less than fifty feet away and heading right for her.

Smiling and waving with her left hand, she slipped her right inside her fatigue blouse and brought out a slim blade, more like a crystal letter opener than a deadly weapon. But the slightest cut would allow the poison to enter his bloodstream, with fatal results. Of course, she would not long outlive her target, compliments of the cyanide capsule hidden in her gums, but that did not matter. As a martyr for the cause, her name would be revered forever, an honor which more than justified her sacrifice.

Angriff strode closer, stopping to salute well-wishers and shake a few hands, showing the famous charisma that inspired such loyalty in his subordinates. Little did they know that within seconds he would be dead, and her only regret was not being alive to witness the hysterical reactions as he convulsed in death spasms.

Cheering along with everyone else, she pulled the knife behind her head to strike. As she drew in a breath, someone shoved a cloth into her mouth. Both arms and legs were pinned in hands like steel clamps and a low voice whispered in her ear, "Not on my watch."

A strong grip pried the knife from her grasp. Fingers grabbed her hair and yanked her head back so a thick collar could be looped around her neck and tightened, like a leash. She struggled as they dragged her away, yet it was done with such precision few people in the crowd noticed anything.

Her captors dragged her into a small side passage, where the man who seemed to be the leader faced her. His lean face was cut by sharp creases, and he had sandy hair and eyebrows. She noticed his eyes most, however. Dark blue and deep set, she had seen eyes like his in other men, men who dealt in death, the eyes of a killer.

"Don't worry about chewing the glass," he said. "We're not going to let you do that."

The cloth prevented her biting down on the capsule, and when she tried to keep her jaws clenched he inserted a metal device between her lips and used a gear to pry her mouth open. Once secured, he reached in and removed the vial.

"Huh." He inspected the glass-and-metal tube. "Now we know who sent you. Let's go find out who else is here and what they've got planned."

She tried to speak despite her jaws being held wide open; it came out as a gargling sound.

"You're already trying to tell me everything you know, right? But if you're not, if instead you're telling me to go fuck myself, well, that will change as we become friends. And just so you know that I'm sincere, I'll tell you my name before I ask you for yours. Call me Ghost."

SECTION 3

Chapter 18

If you must choose between being feared and being loved, choose feared.
  Machiavell, "The Prince"

June 18th, 1951 hours

"I am sorry, General, but there are no exceptions. I cannot sign off on you taking command until I have checked you thoroughly, according to regulations." Doctor Friedenthall might have only been a major, but as the ranking medical officer on the base it was his duty to certify all personnel as medically ready to take up their responsibilities, including the commanding general.

"Schiller!" Angriff yelled. "Get in here."

Just outside the glass office perched high above Central Command, Sergeant Schiller jumped from his chair and double-timed it into Angriff's office, carrying his clipboard. He'd started doing that after the first four times he'd been called for.

"Yes, General?"

"Block me an hour with the doctor sometime between three and seven days from now."

"Yes, sir. Will that be all?"

"No, tell Colonel Walling I want to see him A-sap. And get me some more coffee."

"General—" The doctor paused. "I have to do my examination right now, otherwise—"

"Otherwise what?" Angriff raised his eyebrows in disbelief that a major would dare argue with him. Who cared if he was technically correct? "Three-star generals have always been gods, *Major*, but since I'm now your CO, when it comes to the Seventh Cavalry I'm the only god you've got. I understand you've got your own job to do, but there are thousands who need your attention right now and I've got critical matters that need mine. Savvy, *Captain*? Schiller will let you know when I'm available. And the next time I tell you something, you'd damned well better treat it as an order from God the Father. Is that clear?"

Friedenthall swallowed, and then saluted. "Yes, sir!"

Scowling, Angriff steepled his fingers and stared at his chief medical officer for nearly a full minute without speaking. The air circulators had not refreshed much of the base yet, and the stale air was warm. Sweat ran down Friedenthall's face, but he held his salute and his tongue.

"Two more things." Angriff finally returned the salute. "First, if anybody else says no to his or her mandatory examination, regardless of rank, you tell them it's a direct order from me and noncompliance will be taken as insubordination to the commanding general. Second, in a military organization this large, the medical services are critical, and that's especially true in these extraordinary circumstances. I can't have such a vital component of this brigade under the command of a major; it needs more brass behind it. So go find a silver oak leaf somewhere, Lieutenant Colonel."

Friedenthall was stunned. "Sir?"

"Go, Colonel. You've got a lot of work to do. I want a full report on where we stand in your department within two days."

The newly minted Colonel did not linger. His commander had called him captain when his rank at that moment had been major, and then promoted him. No one could miss the implication—follow orders and all would be well; argue with Nick the A and things wouldn't be. And with the acoustics in Central Command, that message would have been heard throughout.

After Friedenthall almost ran down the ramp and out of the headquarters, Angriff turned to Sergeant Schiller. "Too harsh?"

"Sir, it's not my place to comment on the general's decisions or actions."

Angriff grunted something like *ummp*. "You can't comment to the general's face, you mean, but maybe over a beer to a buddy in the noncoms club. Sergeant, how long were you in the army before you went cold?"

"Twenty-three years, sir."

"Any specialties? What were you good at?"

"Sir, I'm just a line non-com. I like being around the men; I feel most useful there."

"What is your proudest moment, Sergeant? Tell me about that. What makes your dick feel bigger when you think about it?"

Schiller blushed. Impossible to believe the language bothered him. Obscene slang was daily fare among those who humped a pack and slung a rifle. But maybe he hadn't expected to hear it in the sterile office of his commanding general, where everything was chrome, steel, and glass. Angriff waited for him to answer.

"My platoon was lurping through Indian Country in Kandahar when an IED took out the lead Humvee. The terrain was pretty rough; there was a sharp drop of maybe fifty feet on our right and a rocky slope on our left. The platoon commander was in the Humvee that got hit and his right leg got blown off at the knee. As platoon sergeant I took command. The burps had built a sort of wall about two hundred yards up the slope and opened up on us. The whole thing was Charlie Foxtrot."

"Easy to do in Kandahar."

"Yes, sir. Well, the ground between us and them was nothing but moon dust and rocks, no cover at all, but I knew we didn't have a chance unless we could drive them away from that wall. They had slits to shoot through and we were taking heavy fire. I ordered the second Humvee to pick up survivors and gave them two minutes for first aid. We were lucky enough to have an LAV-M with us—"

Angriff held up a hand. "That's a Marine vehicle. Where the hell did you get that?"

"The story I got, sir, was that when the Marines pulled out they left the vehicle for the Afghan Army to use, and somehow we wound up with it."

"Sounds like somebody stole it." Angriff smiled.

"I wouldn't know, sir. The hardest part was getting eighty-one millimeter rounds at the FOB; we mostly used either sixties or one twenties. The platoon also had a Bradley along; I think it was an M3 with the extra ammo. I ordered the LAV to put mortar rounds over the wall on our left flank as suppressing fire. The Humvees were returning fire and hit one burp just as he was about to light off an RPG. When he fell backwards the round must have exploded behind the wall, because the fire slacked off.

"Once our wounded were loaded, I had the Bradley floor it around the wall on our left, their right flank. Two RPG rounds fired while we were moving missed, although my vehicle was sprayed with shrapnel and we suffered a few minor wounds. Within seconds you couldn't see anything because of the dust cloud we raised.

"We turned the corner one after another and shot at anything on foot, but there weren't many targets visible. Not wanting to risk collisions I ordered a halt in place, even though it was a risk. Well, the burps were long gone, only we didn't know it. They had to have gone up the slope and if we had seen them we could have wiped them out.

"We counted 17 dead T-men, then headed home to get our wounded treated. I felt bad about ground transporting them. Our loot was in a lot of pain, even morphined up, but I couldn't call in a Dustoff because we didn't know where the burps were. We got back to the FOB with no further enemy contact. Lieutenant Jaskowitz was medevaced from there. I have to admit, General, I was pretty happy how it turned out."

"You should have been, Sergeant. That was damned fine work. It's too bad Augustus didn't have you at the Teutoberg Forest instead of Varus."

"Sir?"

"Augustus was the first Roman emperor. In 9 A.D., the same thing happened to three Roman legions that were ambushed in the Teutoberg Forest, in what is now Germany. They were commanded by a Roman aristocrat named Publius Quinctillus Varus. Varus was warned that he was in danger, but like most Romans of the period he didn't think his legions could be defeated by the disorganized tribes of Germans. He led them into an ambush exactly like you described, except instead of a drop on one side it was a swamp, with an upslope wall on the other side.

"When his men were attacked, Varus panicked. A good leader probably could have rallied the legionaires, assaulted the wall, and driven off the Germans. The Romans would have suffered heavy casualties, but most probably would have survived. As it turned out, they were massacred almost to the last man. It sounds to me like you were in Varus' position, but you kept your head and won the battle."

"Just doing my job, General." Sergeant Schiller paused. "I'm just a simple infantry sergeant."

Angriff grinned. "Don't try to play me, Sergeant."

"Sir, no, sir, that was not my intent."

"Uh-huh. You're afraid I'm going to stick you with some administrative duty when you really want to be in a combat platoon. The bad news for you is that your combat is right here in this..." He spread his hands and glanced around the glistening surroundings. "...office. I like you, Sergeant. What's more, I think I can trust your judgment. So I want you close to me. I want you running my day-to-day operations. Not the whole headquarters, just my office. Think of it as a liaison with the troops in the field." Schiller started to say something, but Angriff shook his head. "Nope, sorry, Sergeant. Three stars beats three stripes. I need your input and good judgment more than I need you lurping all over Arizona. That's an order, clear?"

"Clear, sir," Schiller said, sounding disappointed.

"But the news gets even worse, Schiller. There's a lot of platoons in this brigade, and at some point I'm going to have to replace one of their commanders. When that happens, I already know who my number one choice is going to be." He pointed at the sergeant. "And while you might like that part, Sergeant, when it happens I'm going to pull those stripes off your sleeve and put a silver bar on your collar."

Chapter 19

Strong leaders listen to cautious advice, weak ones take it.
   Nick Angriff

June 18th, 2218 hours

Ben Walling could not believe he had forgotten his most important duty. Sure, being Officer of the Watch had been hard and Temporary Officer Commanding even more so, and then getting handed the responsibility for the brigade's deployment was the most difficult thing he had ever attempted. He prided himself on doing a superior job, no matter the task, but damn, how could he forget that?

When Schiller waved him in, Angriff pushed back in his chair and rubbed his eyes. He looked tired. "What is it, Colonel? Something gone wrong?"

"No, sir," Walling said. "Well, yes, sir, but that's not why I'm here. In an effort to deploy this brigade as fast as possible, I forgot one of my duties. As Officer of the Watch upon activation, I was supposed to hand this envelope to you as soon as possible." He passed over the large white envelope. "I'm sorry, General. I don't like letting you down."

The envelope was marked COMMANDING GENERAL ONLY. Angriff picked up a bush knife, since of all things it appeared the planners of Overtime had forgotten letter openers, and slit the envelope's flap. A small lump lay at the bottom, wrapped in foam, along with a single sheet of paper. He read the paper and his eyes opened wider. Finishing, he ignored Walling and called for Schiller.

"Yes, General," Schiller said.

"It appears there's another promotion, Sergeant. Would you handle the paperwork?"

"Of course, General." Schiller accepted the sheet and went back to his desk.

"Well, Colonel, that's something I never expected."

"Good news, sir?"

"I've been promoted. Actually, double promoted." He held up the small object and carefully cut away the foam. Walling could see gold. Holding the objects in the palm of his hand, Angriff displayed it so that Walling could see the two sets of five gold stars.

Howard Wilson Dupree worked in the shadow of the Crystal Palace and several times overhead General Angriff's exchanges with others, so he wanted to be certain of his suspicions before he reported them to the NCO. Nobody wanted to meet Nick the A the way Major Friedenthall had, although General Angriff's reputation toward lower ranks was reported as being far more sympathetic. Nevertheless, the brigade had not even fully deployed yet, so who could say for certain how the commander would react in different situations?

At some point, however, you had to do your job and take the consequences. After running the numbers seven times, just to be sure, Dupree approached Sergeant Schiller.

"What have you got, Dupree?" Schiller said.

"I don't know, Sergeant. I think it's a problem, but I'm not sure. I don't want to bother anybody in the middle of the deployment, but I don't want to keep quiet if it's something to worry about."

"Show me."

Dupree led Schiller to his work station and went over the troublesome figures, showing in detail the actual numbers and what they should have been.

Schiller waited until Colonel Walling walked by and explained Dupree's conclusions, asking whether to bring it to Angriff's attention.

"It's a good catch, Dupree," Walling said. "But this isn't the best time. Do this—put all of that in a file, then try to see if there are any other similar anomalies. Give your results to Sergeant Schiller in three days. Sergeant, I'll leave it to your discretion whether I need to see the results. And again, Private, good work."

They watched Walling exit into the hallway and Schiller gave Dupree a shrug

"I think it's a big deal, Sergeant."

"It doesn't matter what we think. We've got our orders. You keep digging, but if you turn up something else, let me know right away."

"Roger that, Sergeant."

Schiller walked away, trying to seem unconcerned, but Dupree's findings troubled him a lot. He could not override a colonel's direct orders without evidence of imminent danger, and he didn't have that. All he had were Dupree's calculations.

But it bothered him. Oh, yeah, it bothered him a lot.

"This is ingenious." Green Ghost examined the blade under a high-powered lamp.

They occupied a small room on the northern fringe of the base, a place of convenience, not permanence. None of them had been awake for more than twelve hours, so there had been no chance yet to set up a proper operations room or even take a shower. Hangover effects ranged from a throbbing headache for One Eye to mild nausea for Vapor.

Green Ghost felt fine. "I'm guessing that's a batrachotoxin in there. What do you think, Vapor?"

"Poisons are your thing, Ghost. You know I prefer sharp stuff. But aren't batrachotoxins contact poisons?"

"Not necessarily. Oh, you're thinking of the frogs in Central and South America, the ones with poison on their skin. IPs smear it on their spears and arrows, and it works. Yeah, that's probably what we've got here." Ghost held up the strange knife. "If it is what I think it is, I have no idea how they kept it potent this long. That's something I'd really like to find out."

Crafted of blown glass, about six inches long and two inches wide at the base, the knife blade tapered to a narrow point. The substance on the tip appeared, to Ghost's trained eye, to be one of the most powerful toxins known to man.

What made the weapon even more dangerous, however, was the pale fluid inside a small chamber at the tip. Undoubtedly it was a second toxin, probably from a different source. Because of its glass composition the knife had no hope of penetrating even the thinnest clothing, but stabbed with force against exposed skin, such as the neck, the poisons would prove fatal.

"That is one nasty piece of work, Private Watts. I don't suppose you'd care to save us all a lot of trouble and tell me where it came from?"

Watts stood on her tip toes, with both shoulders pulled back until the muscles could not stretch any more. Wires tied her wrists to pipes running along the far wall near the ceiling, slicing the skin so that blood ran down her arms and dripped from the elbows. A second wire looped around her waist was tied off to a large hook set into the concrete floor in front of her. If she relaxed to take the strain off her legs, it increased the pain in her shoulders, and vice versa. Ghost knew more complex and painful tortures, but on short notice and without the proper instruments, he'd improvised.

"What kind of dumbass are you?" She grimaced . "I'm willing to swallow cyanide and you think I'm gonna spill my guts to you?"

"Oh, you will. There's no question about that," Ghost said. "See, I don't believe you're just a fellow traveler in whatever group you're running around with. I believe you're a doer. You're willing to kill or be killed. I can respect that. Not that I care about your agenda."

"You wouldn't understand it anyway," Watts said. "It takes more than five brain cells."

"That's the best you've got? Bravado in the face of death, martyr for the cause, hero of the revolution, et cetera, et cetera... I get it. You're willing to die before rolling over on your buddies. You're in deep and you bought into their belief. But you know, to them, you're probably the Saturday night entertainment. Drink beer, plan an assassination, get a blow job from Watts, and just because they're willing to blow a load on your face you think they're in love with you."

Green Ghost's friendly and conversational tone stopped. He leaned into her ear, holding her head between his hands so she could not bite or spit at him, and dropped into a low, hissing tone.

"But we both know they don't give a shit about you. They never did. So now the only question is when you spill your guts, not if, and whether that's a literal statement or not. Vapor over there really does like sharp instruments, and he likes to cut little girls like you into small pieces. He calls it research. "

Leaning against the wall, Vapor smiled at her. "Please tell him he's full of shit. We can have so much fun together."

"It won't be just you, buddy," Ghost said. "I'll get Nipple in on this."

"Ah, shit, Ghost. Not that psychopath."

"She deserves some fun. See, what's worse for you, Watts, is that I've got somebody else who's a real artist at inflicting pain. She lives for it. Like Vapor here, people think she's a psychopath, and they're probably right. Me, I'm not so bloody-minded. I want to give people a different path to walk before hearing them scream to be killed. So which is it going to be, Private Watts? Me, or the psychopath?"

Watts managed a tight grin as her body spasmed from the lactic acid building up in her muscles. "You're both full of shit."

"Have it your way," Ghost said.

Vapor winked at her and picked up a long pipe cleaner with metallic bristles, the kind plumbers used to unclog large drains. He twirled it a few times. "Nipple likes this kind of thing. How long before she gets here?"

"Not long. I'm glad you two will enjoy it. This kind of thing doesn't get me hard," Ghost said. "But do whatever you've got to do to make this bitch talk. Got it?"

"Haven't you been listening?" Watts said, breathing hard. "I'm not telling you shit."

"Me? Maybe not," Ghost said. "My sister? That's a different story."

Chapter 20

Never waste your pain... you paid a high price for it.
    Janine Angriff

June 19th, 0833 hours

    She blinked and rubbed her eyes, then rubbed them harder. Looking straight ahead, things were blurry, but the images had sharpened a little. Her peripheral vision, however, was a halo of spinning colors which created a tunnel effect. When the medical technician spoke to her, she had to twist her head to see him.
    "Other than your eyesight, how do you feel?" he said.
    Even though she sat on the edge of the diagnostic table, she put her hands out, palms down, to try and keep her balance. Nausea welled in her throat, and she hoped she wouldn't vomit. "Dizzy."
    "Vertigo is normal. It should go away pretty quickly." He moved the large waste barrel closer to the table. "Puke in there if you need to. Now, lie down and close your eyes. We'll give it half an hour and check again, but I don't think your vision is anything to worry about."
    "Are you a doctor?"
    "No, but all cases get reviewed by one. Think of this as triage, when not seeing a doctor is good. I'm going to kill the lights. Don't open your eyes until I tell you to. It could slow down your recovery."
    At first the vertigo bothered her—she kept imagining rolling off the table—but after a while it subsided. The nausea also eased. Several times she almost opened her eyes, but decided not to. After sleeping more than fifty years, and as ridiculous as it seemed, she was soon snoring.

Then faint voices filtered into her brain. A gentle shake startled her, and she sat up so fast the doctor leaning over her stumbled backward. His rank insignia identified him as a lieutenant colonel.

"Congratulations, your reflexes are perfect," he said. "I'm Dr. Friedenthall. How's your vision?"

Blinking, she scanned the room. The lights seemed bright, and a few sparkles lingered on the edge of her vision, but focus had sharpened to normal. The clock on the wall indicated two hours had passed. "Not bad, doc. I mean, Colonel. In fact, pretty good. Maybe ninety percent normal. Damn, that's a relief."

Friedenthall looked her over, reviewed her chart, and nodded. "Good, we're about done here. The psych officer has to sign off, then you can get your duty assignment and find a bunk. It's just a formality. She should be in soon."

"Aye, sir."

The wait was quite short. A stout lady in her late thirties or early forties came in, followed by an aide, who handed her a chart.

"My name is Lieutenant Wanda Noshimura," she said, then stopped and started over. "Excuse me, I'm *Major* Wanda Noshimura and I'm the psych officer. I am required to perform a basic evaluation before you can be released to duty. Welcome to this side of warm, Lieutenant—" She flipped the chart back to the first page. "Randall?"

"Yes, ma'am, Morgan A."

"That's strange," Noshimura said. "What's your middle name, Lieutenant? We need a name for the chart. The computer isn't supposed to accept initials; it's a security thing. I wonder how that slipped through. Your middle name isn't Alice, is it? I had a niece named Alice."

"That's not actually my middle initial, ma'am. My middle name is Mary. That's the initial of my maiden name."

"You're married?" The doctor sounded shocked. The whole concept behind the brigade centered on unmarried volunteers with no close relatives. "Widowed, I assume? Or divorced?"

"No, ma'am. I mean, that's why I'm so anxious to get out of here—my husband also volunteered for the battalion. I haven't seen him in a long, long time." She smiled.

Noshimura smiled back, but weakly. "A married couple? From what I was told, that wasn't supposed to happen, either. Oh, and it's a brigade, by the way, not a battalion. What's your husband's name? Maybe I've already cleared him."

"Joe," she said. "Joseph Peter Randall. He's a helicopter pilot."

Noshimura cocked her head. "Captain Joe Randall?"

"Yes, ma'am, that's him. Know him?"

"He's been the Ready Response Team Leader for almost a year. I see him every day. We like the same music, rock and roll."

"That's Joe! So he's in good shape, then. Am I free to go?"

"I can't imagine Joe Randall being married..."

"I'm not sure he could either, Major. May I go now?"

"I still don't understand the army approving a married couple for this assignment. There's something you're not telling me, Lieutenant."

She paused. "I'm being honest, Major."

Noshimura's face hardened. "I'm an accredited psychiatrist and a combat psychologist. I'm paid to read people and I know when somebody is lying to me, and you can't go on active duty without my say-so."

Randall rubbed her lips, thought about it, and nodded. "Okay. I'm not exactly lying, ma'am, and it's not like you can send me back, so here it is. Joe wanted this assignment and I wanted Joe. He didn't have any close family, so he was good to go on that end, but by the time he spoke with the recruiter we had been talking marriage for months. He was the best gunship pilot in the Army and the recruiting officer said they would do anything to get him to sign onto this mission.

"So we made it clear that first, we were a package deal, and second, we had to be allowed to get married, and then we would both go cold together. And the whole thing had to be kept secret. My father would have gone berserk and tried to stop it, and I couldn't face saying goodbye to my mom. So they were told that I died in combat, and they never knew about Joe."

"Dear God, you left your parents behind?" Noshimura said, aghast. "That violates every protocol for this assignment and it jeopardizes your combat efficiency. Not to mention it was a terrible thing to do to your family. What were you thinking? Didn't it bother you, letting them think their child was dead?"

Randall looked down. "It did. A lot. It still does. But I'm a tank commander. They knew I could die at any time. Nobody knew it better than my father. I was torn up about it, and Joe would have turned Overtime down if I had asked him to, but he really, really wanted this assignment. He really believed in the mission statement, so I did what I did, the army met our demands, and here we are."

"And your parents never even knew you got married?"

"No, ma'am, it was better that way. They still had my little sister and she wanted the whole big family thing, baby seats in the SUV, barbeques in the back yard. My dad must have loved playing with his grandkids." Tears filled her eyes, but she fought them back. Tank commanders did not cry. "So now it's time to start the mission, including the mission of being a wife." At that, she smiled.

Noshimura clearly did not like any of this. "Wait a minute. Are you Tank Girl?"

"Oh, that. Yes, ma'am. At least that's what Joe's co-pilot called me. He thought it was funny."

"Don't tell me. Bunny Carlos."

Morgan nodded. "He's quite a character. So Bunny is here, too?"

"He is. You've got quite the welcome committee waiting on you. I will provisionally clear you for duty, Lieutenant Randall, but we are going to have mandatory follow-up sessions later. Is that clear? Mandatory. I think you're going to find that you have more guilt about leaving your family behind than you believe you will. And if you have any issues before we get together, any at all, you come see me. About anything."

"Thanks, Major, will do."

"Just give me your maiden name for the chart and you can get out of here. I don't know how they did it on the front end, but my file won't load without it. Corporal Townsend can direct you to the hangar deck. You should find your husband there."

"Yes, ma'am!" she said, sliding to the floor. "And the A is for Angriff."

Dennis Walling liked being a colonel, even if he did not yet have a bird for his collar. In the middle of deployment, Supply had better things to do than look for spare insignia, so he'd had the metal shop grind a rudimentary nameplate reading COLONEL WALLING and pinned it to his left breast pocket. But as he stood waiting outside the office of his commanding general—a place that already had two nicknames, with the Crystal Palace beating out Heaven's Gate so far—he feared his new rank would prove to be temporary.

At length Sergeant Schiller waved to him. "Colonel Walling, the general will see you now."

Inhaling deeply, Walling walked to the front of Angriff's desk and saluted. The general lifted his left eyebrow, as if sensing something wrong, and returned the salute.

"What is it, Colonel? I'm very busy right now."

Walling licked his lips. "Sir, does your electro-glass work yet? Can you make it opaque?"

"What?" Angriff's expression was a mixture of anxiety and what-the-hell.

"Please, sir, just trust me on this. If your glass works, I think we need privacy."

"Very well." Angriff pushed the button and the glass turned murky. Images on the other side became vague blobs of color. The door slid closed. He reclined in his chair and steepled his fingers. "All right, Colonel, out with it. What's wrong? Tell me it's not the generators again."

"No, it's not the generators. I don't really know how to put this, General—"

"The only way to say it is to say it."

"Sir, half an hour ago Colonel Friedenthall contacted me about a personnel matter. He had just cleared an Abrams commander for duty, and he made me aware of a situation that concerns you personally."

"Which is?"

There was no getting around it. Walling had to plow forward and get it over with. "Your oldest daughter, sir. She was named Morgan, correct?"

Angriff's face drained of color. "You'd better have a damned good reason for bringing up my family, mister." His voice quavered and his eyes burned with anger.

Walling worried the general might hit him. "Sir, I would not ask if it wasn't important. Your daughter's name was Morgan, correct?"

"My oldest, yes." Angriff's teeth clenched.

"And she was an Abrams commander in Iraq and Syria?"

"She was."

"And..." Walling paused; he had come to the hardest part. "...when her tank was hit, it exploded and her remains were virtually cremated. Is that correct, sir?"

"It is."

"And they were too damaged for positive identification. Is that also correct, sir?"

Angriff stood and leaned forward on his knuckles, until Walling could smell the cigar he had finished more than an hour before. "Colonel, if there is a point you'd better get to it."

"Sir, I want you to brace yourself."

"I'm braced, damn it! Why the hell are you asking me this?"

Despite the damping effect the glass had on sound when it was opaque, Walling knew Angriff's yelling could be heard by everybody in Central Command. They would all stop and stare up at the Crystal Palace. Nick the A in action. It was instructive for all of them.

"Sir, it's your daughter Morgan. It appears she didn't die in Syria. She's alive, sir, and she's part of this brigade."

If Walling had smacked him with a crowbar, Angriff could not have looked more stunned. He leaned back, uncomprehending, and sat down without realizing it.

"Morgan, alive?" he said in a low voice. "That's impossible. There's been a mistake."

"No mistake, General. She's waiting outside Central Command. I told her the CO wanted to see her immediately, even before she saw her husband, but I did not tell her that you were the CO. I felt it best that you do it, sir."

"Husband?" Angriff's shoulders slumped and he deflated. For the briefest moment his mind had let him hope for a miracle. "It's not the same Morgan, Colonel. There's been a mix-up. My daughter wasn't married."

"Apparently she was, sir. She said they kept it secret."

"Why would she do that?"

"So they could both join the brigade. She said if you had known any of this you would have stopped her and she would have lost her husband."

"Where is she?"

"In the hallway outside, sir, by the elevators."

Angriff was around his desk, through the clutter of the surrounding office platform, and halfway down the ramp before Walling could move. He followed, and when Sergeant Schiller spread his hands in a what's-going-on gesture, he shrugged.

"Please God, please God," Angriff whispered as he took long strides down the ramp. He stumbled once, grabbed the handrail, and sped up. Bewildered personnel saluted and glanced at each other when he did not notice.

Walling trailed behind. Many more people crowded the hallway than the previous day, saluting Angriff as he passed. Angriff didn't seem to see them, either, looking desperately around through the crowd. His gaze froze on the slim blond woman fifty feet away, across and on the other side of the wall. She faced the other direction, but his face softened.

Pushing forward, he closed within feet of her before she noticed him. Her gaze fastened on the five stars on his collar and she came to rigid attention, giving a sharp salute. Only then did her eyes creep up from the barrel chest at her eye level to the craggy jaw line above the collar, then to the face and the moist eyes filled with tears. It took a full three seconds.

"Daddy?" she said.

Chapter 21

Burrow, burrow, down and deep,
Burrow, burrow, gnash and weep.
Deep beneath the granite heap,
Deep beneath the ground we sleep.
    Old German children's rhyme

June 19th, 1202 hours

    Terry Bettison placed his right thumb on the elevator's security pad and waited for identification. Overtime had three restricted access elevators, but those three were equipped with high-security technology and Bettison knew the protocols better than anyone else because fifty-nine years ago, he wrote them. More importantly, he also knew the security bypasses, information known only to a select few others.
    His eyes itched, a common hangover effect from Long Sleep, and he leaned against the elevator wall to offset mild vertigo. But time was of the essence and he could not afford the standard six or eight hour standdown after waking up. More than a full day had passed since activation, but Bettison had taken longer than average to regain consciousness. Although he hated the greasy hair and beard, and the awful metallic taste left over from the cryogenic storage chemicals, he ignored his discomfort and pressed on with his mission.
    Less than one hundred people had access to the entire base, and as Chief of Security Bettison topped the list. But soon his duties would make disappearing for more than a bathroom break noticeable, so finishing his own mission before then was critical. Only one other person in the entire

base knew of that mission, because that person's mission mirrored his. Neither knew the identity of the other.

Once his identity had been authenticated, Bettison pushed the lowest button in the left-hand column, a yellow button labeled Sub Floor 11 Authorized Personnel Only. Located deep underground, SF 11 had originally been intended as a storage area for non-essential items and a potential area for growth if more space became needed. As construction on the base progressed, however, it turned into a dumping spot for all kinds of things that seemed too valuable to throw away but which served no immediate purpose, such as the two warehouses filled with riding tack. Emergency access tunnels leading to the hydroelectric generators, reactors, and water pumps could also be reached from SF 11.

Bettison's thoughts turned to another passage, hidden and secret, a shaft leading even further underground and known only to him and his unknown counterpart. During construction he'd followed the shaft all the way to its end. The memory made him shudder.

The elevator doors opened into a wide, sparsely-lit corridor running in both directions, with another branch tunnel directly ahead. He looked both ways before exiting to be certain he was alone. Discovery itself presented no problem, but if someone else roamed the hallway, he could not complete his time-sensitive mission.

On sub-level 11, no security cameras monitored the floors—deliberately. His mission formed part of the base's DNA, the planning dated from the first conception of Operation Overtime, but prying eyes could still jeopardize everything he had worked for. Anxious and excited, he walked down the long central corridor to his right.

Despite long familiarity with the area, Long Sleep hangover made it hard to concentrate and he paused several times to get his bearings. Unlike most people, whose memories fade with time while imagination fills in the gaps, Bettison had been trained by the FBI never to forget details. However, far more miscellaneous stuff crowded Sub-Floor 11 than before he went cold, and it took him a while to get oriented.

It took him twenty minutes to find the right room, and in it nothing had changed. The clock sat right where he'd left it all those years before, with the hands pointing to straight-up twelve, meaning his counterpart had not already completed the mission. Bettison had always assumed it would fall on him, since he was in the first wave of wakeups along with the highest-ranking officers and essential personnel.

Moving across the storeroom, he opened the large metal cabinet against the far wall. Stepping inside, he closed the doors, knelt in the darkness, and felt around for the pressure lever in the right rear corner.

When he pushed down with his right thumb, a two-inch square switch lit up in the cabinet's rear wall. This he depressed with his left thumb while maintaining pressure with his right.

A light flickered on, outlining a doorway in the rear of the cabinet, five feet tall and three feet wide. Bettison pushed and it swung inward with a faint squeal. A short crawlspace, lit by blue LEDs, ended in a square opening in the floor. Once there, he looked down. A shaft disappeared downward, with a ring ladder down one side and the same blue lighting. That was the part Bettison had been dreading. He hated ladders. But he climbed down.

Sweat matted his armpits despite the chill air inside the shaft. Eighty feet below, he found a recess in the side and stopped, although the ladder kept going down into places deep and dark. Bettison knew it led a long way down, and then a long way out. But he only wanted to finish the job and get back upstairs. The recess measured four inches square and he opened it by pulling a tiny metal handle. In the semi-darkness it was impossible to spot unless you were looking for it.

Bettison flipped a red toggle switch, identical to an electric breaker, from left to right, closed the panel, and started his ascent. Mission accomplished. On the way back to the elevator he stopped and adjusted the hands of the alarm clock to read six o'clock. Whoever his mysterious fellow traveler might be, he owed Bettison a huge debt for not having to endure the nightmare of the shaft.

Chapter 22

Nothing great was achieved without risk.
 Machiavelli, "The Prince"

June 19th, 1549 hours

"I'm too old for this," Norm Fleming said. "Are you sure I'm not dead and this is hell? I feel terrible."

An hour before Angriff might have sympathized with his old friend and maybe even agreed. But the shock from regaining Morgan had not yet worn off, and he knew sooner or later the shock would be replaced by anger. For the moment, however, he tried to stop grinning like a damned fool.

"It ain't hell, Norm, although you do look like it. You've just got a really Long Sleep hangover. What can we get you? Sergeant Schiller's brewing some more coffee."

"Maybe when my stomach settles. For now some water would be fine."

Schiller brought two cups of coffee anyway, and water for them both. He also brought Fleming two of the pink tablets that were supposed to help with Long Sleep hangover. While giving him a minute to rehydrate and collect his thoughts, Angriff wondered what to divulge first—his unbelievably happy news or his growing misgivings about the whole project. He settled on something neutral.

"What have we gotten ourselves into?" he said.

"This was your idea, not mine." Fleming drained his glass and poured more from the metal carafe. "I left an important command for this."

"That's right, I forgot that I dragged you out of Paradise. Centipedes, fleas, and puff adders, every man's concept of Heaven."

"You didn't say that when it was your command."

"That's because I like that kind of stuff," Angriff said. "But we both know that you don't, so don't pretend that you do."

Fleming smiled, but that faded. "Something odd happened when I was climbing out of my CHILSS. One of the hand railings from a deck above mine fell and missed my head by inches. A little closer and you'd be looking for a new S3."

"How heavy?"

"Forty or fifty pounds."

"That could have killed you."

"I know. I wouldn't have liked that."

"No." Angriff rubbed the point of his chin the way he did when thinking. "I'm sure you wouldn't. How does a railing just come loose?"

"Shoddy construction?"

"Somehow I doubt that. Steeple was in on this from the ground floor and while I never much cared for the man, one thing he was not was sloppy. You knew him better than I did. Of course, you were a better ass-kisser."

"The only ass I kissed was female."

"Doesn't that describe Steeple?"

Fleming stared at his friend, as if trying to convey with his face his total lack of interest in trading quips.

"All right, I think we agree that Steeple was a careful man, he would not put up with shitty work, and that everything he did had a purpose. But you know, looking back now I don't trust a damn thing he told me. So I want our engineers finding out what happened with that rod. If it was an accident, I want to make sure it doesn't happen again."

"And if it wasn't?" Fleming said.

"Then we have a big problem."

"I have a feeling there's a lot about this place we don't know yet."

"Since you brought it up, that reminds me of something else you don't know, and in this case it's kind of amazing."

"Oh? I can't remember the last time I was amazed," Fleming said. "Can it wait until I've had a nap?"

"No. Now, get ready." Angriff buzzed for Schiller. "Bring her in, Sergeant. I want you to meet one our officers, Norm, and afterward I want you to go get squared away."

"You're the boss."

Schiller came in within seconds, followed by a short blonde lieutenant. She snapped to attention and offered a sharp salute. Fleming blinked and sat there, unsure of what to do or say. At last, he turned to Angriff and put out his hands in a what-the-hell gesture.

"Lieutenant General Fleming, I'm sure you remember my daughter Morgan?"

"Morgan?" But Norm Fleming did not stay flummoxed for long, even when faced with the impossible. He returned her salute. "Should I point out that you're dead? I was a pallbearer."

She relaxed into at ease and tried to convey an apology with her smile. "Hi, Uncle Norm."

Joe Randall was fucked. The CO wanted to see him on the double, but not the rest of his team, not Plotz, Arnold, or Carlos, just him, which meant things were about to go from really good to really bad in a hurry. So when Sergeant Schiller showed up to escort him to a meeting with the CO, he followed like a condemned man being led to his execution. They boarded an Emvee and Randall could feel Alpha Charlie heading right for him.

Schiller drove and Randall tried to pry loose some intel. They knew each other from their shared wakeup tour and had become friends. Schiller was a likeable guy, and when you're stuck underground in more than seven hundred miles of tunnels, rooms, and giant chambers, with only twenty other people around, loneliness tended to blur the lines of separation between officers and enlisted personnel.

"Any chance we could stop for a sandwich, J.C.?"

"Captain, we don't have sandwiches yet. Just PSBs, like we've had all along."

"Fine, let's stop for a PSB."

Schiller half-smiled, and Randall had the feeling the Sergeant knew why the CO wanted to see him. "I don't think that's a good idea, sir."

"What about a drink? I'm buying."

"Sorry, sir. No Officer's Club yet."

"Right. Look, I've never met a sergeant yet who didn't know more about what was really going on than anybody else in the unit and I have a feeling that's doubly true for you. So be honest with me. How fucked am I?"

Schiller looked at him like he would a favorite child who was on his way to a spanking. "I wouldn't know, sir, I'm just a sergeant."

Schiller came out of the door and motioned him to enter. As Randall slipped past him, Schiller whispered, "Good luck, sir."

Angriff stood with his back to the door, staring through his office glass out the huge observation window facing eastward from the mountainside, an unlit cigar stuck in his right jaw. Over Angriff's shoulder, Randall could see across the broad valley below all the way to the mountains across the valley, some seven miles distant. The panorama was spectacular as the setting sun lit the desert in reds and yellows, and far overhead a prairie falcon soared on the hot winds.

Randall chanced a glance to his right, where a small blonde lieutenant stood at rigid attention: Tank Girl herself. His heartbeat sped up and he tried to signal her, but she did not move, eyes fixed rigidly ahead, not even blinking. In the excitement of seeing her again, he forgot everything else.

But then his brain filled with the memory of her naked in the shower. He remembered where he was and knew why the CO had sent for him. He came to ramrod-straight attention, and without warning the glass around them turned gray, blotting out everything beyond the office.

Oh, shit.

Angriff spoke without turning around. "Captain Randall, I'm told that you are our best Comanche pilot, both as commander and tactician. So good, in fact, you don't even have a backup crew to share your aircraft with. I hope for your sake that's true." He turned around and Randall got the full force of Nick the A's legendary glare. "Because I've got a long memory, and if you aren't the hotshot everybody says you are, then you're just a fuckup, and my quota for fuckups is full. Is that understood?"

"Yes, sir."

Angriff's footfalls rang on the metal floor as he got right into Randall's face, an angry DI with a raw boot. He took the cigar out of his mouth and used it as a pointer, and it felt like a well-rehearsed theatrical act. Nick the A had probably done this many times over the years. Or at least Randall prayed it was an act.

"Captain, I have to deal with a grave matter. You see, I have to decide whether you have put this command in jeopardy or not. Do you think that when I woke up this morning that was the number-one priority on my agenda for today?"

"No, sir."

"You're damned right it wasn't! For your own selfish purposes, you put yourself and your wishes above the well-being of this brigade. And if that's not bad enough, you dragged somebody else into it—a fellow officer, no less." He turned from Randall and took two steps toward Morgan, but Randall heard the intensity in his voice drop a notch. "As for you, Lieutenant... what do I call you? Angriff? Randall?"

"Randall, sir." Her eyes stayed fixed on a spot across the office.

If Randall had never been chewed out by a general before, surely his wife had, countless times. It still angered Randall to see his Tank Girl subjected to such treatment.

But Angriff stopped speaking and, try as he might, could go no further. He wanted to chew his daughter out worse than ever before, even worse than when she joined the Army without telling him, to let her know the agony and grief her reported death had caused not only him, but also her mother and sister. Her irresponsible and immature decision had possibly compromised the most important mission in the history of the U.S. Army and she needed to understand the potential consequences. He needed to get in her face and put the fear of God into her, to vent the incredible pain he'd lived with every second of every day since told that she'd died in combat.

Yet he could not do it. Not only had seeing his baby girl alive again rejuvenated some part of him that had died with her, but also...

Arms crossed, he retreated two steps. "At ease. Sit."

Moving behind his desk, he slumped into the oversized office chair and reached behind, adjusting the lumbar support for his aching lower back. When Schiller had found his supply of cigars, he'd begged Angriff not to smoke them in the office because it would gunk up the filters. Now he cut the ends off the Cubana Monte Cristo Especiales Number Three he'd been using as a prop, toasted the foot, and lit it. Taking a long draw, he leaned back and found the first pull delicious, even after all those years.

"So, you're married?"

Morgan didn't squirm. "Yes, sir. A priest and everything."

Angriff motioned with the Cubana. "And this is my son-in-law?"

"Yes, sir."

Angriff pointed at his daughter with his free hand. "All right. You and I have to have a family conversation. Dad and daughter. Since he's your husband, he can listen in." He turned to Joe. "But conversations between you and I remain strictly military. Is that clear, Captain?"

Morgan roused. "Dad, that's not fair. This was all my idea. Joe tried to stop me."

"He should have tried harder."

"You can't blame—"

"Stop." Angriff raised his right hand and spilled cigar ash on his desk. "I don't want to fight. I... I thought you were gone forever and now..." Unsure what to do next, he rubbed the bridge of his nose and closed his eyes. "There's something you need to know, something terrible, and I'm not really sure how to tell you."

Morgan leaned forward. "Daddy? What is it?"

After Angriff ceased speaking, Randall's heart ripped in two at the agony on Morgan's face.

"Dear God," she whispered. "Oh my dear God... Oh my God, oh my God, is this my fault?" Tears started flowing.

Angriff knelt beside her chair and put his arm around her. "No, sweetie, this wasn't your fault. You can't blame yourself. You didn't murder them, and I didn't murder them, even though this happened because of who I was.

"I couldn't do anything to avenge you, but I vowed to track down the bastards who killed your mom and sister and torture them like they torture others. But then I was offered command of this brigade. At first I turned it down. What I really wanted was revenge. I wanted to wipe out every Muslim terrorist on the globe, single-handed if necessary.

"But then I looked at the big picture, the greater good. Regardless of how many burps I killed, there would always be more to replace them. I prayed like I've never prayed before, and asked God for guidance. Hell, I even went to Confession. I came to understand that my place was here, in the future, where I might be able to make a real difference. So I accepted this command.

"And now, just when I thought I'd lost everything, I have you back again. And—" He finally looked over at Randall, met his gaze. "—it looks like I've gained a son-in-law, and apparently one who can shoot straight. So sweetie, at the end of the day, it's hard not to see the hand of God in this. If you had still been alive after I buried your mom and sister, then I would not have taken this assignment. But by taking it I got you back and picked up a son. That can't just be an accident."

With savagery Joe had never heard in his wife before, she looked her father in the eye. "Did you get them?"

Without prompting, Angriff knew what she meant. "I personally took care of the guy who leaked their itinerary. It wasn't random; they were targeted. He worked at the NSA."

"I need details, Dad."

He nodded. "I followed him after work one night. I called in a favor and certain cameras had a malfunction in the parking lot, and some guards turned away from a shadow that slipped through the gate. I caught up with him, dragged him behind a big SUV, and poured pig's blood down his throat. He choked on it and tried to scratch me, but I knelt on his chest. He cried and pissed in his pants and begged me not to kill him. Then I strangled the bastard with my bare hands. I looked into his eyes as his life drained away. Some friends had offered to help, but I had to do this all on my own. They got rid of the body for me and cleaned up the evidence."

"So he suffered?" she asked.

"Oh, yeah."

"Good. Joe, none of this leaves this room."

Randall had never seen his wife like that before. The bouncy, happy-go-lucky Tank Girl he fell in love with was nowhere to be seen. Instead, Lieutenant Morgan Mary Angriff Randall, veteran tank commander and trained killer, sat in her place. For the first time he saw the father in the daughter.

"I wouldn't dream of it," he said, more than a little aroused.

Bunny Carlos wanted to hit somebody. Two days ago, the enormous hangar had been dark and quiet, not counting when Joe cranked up his music. Carlos could tinker and clean and let his mind wander without worrying about tripping over somebody. In the past forty-eight hours, everything had changed. Talking, shouting, air tools, music, engines revving, different music, metal on metal, another kind of music... the relentless cacophony rang in his ears. And where the hell was Joe? He'd been gone for hours.

Six ground crewmen stood at attention beside the Comanche, four women and two men, in clean new coveralls. None of them knew each other or him. In practical terms, he and Joe were supposed to trust their lives to six strangers whose competence was unknown and who had never worked together as a team. Carlos had no intention of letting that happen. He and Joe knew their Comanche inside and out. They had maintained her by themselves for the last eleven months and could keep doing so if necessary.

"How many of you have experience working on AH-72s?" he said.

"I do, sir," said the E-8. "I was crew chief on AH-64s and 72s in Malaysia."

"Malaysia?"

"Khota Baru, sir. When ISSA launched their final offensive?"

"Must have been after I went cold." Carlos leaned sideways and examined the stripes on the sergeant's sleeve. He straightened up with a new respect for her. "What's your name, First Sergeant?"

"Rossi, sir. Frances J."

"You worked on Comanches in Malaysia, Sergeant Rossi?"

"Mostly Apaches, sir, but Comanches too, for a little while. The brass called them Golden Eagles, but we all thought that name sucked."

"A tropical environment? Tell me about the conditions."

"Conditions weren't too bad to start, sir. We moved in on the third day of the attack and used the Malaysian Air Force's base in the area. It was near the coast and the salt air was a problem from the get-go. We had to pay special attention to look for corrosion, mostly on contacts, O-rings, rubber gaskets, and in the ordnance pods.

"Bugs were an issue, too. There were clouds of mosquitoes and flies and they were constantly clogging the filters. Centipedes, too, they crawled into everything and if they stung you, you were down for the count. The airfield itself was grade-A. Hard surface, hardened bunkers, good workshops and equipment, it was pretty much the same as flying from one of our own bases.

"That lasted for about a week. Our birds flew seven to ten sorties every twenty-four hours, day and night, and it took a toll on the aircraft and crews. Then the jimbangs broke through and we had to second-wife it in the pitch dark. It was a real soup sandwich—"

"Jimbangs?"

"Yes, sir, the ISSA foot soldiers. The Malaysians called them *jembalangs*. In English that means goblins. They were ugly fuckers, big noses and chins; they looked like goblins. Somewhere along the way it got changed to jimbangs. Some of our older guys called them Ali Babas, burps, ceefees, walfers, all kinds of names, but jimbangs is what stuck."

"Jimbangs," Carlos said. "I like that. What was that other one, walfer?"

"Walking fertilizer, sir."

He smiled. "Go on."

"Not much else to tell, Lieutenant. It was pretty kinetic. We retreated from base to base for the next three weeks until we wound up back at Singapore, where we got evaced to Guam. Most of our combat time was out in the jungle, but the engineers did a thumbs-up job chopping landing zones out of the forest. It rained all the time, there weren't any spare parts... what else? Oh, yeah, once we were grounded because of no fuel, but we hijacked an air force convoy and un-assed it down the coast. That was close, too; the jimbangs were biting our butts. We finally had to start cannibalizing the less airworthy birds just to keep the others flying.

"The attack battalion went into combat with a full load of Apaches, twenty-four of them. We came out with three and those were held together with duct tape. We burned them on the tarmac at Singapore just before wheels-up to Guam. We all got Bullwinkle Badges out of it, although nobody gave a shit. We left seven buddies over there, but we should have lost more. Our zoomies were top notch and brought a lot of guys out who should've been dead."

"Zoomies?"

"Rotorheads, Lieutenant. Helicopter pilots?"

"Rotorheads I know, Sergeant. We called jet pilots zoomies."

Rossi shrugged.

"It seems like I missed a lot."

"If you mean combat, sir, I would say that's probably a big roger."

"Thank you, First Sergeant Rossi."

Rossi appeared to be in her mid thirties with a small frame, but Carlos knew fire-hardened oak when he saw it. Something about the way a person carried herself let you know if she had a steel core or was just pretending, and Carlos knew Rossi was the real deal. If she could service combat aircraft under enemy fire while simultaneously running a crew, working in the safe confines of Overtime's spacious hangar should be a piece of cake.

"Ten-hut!" Rossi said, in the same way non-coms had barked in every war since Helen took a boat ride to Troy.

Carlos looked over his shoulder and then turned completely around. Joe Randall had come out of the tunnel leading from the inner base and had already started down the stairs, preceded by a short blonde lieutenant. Carlos put his hands on his hips, cocked his head, and watched them climb down. Recognition dawned. Folding his arms, his face creased into in a frown and then a glare. "I'll be dipped in shit."

Morgan Angriff Randall stood on her tiptoes and kissed him on the cheek. Red puffiness ringed her blue eyes. "It's nice to see you, too, Bunny."

Behind them, Sergeant Rossi held her salute and did not move or flinch. But somehow Carlos knew the nickname had not passed unnoticed.

Seeing her audience, Morgan said a little louder, "Hello again, Lieutenant Carlos."

"Nice to see you, Lieutenant... Angriff, right?" He glowered and didn't take his eyes off Randall. "I hope you're well."

Avoiding Carlos' glare, Randall walked past them both and over to the line of technicians. "Who do we have here, Lieutenant Carlos?"

"Our ground crew." His terseness underscored his dislike of surprises, particularly secrets kept from him by his best friend.. "First Sergeant Rossi there is our scud-running trunk monkey."

Randall returned her salute. "At ease. Rossi, is it? Any relation to Dan Rossi, Air Force pilot? No? Well, it's a big world. Lieutenant Carlos and I will want a private meeting later to make sure we're all on the same page as to what will be expected of you and your crew. It's not that we doubt your abilities or your crew's skills, but we don't know you. So in the meantime, you and your people will touch nothing, and will start memorizing every technical manual we have on the AH-72. It's similar in some ways to the Apache, but it also has its differences."

Carlos interrupted him. "Sergeant Rossi has combat experience with the AH-72, Captain."

The two men exchanged irritated glances.

"Does she now? Combat experience or not, I don't even want you breathing on my aircraft until I say you can. You and your crew have one and only one mission, and that is keeping Lieutenant Carlos and me alive. To that end, you are to learn anything and everything you can about this world-class weapons platform you see before you. Capiche, Sergeant?"

"Aye, sir," Rossi said.

"You are to know this gunship better than I do, from the box office to the tourist killer. Then and only then will I permit you the honor of servicing this magnificent machine of war. Are there any questions?"

"No, sir."

"Good, get to work. Dismissed," Randall said.

When their crew was out of earshot, Carlos re-crossed his arms and tapped his toe. "Let me guess. You two meeting here isn't exactly a coincidence."

"You could say that," Randall said.

"I always wondered why her picture was on the bird. And that whole thing in Tel Aviv was, what? An act? A smokescreen for my benefit? 'Where's Tank Girl,' I said. 'Gone,' you said, 'and she's not coming back.' I guess technically that wasn't a lie, now that I see where she went. But shit, Joe, I thought we were friends. You couldn't tell me about this, that Morgan was going cold, too?"

"That much I could have told you, Bunny. It's the rest of it I had to keep quiet and you're not much at leaving things alone. If I told you any of it, then I'd have had to tell you all of it."

"So there's an *all of it*? Awesome. Let's hear it."

"Her name isn't Angriff."

"She's not Lieutenant Angriff? That was a lie, too? I thought you said *Tank Girl* was Nick the A's daughter. Sorry, Morgan."

She held up a hand. "I've called him worse."

"Oh, she's his daughter, all right," Joe said. "But Angriff is her maiden name. Her married name is Randall."

"Well, fuck me sideways," Carlos said. "You two got married and didn't tell me? This is really fucked up, Joe, you know that? This really pisses me off, man."

"I couldn't tell you, Bunny. I couldn't tell anybody. Shit, do you know what the army went through to get us here? They faked her death in combat. They blew up a fucking M1, then they told her parents she was a crispy critter. A dead crispy critter. Dead—do you hear me?—as in not alive? The army told her parents, including the father who is now our commanding officer, that she was incinerated in the explosion. All they ever got to bury was a jar full of ashes they probably scraped out of some haji's cook stove. That's one helluva big pile of shit ready to fall on your head if somebody found out, and you really wanted to be in the loop on that?"

Carlos paused and thought about it. "You were protecting me?"

"Fuck, Bunny, you're the last person in the world I would hose. And you're the only person I wanted to tell about this, but I couldn't do that to you."

"So who was your best man?" Carlos said.

"There wasn't a best man. There wasn't even a wedding. Five minutes with the chaplain, two civilian contractors as witnesses. That was it."

"Straight up?"

"Straight up," Randall said.

"Where did you go on your honeymoon?"

Randall stepped back, smiled, and spread his arms. "Sunny Arizona, my brother."

"If we're brothers, what does that make her?" Carlos pointed with his thumb at Morgan, busy inspecting their Comanche. "Is she like my little sister now?"

"You're the creepy uncle," she said. "And did you really tell him that if he married me I'd swell up like a dead cat in a ditch?"

"I'd never say anything like that about you, Morgan." Again Carlos looked at Randall with the nastiest expression he could muster. "And if I did, I sure as shit wouldn't expect him to tell you."

"Unless you're gonna start sleeping with him," she said, "I wouldn't tell him anything you don't want me to know."

"He should be so lucky."

"You don't romance me like she does," Randall said.

"Hey, you two!" Standing beside the Comanche, Morgan pointed at the lewd image of Tank Girl on the helicopter's side. "If that's supposed to be me, the ass isn't round enough and that sword needs to be a lot bigger."

Chapter 23

I cannot trust that a man will control others if he cannot control himself.
  Robert E. Lee

June 19th, 1921 hours

The small room did not appear on schematics of Overtime Prime. Air circulation for the past fifty years had been minimal. The cool temperature resulted from being underground, as did the nauseating smell of mold. The condensation of so many people exhaling began warming the room.

"Hello, boys and girls," Terry Bettison said. "Welcome to fifty years later."

Laughs told him everyone was in a good mood. "Raise your hand if you really thought we could pull this off... nobody? It does seem incredible, doesn't it? Here we are with a chance to rebuild our country in the way we know is for the best, with a brigade of soldiers that everyone in this room hand-picked for this assignment—"

"Except for the commander," someone said.

Bettison nodded. "I don't get that one, either, but Steeple was damned certain he was the one. I repeatedly told him it was a bad choice, we argued about it all the time, but he won, simple as that.

"Look, I know Angriff is a pain in the ass, but at the end of day he wants to rebuild the country, same as we do. He'll listen to us; he has to. We're half of his command staff and each one of us is a specialist. We're good at what we do. He won't throw that away—whatever his flaws, he knows how to use talent—and if it comes to fighting, which it might, the guy really is the best we've got."

"How can you be so sure he'll listen to us?" the same man said. "I served under him once. The man's a tyrant. It's his way or the highway. We spent months and years drafting ROEs and regulations, and he ignored all of them."

"They don't call him Nick the A for nothing," Bettison said. "This is new territory for all of us. You can't argue with his track record, though. Angriff isn't stupid. He'll listen. Plus, Fleming is with him, and Fleming's a practical man. It'll be fine."

"Fleming is good," a woman major said. "I've known him a while. Very level-headed."

"That all sounds great, but what if it isn't fine?"

"If it's not... then we'll have to take other measures."

The shower was what Tompkins would never forget. The MREs, formulated for near-permanent storage and which everybody else hated, to him tasted delicious. The sight of young, healthy, uniformed American military personnel overwhelmed him, as did their shiny new equipment.

Weeks would pass before he'd stop searching for ambushes at every tunnel junction or behind every object. The pleasure when he first lay on a real bed with clean sheets caused him to spend that first night moaning in pleasure.

Yet as wonderful as all those things proved, nothing matched the stream of high-pressure hot water firing into the knots in his back, neck, and shoulders, or steam opening his nasal passages.

Dennis Tompkins did not step out of the shower until his skin turned lobster red and he gasped for breath. Once toweled off, he put on the first clean underwear in years, sat on the side of his bed to finish dressing, and slumped over, sound asleep.

From the dimmest depths of antiquity to modern battlefields such as Iraq and Syria, armies have depended on non-commissioned officers as their fighting heart. Hannibal would have recognized the modern concept of the strategic corporal, as would the lowliest centurion serving with Scipio Africanus at the Battle of Zama in 202 B.C.

At Zama, Scipio crushed the previously invincible Hannibal Barca once and for all, but only the unflinching courage of the individual centurions held his hard-pressed army together at the critical moment. Although outnumbered more than two to one, Scipio's centurions maintained discipline long enough for the Roman cavalry to ride to the rescue after dispersing the Carthaginian cavalry.

But the influence of non-commissioned officers did not only flow down to those they outranked. The respect wise officers have always shown their veteran non-coms gave them influence far beyond their rank. Kings, queens, and emperors have asked the advice of a grizzled sergeant, and so did five-star generals. So when First Sergeant Schiller insisted Angriff eat something, his subtle approach implied the general would be letting down his command if he didn't.

"The men are being fed in shifts, General," Schiller said. "The mess hall isn't cooking food yet, so for a while we'll be living off LSL-MREs. Colonel Friedenthall issued an order mandating no less than 2500 calories per day for men, 2200 for women, no exceptions."

"Good," Angriff said. "With all the work that needs doing, I don't want any accidents because somebody wasn't sharp or their blood sugar got too low."

"Aye, sir. Does the general have a preference on what he would like for supper?"

"Peanut soup."

"Peanut soup, sir?"

"Yes." Angriff looked up over his glasses. "Love the stuff. My mother served it at least once a week when I was growing up. She had her own recipe and passed it on to my wife. It's very popular... it *was* very popular in Virginia."

"I don't think we have peanut soup, General."

Angriff waved at him. "I'll eat something in a little while. Right now I'm busy. Can you believe that I'm supposed to decide what crops to grow in the hydroponics farm? Hell, I've never even seen it, and I'm sure as shit not a farmer. What do you think, Sergeant? Do you prefer black beans or chickpeas?"

"I'll eat whatever the mess serves, sir."

"But if you had a choice, which one would you pick?"

"General, I'm not qualified to—"

"Pick one, Sergeant. That's an order."

"Black beans. I'm not much for chickpeas."

"It's the texture, isn't it?"

"Yes, General."

"I'm with you. Middle Easterners love chickpeas, but I don't get it. Black beans it is, then. Maybe we'll get chili."

"As you say, General, but speaking of food, maybe just something to tide you over? You look a little tired, sir, if you don't mind my saying so.

All you've eaten since you woke up is energy bars. I worry about your blood sugar dropping too low."

Angriff gave Schiller a sideways glance. The sergeant had used his own words against him. "Oh, very well."

When Schiller returned with a square tray and yet another cup of coffee, the napkin was actual cloth and the silverware made of stainless steel.

The smell caused Angriff to turn his nose. "What is that?"

"Steak and potatoes, General, with green beans and a roll."

"It smells like rancid motor oil." With considerable effort, Angriff sliced off a thin strip of grayish meat and tried to chew it. "A rifle sling tastes better. What animal is this supposed to be?"

"Presumably a cow, general."

"This is awful. And we've got to live on this stuff?"

"For a while, sir. The troops don't like them much. Perhaps if you pointed out you eat them, too, and said they aren't so bad, it would make them easier to swallow."

"I'm not sure that's possible. So you suggest that I lie in my first order of the day? Probably for the greater good, but between you and me, this is virtually inedible."

"The men call them PSBs, General. Petrified stomach bombs. The breakfast with link sausage they call FTDs, fossilized dinosaur turds. Except the Marines. Apparently they call them the four dicks of death."

Angriff laughed and almost spilled his coffee. "Oh, I'm promoting somebody. I need it done A-sap so I can sign off on it. This is a priority."

Schiller nodded; there had already been a rash of promotions and he knew the paperwork by heart. "Of course, General. Who is being promoted and what is their new rank?"

"New rank is sergeant major of the Army. Congratulations."

Dupree rested his head on his right hand and stared at the computer screen. The hologram generators were not up and running yet, but he did not need them. Data did not lie, exaggerate, or have an agenda. Data reflected reality. The art came in knowing what story the data told, but Dupree knew damned good and well what his data said. The only question was, would anybody who mattered care?

Again he found Sergeant Schiller. The sergeant sat at his desk on the outer ring platform of the Crystal Palace. The ancient major they'd saved the day before yesterday stood beside his desk, while dozens of other officers milled about like at a cocktail party. Dupree saluted the closest officer, the major.

It took the old man a moment to remember the protocols of military life and return the salute.

"Sergeant Schiller," Dupreee said, "you told me to come to you right away if I found something, and I did. Something I can't explain."

"You're sure it's important, Dupree? This isn't the best timing in the world."

"I think it is."

"You're putting both of our asses on the line. No offense, Major."

"What? Oh... none taken, Sergeant," Tompkins said.

"Run it by me," Schiller said.

Dupree did.

When he'd finished, Schiller looked around the platform at General Fleming, the other milling officers, and the CO, reading something in his office.

"Tell you what, Dupree, go back to your station and run it all again, from the beginning. If you get the same answer, come back right away."

"I've done it four times, Sergeant."

"Then do it five."

"Welcome back, Colonel," Friedenthall said. "Your recovery took longer than expected. We were starting to worry."

The colonel raked fingers through thin blonde hair streaked with white. His pallor had worried the medical staff, but when his vitals normalized and his skin remained pale, they'd decided it was his normal state.

"How long have we been active?" he said.

Friedenthall glanced at the clock. His own face was drawn from a lack of sleep. "Day three; is that right? Yes, third day, that's right."

"Then I can see why you were concerned. Am I cleared for duty? The CO is probably wondering what happened to me and I have no idea what the status of my department is."

"You're the S-4, right?"

"That's what they tell me, so can I go now? I'm way, way behind on my duties."

"Of course, Colonel. I'll have someone take you to the quartermaster so you can get fitted out, then to Central Command. In the meantime, I'll inform General Angriff's office that our S-4 is on his way up."

"Nick Angriff is our CO?"

"Yes. Do you know him?"

"Only by reputation. We've never met. This should be interesting."

"At the very least," Friedenthall said. "One more thing, Colonel. Your last name, Schiller—are you related to Sergeant J.C.?"

"Yes, he was my brother. Did you know him?"

Chapter 24

I fear no man and I fear no god, but I do fear myself.
   Disputed quote that legend attributes to Flavius Aetius

June 19th, 1927 hours

Dennis Tompkins had trouble processing everything he had seen, heard, and felt the past two days.

He stood at the threshold of Central Command, trying to understand what he was seeing. Sentries stood at either side of a ramp leading upward to the huge glass dome overlooking the vast space below, a semicircular amphitheater overflowing with personnel. Work stations covered the length of each hemispherical terrace, each with someone seated before a bank of instruments. Other soldiers seemed in a hurry to get somewhere, but Tompkins had no idea where they could be going. He had not seen so many people in one place since The Collapse. The futuristic design made it more unfathomable. He felt like a gawking hick at a county fair.

In the space of a few hours, he'd gone from facing death to being thrust into one of the wonders of the world. The surreal experience had left him muddled and feeling out of place, but when the commanding general requests your presence you present yourself, ready or not.

A sergeant came down the ramp and saluted. "Major Tompkins?"

"Yes, that's me."

"I'm Sergeant Major Schiller, sir. General Angriff is expecting you, but he's been delayed for a few minutes. May I get you something while you wait?"

"No, thank you. I'm fine."

As Tompkins topped the ramp, a gaggle of officers milling on the platform turned and stared, as if trying to decide if he might be important. Then they turned away. Tompkins did his best to be invisible.

Moments after the private left to run his calculations for the fifth time, Schiller's phone buzzed.

"The general will see you now," Schiller said.

Tompkins nodded and, turning, saw Angriff watching from behind his desk. He hurried after Schiller. Hopefully he had shaved close enough to pass muster.

Standing before Angriff, he came to attention, ignoring the officers on the platform watching them. The general came to full attention, snapped off a sharp salute, and held it for a second as a sign of respect. Then, after both men relaxed, Angriff walked over to his desk. He pushed a button and the glass became opaque.

"Thank you for coming so quickly, Major Tompkins. The medical staff says you're in great shape, but very underweight and in need of a long rest."

"I'm all right, General."

"Good," Angriff said. "Because I'm going to put you to work."

"General, I... I can't imagine what I'm good for, sir. I'm an old man now and all this is like some fairy story to me."

"So you don't want to help?" Angriff sounded surprised, and maybe a little hurt. His voice carried the perfect inflection for producing guilt. "It's your call, Major. You've been on active duty for more than sixty years and you've certainly earned the right to retire. So if that's what you want..."

"No, sir, that's not what I meant," Tompkins said. "I owe you my life and the lives of my men and all those women and girls. If there's anything I can do to help this command, then I'm ready and gung ho, sir. I just can't imagine what I've got to offer."

"Sit down, Major, and let's have a talk."

Sergeant Major Schiller appeared from nowhere, carrying a tray loaded with coffee and cigars. Angriff's sudden smile seemed surprised. After pouring coffee for both officers, Schiller left.

Angriff picked up a cigar. "Do you smoke, Major?"

"Not for a long time, sir."

"But you did?"

"Sometimes."

Angriff smiled, nodded, and trimmed a Cubana Monte Cristo Especiales Number 3. When the cigar was lit, he handed it to Tompkins and started prepping his own. For the next five minutes, the two men savored the rich smoke in silence. On the platform outside, the gathered officers sniffed and looked at one another, as if disgusted by the smell.

"Good?"

"I don't think that's quite the word, sir. I'm not sure there *is* a word."

"I'm truly glad you're enjoying it. Nobody deserves it more. Major, you asked me what you could do to help this command. Did you mean that?"

"Yes, sir." Tompkins was starting to feel a little sick. The cigar was delicious, but after decades without tobacco, it was too much of a good thing. He held it away from his face, hoping not to be obvious. "If there's something I can do, I'm all in."

"Do you know our mission, Major, why this place exists?"

"Scuttlebutt is all, sir. Just rumors."

"Really? Those activation codes were above top secret, yet you were given a copy. How did that happen?"

Tompkins rubbed his chin. "One day, a month or two after The Collapse had begun, out of nowhere this messenger shows up with a packet from General Steeple. Inside it were the codes and instructions on how and when to broadcast them. Nothing else. I did as ordered, too. I must've broadcast those things every day for ten years and nothing happened, so eventually I quit. I figured that whatever Overtime was supposed to be, it didn't work out."

"When did you start broadcasting them again?"

"I didn't, General. I forgot about them. My sergeant, John Thibodeaux, he asked me to try them one more time. I didn't put any stock in them, but John had followed me for most of fifty years and if he wanted me to do it, I was going to."

"Fair enough," Angriff said. "But ever since I got involved in this project something has been nagging me, like I missed something, except I don't know what. This is just one more thing that doesn't add up." He set the cigar aside; maybe he'd noticed Tompkins' nausea. "This base is called Overtime Prime, and it was built to reclaim America from the barbarians who have overrun her. It's the best equipped self-sustaining military base in the world. We have everything we need for our mission, with one exception. We have no idea what is outside the walls of this mountain."

"And I do," Tompkins said.

"And you do." Angriff nodded. "You survived more than fifty years out there. You come across as this aw-shucks good old boy, but you led men in a combat situation for five decades and brought some of them out alive. That's leadership. I need that on my team... I need you on my team.

I want you to be a special adviser reporting directly to me. As such, you'll have free rein of the base and access to me at any time. This will be a command staff level position, so you'll be expected to attend all meetings, starting with the one tomorrow. So you'll take the job?"

"General Angriff, I'd have been flattered if you'd asked me to sweep the floors. If my men want to, can they help me in this?"

Angriff reared back as if speechless. "Of course they can. You can pick anybody for your staff you want. I'll have Schiller find you and your men some office space. And your first duty is to give us everything you have on the people who attacked you on that ledge."

"The Sevens?"

"Right. In your initial debrief you said they came from a caliphate somewhere to the south? Did you mean an Islamic caliphate?"

"Yes, sir. Sort of. I'm not sure what they are, exactly. I don't think they're traditional Muslims. It's more like a cult. It started in Texas and spread west."

"Write down everything you know about them. Oh, one more thing. Since you've been on active duty for more than sixty years you're overdue…" Angriff walked over to the couch and Tompkins stood. Reaching forward, Angriff pinned two stars on each collar of Tompkins' shirt, stepped back, and saluted. "Major generals don't sweep floors. But they do get to issue promotions to their own men, so you do whatever you feel is right and let Schiller know so he can take care of the paperwork. Anything you need, you come see me. Welcome to the team, Dennis," Angriff said. "Now let's get to work."

Tompkins just blinked. "Yes, General."

Angriff shook Tompkins' hand. "Call me Nick."

Schiller nodded. "Allow me to offer your first salute, General Tompkins."

Still stunned, Tompkins' return salute resembled a wave.

Schiller had already processed the paperwork, so Tompkins' promotion was no surprise. "I'll find an office for you right away. Would you please follow me, General?"

When they emerged onto the crowded platform, no one moved to let them through, the crowd of officers oblivious. Schiller tried to be polite, but in the end he had to push their way through the officers and aides assembled for the first staff meetings with the CO. Most ignored Tompkins and none moved out of his way, leaving Schiller to squeeze between them with a lot of *Excuse me, sir.*

Tompkins understood their behavior. It wasn't so much rudeness as it was a cold-blooded calculation. During the years leading up to The Collapse, a well-developed political sense had been necessary for those breathing the rarified air reserved for officers above the rank of lieutenant colonel. In the twenty-first century American military, promotion had depended on political acumen, not battlefield ability, in a Byzantine system of favors and obligations.

The brigade's assembled command staff had seen Tompkins' major's bars on his way into Angriff's office. Majors had no political relevance in the command staff world they had all thrived in. Majors existed only when receiving orders or making a report.

Tompkins and Schiller were at the ramp when a deep voice boomed over the droning chatter.

"Attention!"

Everyone turned. Angriff stood in his office doorway, face red and fists clenched. Every man and woman within earshot came erect, including those in the Clam Shell below.

Angriff moved slowly, taking time to stare into the face of each officer he passed. His smoldering cigar jutted from his jaw. He made his way through the crowd until he stood beside Tompkins. Reaching over, he tugged on Tompkins' collar, pointing at the two stars.

"Don't you people know to salute a superior officer? Well, don't you?" Immediately, everyone snapped a salute. "I'm buried in work, and I didn't expect to have to instruct you people on military etiquette!"

"What should I do?" Tompkins whispered, embarrassed.

"That's up to you, General."

Trying not to make eye contact with anyone, Tompkins returned the salute. "As you were."

Angriff nodded and then glared at his officers in turn. "We will discuss this further in the staff meeting." His tone was not conciliatory. "But I'll tell you this much now. You'd damned well better get your noses out of each other's asses and start paying attention to what's going on around you. That goes for every last member of this command."

Angriff turned and stalked back to his office. More than one officer glared at his back.

SECTION 4

Chapter 25

Never stop your enemy from making a mistake.
  Napoleon Bonaparte

June 20th, 0735 hours

Angriff preferred reading hard copies. Digital readers gave him a headache, whether a desktop, laptop, or tablet. Something in the tactile feel of paper made it easier for him to visualize the subject. The huge viewing window filtered bright morning sunshine onto the staff list he currently read. It would be a long day of meetings, questions, and decisions. The most urgent matter was meeting his command staff in preparation for tomorrow's conference, followed by writing his address to the brigade.

On paper, he had a first-rate staff, despite their proclivity for kissing ass and playing politics. He read their qualifications and career achievements twice, jotting down a few questions for clarification, until he came to his S-4. He stopped, saw Sergeant Schiller's empty desk on the platform surrounding the office, and again studied the attached photograph of his logistics officer.

"Sergeant Schiller, can you come here, please?" he said into the headphone mike.

At a light knock, Angriff turned from his notes. Corporal Juan Diaz stood in the doorway. "What is it, Corporal?"

"Sergeant Major Schiller was called away, sir. Is there anything I can do?"

"Thank you, Corporal. Where is Sergeant Schiller?"

"Colonel Walling needed him, sir."

"Tell him to see me as soon as he returns."

Again Angriff squinted at the roster of his command staff. Dry data could not convey everything he needed to know about the people upon whose competence all their lives would depend. The nature of the brigade dictated he had only been able to go cold with his executive officer, Norman Fleming. Other officers he knew and trusted had families and thus were disqualified. So his brigade staff had been picked by others, making him dependent on their judgment to provide him a competent group of subordinates.

After re-reading the name and summary resume of his supply officer three times, he leaned back and stroked the bridge of his nose.

"You wanted to see me, General?" Schiller paused in the doorway.

"Did you and Colonel Walling get the situation handled?"

"We did, sir. Would you like a report?"

"Maybe later." Angriff motioned him inside. "Sergeant, didn't you say you had relatives in the army?"

Schiller looked confused. "I did, sir. I had two brothers in the army and one in the navy."

"The navy doesn't count," Angriff said with a small grin. "But the two brothers in the army, what were their names?"

Confused, Sergeant Schiller answered warily. "Bob and Bill, sir."

"One was named William? What was his middle name?"

Schiller had to think about that. "Emerson, sir. General, did you know my brother?"

"I don't believe so. Tell me about him, Sergeant. What was his rank, did he have a specialty, what kind of man was he? And if you don't mind my asking, what did he die from?"

"I had four brothers, General. Bill was the youngest. Our mother died when he was only four. He wasn't as big as me, didn't talk as much. More brains, less nose. He was born to be an officer and me, I was born to be a non-com. When he was just starting in the Army, the South Vietnamese awarded him several commendations for working logistical wonders during some operation. I know his master's thesis dealt with Bolivian mining resources, or something like that."

"Which college was that?"

"His undergrad was the University of Arkansas, his masters was from Oklahoma."

"Boomer Sooner."

"Uh, yes, sir. He died during surgery to have his appendix removed. Apparently he was allergic to the anesthesia. General, may I ask what this is about?"

"You attended his funeral?"

"I did, sir. He was a full bird by then. They put him in Arlington ground, back when they still did that. They put me in the mausoleum near my wife."

"I didn't know your wife was buried there, too."

"She was a wonderful girl, sir. English, very petite. Her name was Louise. She was from London, Kensington, to be exact. I was lucky to have her as long as I did."

Angriff nodded. "I know, Schiller. We're the ones who signed up to get shot at. Somehow it doesn't seem right that we outlived our wives."

"No, sir. I miss her a lot."

"Sergeant, do you remember the other day when I found out my daughter was still alive?"

"I do, sir."

"Had you known in advance that she was alive and that I would shortly find out, what would you have said to me?"

"I don't understand the question, sir."

"It's not a trick question. What would you have said to me?"

"Uh, just that your life was about to get a whole lot better, in a way you didn't think was possible?"

"That's great, it really is. Perfect. That's why you're the sergeant major of the Army, because you are a wise man."

"Begging your pardon, General—"

"Your life is about to get a whole lot better."

Chapter 26

For I have seen the face of Death, in all his many guises,
I have been his tool of fate, killed men both slow and wise;
He the hammer, I the nail, a wake of blood I trail,
For I have seen the face of Death, his shroud's my Earthly veil.
    Unknown author, found on Guadalcanal, early 1943

June 20th, 0911 hours

Colonel Walling pressed the accelerator of his Emvee harder, although it already scraped the floor. He was late for a mandatory meeting with the CO. He hoped Schiller would cover for him, but until the techs had the internal network up and working, the only way to do that was to stop and call Central Command. That would mean running even later. So he pushed the electric vehicle to its limit, weaving in and out of hallway traffic, while heading for the nearest elevators.

When the doors opened he drove straight in. Two female soldiers were already there, both holding rifles. A medium-sized soldier in non-reg black-and-green camos followed him on and stood in the corner with his head down. Walling turned the Emvee around to face the doors.

Halfway through backing and filling, Walling noticed the two women glanced at each and nodded. The left one took a step forward and pushed the STOP button. The other stepped back two paces. The elevator jolted to a halt.

Without warning, the second one lowered the muzzle of her rifle and aimed at the soldier in the corner. Her companion pointed her M-16 at Walling. The maneuver was well choreographed and they moved like trained soldiers should move, quick but not fast, and with confidence. Walling was taken off guard.

The other soldier was not.

Even as the rifle leveled out, aimed between his eyes, the soldier crouched in a swift, compact move. His right hand shot upward and grabbed the rifle barrel, while his left drove a long stiletto under the woman's left ribcage and up into the heart. She opened her mouth in surprise but no sound came out. Her legs buckled and she collapsed.

Her killer swung the M16 out of her hands, twisted to his right, and brought the rifle into his shoulder in one fluid motion. The second woman turned. He put a bullet into first her left shoulder, and then her right. At point blank range such high-powered rounds should have gone straight through and ricocheted in the metal cage of the elevator, endangering Walling and his savior. Instead, both exit wounds were the size of softballs, the signature of super hollow points.

The alarm siren began to wail.

The impact of the rounds slammed the woman backward into the closed doors. She slid to the floor. Blood spurted from both front and back. Her head lolled and more blood trickled from her mouth and nose. Walling froze in place. The last man standing jumped forward and reached for her mouth.

Too late.

There was a slight crunching sound. The woman went into spasms and foam mixed with the blood running out of her mouth. With a shudder, she died. The blood pouring from her shoulders into the sticky puddle coating the elevator floor soon stopped.

Walling sat in the Emvee, stunned. Fear twisted inside him. Would he be next?

The killer crouched beside the dead woman, rifled her pockets for anything significant, and then pulled up her left pant leg. Near the ankle was a small, ornate tattoo.

Pointing at the tattoo, the killer looked up at Walling. "That says RSVS, for *Rabota sdelayet vas svobodnymi*. That's Russian."

"Russian?" Walling said, not comprehending. "Are you going to kill me, too?"

"It means work will set you free. I need to see General Angriff immediately."

"General Angriff? I'm not going to let you kill him, too. If you think I am, you might as well shoot me now."

The killer stood. Walling studied his face, trying to read what might happen next, but there was nothing, no twitch, no blink, no tell whatsoever.

"I need to see General Angriff. It's urgent. Tell him it's Green Ghost."

"You remind me of a human being," Angriff said.

"Haven't I heard that somewhere before?" Norm Fleming's melodious voice had regained its fluid and commanding resonance after sleep, food, a shave, and a long shower. The barber insisted on taking the brigade's executive officer before others. Fleming had always endured the grime of his profession with stoic patience, no matter how much it irritated his fastidious nature.

"Colonel Walling's giving me an update on the deployment soon. I'm glad you'll be here for it."

"Good. So far I feel like I'm in the middle of somebody else's movie."

The lingering after-effects of Long Sleep reminded him of a virtual reality simulation, like command programs he'd gone through at the School of Advanced Leadership and Tactics. People seemed to be moving in jerky motions, sometimes too fast, sometimes a tad too slow, and the disorientation did not appeal to his logical mind. As he walked up a ramp, leading to the crowded metal platform surrounding what looked like a glass geodesic dome, he half-expected hairy men with AK-47s to drop from the ceiling. Disorientation did not appeal to his logical mind.

Ten feet from the top of the ramp he stopped and stared. Someone pushed past him but he kept staring at the sergeant who stood at the top of the ramp, arms folded, wearing a deep scowl. The light was at his back but enough features were visible—a fleshy face, large nose. The image could only be another manifestation of Long Sleep Hangover, a hallucination.

And then the hallucination spoke.

"I know what you're thinking," the apparition said, sounding just like his brother J.C. "You're thinking that you're seeing me because of all the chemicals flooding your brain for the past fifty years. They scrambled your synapses and you haven't come out of it yet. But you're wrong. Your brain is working just fine."

"No," he said. "I think medical cleared me too soon."

"That could be true, but it doesn't change the fact that I'm really standing here."

Chapter 27

Men tend to worry more about what they cannot see, than what they can.
    Julius Caesar

June 20th, 1006 hours

The time had come, Dupree decided. He left his work station on the top level of the Clam Shell and found Sergeant Schiller having an animated conversation with a colonel near the bottom of the ramp leading to the Crystal Palace.

"What is it, Dupree?" Sergeant Schiller sounded annoyed at the intrusion.

"You told me to run it again, or come to you if I found anything else, Sergeant. I really think we need to at least run this by security."

"S5 isn't up and running yet, if we're going to have one at all. What have you got?"

Dupree moved just his eyes to look at the colonel.

"This is my brother, Colonel William Schiller. He's our S4, Dupree. I'll vouch for him."

"No need," the colonel said. "If General Angriff is busy, I'll go clean up and get situated. Do you know where my quarters are?"

Dupree waited, feeling awkward, while Sergeant Schiller gave Colonel Schiller exact directions to Officer's Country, then grinned as he sloughed off down the hallway. It looked strange, then Dupree realized he hadn't seen the sergeant grin before.

"Now, what were you saying, Dupree?"

"We've been breached," Dupree said.

"Explain that."

"We have a data leak. Someone else is accessing our data."

"That doesn't make any sense. There isn't anybody else."

"Apparently there is. Added to those power usage stats I showed you, I think we need to get the CO involved."

"You ran the power usage again?"

"Yes. Same result. Sergeant, if you want to show him this without me there, that's okay by me."

Schiller studied him. "Come with me."

Dupree walked up the ramp like a man heading for the gallows. For twenty-four hours he'd dithered over whether his evidence was strong enough to show the CO. Now, finally committed... maybe he'd oversold it to himself. Screwing up in front of a five-star general was like a mouse annoying a lion.

Angriff waved them in and Dupree tried not to hyperventilate. When he saw another general in the room, Fleming, heat rushed to his face.

"I'm sorry to bother you, General," Schiller said. "Private First Class Dupree is one of our communications specialists. His duties include auditing performance parameters and making sure everything is operating correctly, and he found something that he thought you might want to know about. He was on watch when the activation code came in."

"Were you? That has to be a moment you'll remember the rest of your life. Does this have anything to do with getting the internal network up and running?"

Schiller turned to Dupree as if to say *It's all yours now.*

"Ummm... no, sir, General. Not exactly." He saluted first Angriff, then Fleming. "I'm actually not directly involved in that, although this did come from me trying to help."

"Relax, son," Angriff said. "I don't know what you've heard about me, but I only bite lieutenants and above. Privates are safe. Take a deep breath and then tell me what you've got."

Dupree paused, closed his eyes, and gathered his thoughts. "Like Sergeant Schiller said, I had the watch when the activation codes came in, and part of my deployment checklist was to monitor and audit power usage. I had been doing that all along, but when the base was shut down we never ran at more than point eight percent of maximum power, and that was with the hydros and reactors off line. They more than tripled our capacity, so there was never an issue with Overtime using too much power.

"I did a weekly audit as called for in my duties, but it never varied more than one percent up or down, and that's one percent of point eight percent. But I never checked where that power was actually going, what was using it, because that wasn't part of my duties. When Deployment Plan A was implemented, that changed."

"Good, good, you're doing fine, son," Angriff said. "Did I miss where we're going with this?"

"Oh, no, sorry, General, I was just kind of giving some background. I took a reading of power usage twelve hours after we powered up, as called for. The CHILSS each use a certain amount of power and with everybody waking up, that amount would go down to almost zero, which it did. There were still some CHILSS online, livestock, I think, so I knew the wake up wasn't one hundred percent, and that was normal.

"Anyway, we're supposed to manually verify everything, so I took the power usage of one CHILSS and multiplied it by our roster. Then I subtracted the CHILSS still active and drawing power. Allowing for variables, it should have come out within seven ten-thousandths of a percent up or down. Except it didn't. Before they powered down, the CHILSS were using nearly a hundredth of a percent more power than they should have been.

"I know that doesn't sound like much, but it is. I ran every test I could think of to try and explain the anomaly, but when that didn't work I took the raw quantity of extra power usage and divided it by the average necessary to run one CHILSS. That's when I got my answer."

"I'm not a computer analyst, Dupree. You're going to have to spell it out for me."

"Yes, sir. The exact extra power usage exactly matched the quantity that would be needed to run forty-three CHILSS."

Angriff leaned his chin on folded hands. "Are you saying we have forty-three people on this base who are not part of our duty roster?"

"That's really not for me to say, General."

"Say it anyway. Best guess. You won't be held responsible if you're wrong."

"If you twist my arm, General, then yeah... yes, sir. There's forty-three extra people running around."

Fleming and Angriff exchanged glances.

"Dupree, you've done a great job. This is outstanding work, son. I am truly grateful for your dedication." Any private in any army would have recognized the tone in Angriff's voice: great job, thank you, now go away.

"Umm... thank you, sir, but that's only the first thing."

"There's more?"

"Well, it's not a power issue, but we have a data leak."

This time there was nothing dismissive in Angriff's manner at all. "How do you know we have a data leak, Private?"

"Like I said, sir, I'm not directly involved in getting the network up, but I am running scans on peripherals to look for anomalies. I was checking to see if there were any issues in memory storage, and also to see what communications were available and which weren't. I manually traced the largest data dumps to see who was able to access records and who wasn't, then cross-referenced it with a list of end users, hoping we could isolate the issue. Yesterday, a new user came online suddenly, but with no identification of who it was. One second it wasn't there, the next it was. And within thirty seconds it downloaded a massive amount of data."

"Did he get it?"

"The data? Oh, yes, sir. At least, the computer sent the data. Whether or not he actually received it, I don't know."

"And we have no idea who it is?"

"I don't, General. There's no way to trace it from my end. But I've been thinking about it, and I have a theory that this was some sort of tap."

"Tap?"

"A hard line, a land line. I think someone connected directly to our mainframes. That would never show up in standard communications audits, and I would never have found it if I hadn't been thinking outside the box trying to get the network running. It was just an accident I found it at all."

"You mean someone made a physical connection to our computer system?"

"Exactly, sir."

"Through some sort of cable, I assume?"

"Yep... I mean, yes, sir, high-capacity fiber optic cable, judging by the quantity of data accessed and the speed. It's the only way I can explain it."

Angriff leaned back, rubbing his jaw as everyone in the room watched him. "Could this have been done before we went active? What I mean is, could this hypothetical cable have been connected before yesterday, or is this new?"

Dupree considered that. "It could have been done any time, sir. Just because the data leak started yesterday, that doesn't mean the connection was made yesterday. It's like a water faucet—the water doesn't come out until you turn it on."

Angriff started to respond, but stopped as four armed men ran up the ramp toward his office. Schiller put his hand on his sidearm, but it was the headquarters company sentries, led by Juan Gonzales.

"What's wrong, Corporal?" Angriff rose.

Gonzales was breathing hard. "Gunfire, General, southeast elevators near the seventh floor. Colonel Walling called on an elevator phone and said to secure your headquarters."

"Gunfire? Did he give any details?"

"No sir. He said he was on his way and should be here shortly, and we were to protect your person."

"He said I'm in danger?"

"He did, General."

"Me, personally?"

"You personally, sir. And General Fleming."

Angriff reached into the bottom drawer of his desk and pulled out his beloved Desert Eagle pistols. He laid them next to his computer, chambered a round in each, and arranged them within easy reach.

"Want to borrow one?" he said.

Fleming cocked his head. "I haven't changed my opinion."

Angriff sat back down. "Dupree, I want you to track down this tap or whatever you call it, find out where it is and where it goes, and if possible how long it's been there. You have authority to do whatever needs doing. Use my name if you have to. I'm counting on you, son."

"Uh... yes, sir. Should I wait until things calm down?"

"Hell, no, son, there's no reason to wait. I don't even want you to sleep if you can help it. But if you're worried about getting shot, you have my permission to carry your service weapon with you. Have you ever shot it?"

"No, sir." Dupree swallowed. "Well, in basic."

Chapter 28

I chose my path, I chose my tests,
To mine own self was true;
With faith in God and no regrets
I gave my all for you.
      Nick Angriff

June 20th, 1048 hours

Within ten minutes Colonel Walling came striding up the ramp, followed by a lean man in dark camo. Shadows hid his face under a weather-worn boonie hat.

Two of the sentries stood at the head of the ramp, while the other two flanked the door to Angriff's office. They all stiffened at Walling's appearance, with crossed spurts of dried blood on his face and cheeks, and more on his uniform. However, it was the man following Walling who scared them. Although not physically imposing, when he looked up, under the brim of the hat gleamed the cold eyes of a killer.

Walling held up his hand for the man to wait outside the office, and then he went in. "We've got big problems, General."

Angriff looked him over. "None of that blood is yours, is it?"

"No, sir. I'm fine. No thanks to me. I got on the elevator and two assassins were waiting. Fortunately, my guardian angel followed me aboard. Neither one of them survived."

"Guardian angel?" Angriff said. "I'd appreciate you not speaking in riddles, Colonel, I don't like it."

"Sorry, sir." He stepped back a pace and waved the strange man in. "But I think the term fits. I'm told you two know each other."

When the killer rounded the doorway, Angriff's jaw dropped for nearly two seconds.

"I should have known," he said. "Damn it, I should have guessed... you have no idea how glad I am to see you, Ghost."

"Yeah, ditto. You've got assassins on the loose, Saint. I need you to come with me right now. The shit's about to hit the fan, and we need to be out of the way if it does."

Schiller and Walling both started to correct Ghost's insubordinate language, but Angriff spoke over them. "That bad?"

"Worse. I don't know what you were told about this place, but I don't think much of it was true. We've got to saddle up. Let's go."

"Where are we going?"

"To a part of this rat's maze I'll bet isn't on the schematics. It's a defensible position and I'm holding somebody you need to meet while you can, but she's not going to last much longer."

"Who is she?"

"One of the assassins sent to kill you."

"Who stopped her?"

"Who do you think? I'll explain that on the way. We need to hurry."

Angriff pulled shoulder holsters of out his desk. With the perfected movements of long practice, he strapped them across his chest. "She's dying?"

"You can't make sushi without carving up the fish."

Chapter 29

Save me from the lion's mouth...
Psalm 22:21

June 20th, 1126 hours

When Angriff and Green Ghost left the Crystal Palace, two of Ghost's men joined them. Angriff recognized both of them from a dozen operations, including the final one in the Congo. Both men saluted Angriff, a rarity done only when they respected the officer, then Vapor took point and Wingnut was rear guard. Trailing behind were two of the headquarters sentries.

With unknown assassins roaming the base, unauthorized personnel on hand, and a small circle of people he knew he could trust, Angriff ordered Fleming to stay at the Crystal Palace with Walling and Schiller, and to have Dennis Tompkins join them. They were to arm themselves and not leave until the situation became clear. Everyone's duty was to protect the chain of command in case Angriff died. Personal safety issues were secondary to their mission of resurrecting the United States.

"Sorry, boys, we walk," Green Ghost said. "Vehicles can be rigged to explode pretty easily, and even if they don't, if we move too fast we can't avoid an ambush."

"How far is it?" Angriff said.

"Not that far. None of us are recovered from Long Sleep yet, but I don't see a safe alternative. Sorry, Saint. Vapor, get far enough ahead to be a tripwire. Twenty feet should do it."

As they moved toward the northernmost elevators, Angriff did not ask any of his thousand questions about what happened after he went cold, or how Green Ghost and his men wound up as part of Overtime.

Some things, however, could not wait. "What am I dealing with, Ghost? How bad is it?"

"Has your Chief of Security not briefed you yet?"

"What Chief of Security?"

Green Ghost shook his head, but his eyes never stopped roaming. "That's what I was afraid of. You have a Chief of Security. He's a civilian, but on paper he has authorization to access anybody and anything anywhere on this base. He has total authority over military personnel. That he hasn't introduced himself yet confirms my thinking."

"Care to tell me his name?"

"This is gonna blow, Saint. You're not going to be happy. Your Chief of Security is Special Agent Terry Bettison."

Few things could stop Nick Angriff, but that did. He pulled up short and Vapor almost ran into him. "The same Terry Bettison who couldn't find my family's killers? Who screwed up the investigation into who took pot shots at me? That Terry Bettison?"

"Let's talk while we walk. Yeah, that Terry Bettison. When you disappeared, I thought you bit the glass, skied into a ravine where nobody would ever find you. It didn't seem like something you'd do, but I couldn't blame you. Losing the last of your family is tough."

"You sound like you know that first hand."

"Yeah, I do. Sort of. The boys and I even wrote this ode..."

"The Legend of Nick the A."

"You've heard it?"

"Not yet. I'll let you recite it later."

"No chance."

"I'm still your boss," Angriff said. "I'll order you to do it."

"And I'll disappear."

They came to the elevators and deployed in a tactical formation, since the open octagon made for a perfect ambush. Angriff held one of his pistols and rotated, looking for a target, as did the others. When the elevator arrived Vapor swept it for explosives using a hand-held device, then flashed thumbs-up.

Once on board with the elevator going down, Angriff and Green Ghost continued.

"It was a couple years later and I was back in the States. When you died, I made you a promise that I would get revenge on whoever killed your family. I started sniffing round the investigation. I talked to a few people. Some of them didn't want to talk but I didn't give them a choice. Once I used a special interrogator I know who gets results. You'll be meeting her shortly."

"You didn't kill anybody," Angriff said, and it was not a question.

"When I kill people, they've earned killing. I'll bet it's no shock to you, but Bettison never tried to find out who killed your family or who shot at you. It was all smoke and mirrors. I don't know why. And while I was sniffing around, I got wind that your death may have been faked, and that led to this place."

"Why wait to tell me you're here?"

"We're not on the books, Saint. There's something fucked about this whole thing. I don't know exactly what it is, but something doesn't add up."

"I've felt that way since my family was killed."

"Your instincts are right."

The elevator stopped. They hugged the sides as the doors slid open, but nobody waited to spray them with automatic weapons. At that level, the tunnels walls were bare granite and much rougher than higher up, since nothing but warehouses occupied the deepest floors. Down there lighting did not dispel all the shadows.

"This is sub-level nine," Ghost said. "We've secured this part of the passage, but there's bad juju down here, bwana."

"Why do you say that?"

"You'll find out in a minute."

"We were talking about Bettison," Angriff said. "What have you found out about him?"

"You can talk to Watts about that. Well, you can try."

"Watts?"

"Our guest, Rita Watts. Rita's a dues-paying member of something RSVS, a terror group that started in Russia, although she's American. Best I can tell, they're a hybrid communist-Nazi group that took hold in the NSA at some point. The name RSVS is an abbreviation. It's the Russian for *work will set you free.*"

"Arbeit macht frei?" Angriff said, stunned. "That's the slogan over the gates of Dachau."

"Yeah," Ghost said. "I know. These people are true believers, real hard cases."

"I've heard that name before, I think Steeple said something about them, but Nazis? I thought those days were gone."

"I don't make this shit up, Saint. I don't think these are old style Nazis or communists, not exactly. Best guess is they were butt buddies with the radical leftists, only more militant."

"Like the former president?"

"Which one?"

The corner of Angriff's mouth turned up in a smile. "I keep forgetting that I slept through nine years of history. The one who pretended to fight radical Islam while letting them run wild."

Ghost turned and laughed. "Which one?"

"Oh," Angriff said. "So does this RSVS hate Jews?"

"Not that Rita's brought up, but they are pro-ISIS in that they approve of their methods. So anti-Semitism might follow. I don't know. They hate the Israelis, but I don't think it's because they're Jews."

When they rounded a corner, the corridor ended in a blank wall of stone.

"This is where your blueprints and schematics end, and everything you're not supposed to know begins."

"As if it's not enough to rebuild a whole country, now I've got to figure exactly what I've walked into."

Green Ghost touched four spots on the wall that appeared as nothing more than flaws in the stone. If done in the wrong order, nothing happened. When done in the correct sequence, however, the light blue outline of a door glowed on the side wall. Ghost pushed four spots on that rectangle and a door squealed as it swung inward.

Angriff was struck by the musty smell of long-sealed rock and dirt, reminiscent of the catacombs of St. Callixtus, on the Appian Way near Rome. He and Janine had accompanied Morgan on a high school student tour of Italy. Since she attended a Catholic school, the director of the catacombs, a priest named Father Ottavio, insisted on conducting the tour himself. Praying at the Crypt of St. Cecilia, with the rich brown dirt under the kneeler, was a moment Angriff would never forget. Nor would he forget the earthy smell.

Beyond, the corridor was lit only by glow-sticks. After fifty feet it ended in a wider tunnel lit by green LEDs, with rooms every twenty feet on each side. Many of the rooms had tiny windows with revolving trays built into the door.

"A prison?" Angriff said. "Who built this? Who were they going to put in here?"

Ghost kept walking, speeding up as they entered secure territory. "These cells were probably meant for you. And anybody who supported you."

The implications were clear. Underground construction required geologic surveys, heavy machinery, and a lot of manpower. Sub-floor nine was at least two hundred feet below ground level. The hidden section must have been part of the original plan, meaning omission from the schematics could not be an accident.

"None of this was an afterthought."

Ghost nodded. "Don't worry. It gets worse."

A tall woman with a nasty scowl and M16 stood guard on a cell with dim red lighting. Green Ghost whispered in her ear and she shook her head. He waved to the group.

"She might still be alive." He pointed at the headquarters sentries. "You're backup for my guys. They're going to check something out. Go with them."

Even though he wore no rank insignia, or even a proper uniform, neither sentry objected. Angriff didn't blame them.

Following Ghost, Angriff entered a small chamber with a raised rectangle carved from the living rock for a bed. A small hole in the corner served as the latrine. The only furniture was a metal chair with a naked woman tied to it, with her wrists tied to her ankles. A second rope looped around her neck ran first around her left foot and then the right. She'd leaned forward to relieve the strain on her back muscles, which had increased pressure on her neck. It would feel like hot coals seared the flesh from her temples to her shoulder blades. Her body was swollen and red, except around the ankles, knees, and wrists, where pooling blood turned them purple.

Standing near the chair, a small woman with blonde hair, freckles on her nose, and white teeth flashed them a girl-next-door smile. Aside from the long pipe cleaner with metallic bristles dripping blood in her hand, Angriff thought she looked about thirteen years old.

"The boys are back in town," she said cheerfully. "You missed the best part, Ghost."

"Saint, meet the newest member of the platoon, Nipple. Behave, do you hear me?"

"I always behave. Heard a lot about you, Saint. More than you might think."

"Watch it." Green Ghost clenched his teeth.

"Nipple—that's your name?"

"Yep. Wanna see why?"

Angriff put up his hands. "No, that won't be necessary."

"Focus," Ghost said to her. "What's the latest with lovely Rita here?"

"Rita's had better days... in fact, I think she's dead. But it doesn't matter; she gave up everything."

"I asked you to keep her alive until Saint got here."

Rita shrugged. "I tried to... okay, not really. Sorry, I couldn't help myself. But there was nothing left for her to say."

"Next time, do as I say," Ghost said. "Nipple's the best interrogator I've ever met, Saint, but she gets a little carried away. She likes her work too much. So, what don't I know?"

"A lot. These RSVS turds are gathered not too far from here, but down a level. After poor Rita, it looks like there're ten others. She didn't want to give it up, but there were no contingency plans if she failed to kill Saint Nick here. They only got into this dirt hotel at the last second. It wasn't some grand plot or anything. Before we all took a nap, their influence wasn't as much as it had been."

"Their influence was waning?" Ghost said.

"Waning? Did you really say waning? Sounds like wanking. I never paid attention to any of that political shit before, but she did say something about the stiffs at the top getting jumpy that they were too radical."

"Lines up with what I know," Angriff said. "Those who openly wanted to fight terrorism got the boot. It almost happened to Norm Fleming and my days were numbered, so ditching radicals on the other side makes perfect sense. Those politicians promoted within the armed forces to support their personal agendas wouldn't want some died-in-the-wool communist or Nazi to try and co-opt their power play. They couldn't entirely throw them out, either; they must have been useful. I never heard of this group before, but as I think about it I can see their influence."

"One more thing," Nipple said. "The plan to kill that colonel took Rita by surprise. I don't know how you figured out they were gonna hit him, B.B.; it was news to her. She thinks the rest of them are down there trying to figure out what do next, so a quick strike might get them all."

"Anything else?"

"Just the bigger news."

"Give," Angriff said, already tired of Nipple. Dealing with dangerous people meant making allowances for their quirks and often bizarre behavior, but there was still a line they should not cross. Being coy to a general crossed it.

"I always knew he'd be a prick." Nipple pointed at Angriff.

"He's a five-star general. If he wants to be a prick, that's his privilege." Ghost turned to Angriff. "I forgot to tell you she can be a little psychotic."

"I'm mostly insane, with horrible periods of sanity in between," Nipple said.

"Quoting Poe doesn't impress me," Angriff said.

Before he could say anything else, her tone changed. Her voice lost its cheerful girlishness and dropped an octave, and he heard something in it that actually scared him. "This RSVS isn't the real problem, unless they actually kill somebody. They're dedicated enough; Rita here lasted longer than most. And they have some tricked-out stuff, like that dagger they tried to use on asshole here, but their presence wasn't planned. They snuck in just as the doors were closing. If you round them up downstairs, I think you're done with them. They might run away first."

"Then what's the real problem?"

"The other group."

"Other group? What other group?" Angriff said. "What do they want?"

"I haven't learned to answer three questions at once yet," she said, only this time it like a snarling dog.

Angriff mentally ran through the patience drills he had worked on over the years. When his heart-rate slowed, he tried again. "Who is the other group, Nipple?"

"That's easy." The all-American grin came back. "The people who built this underground theme park."

Back in the hallway, Angriff had a hard time suppressing his anger.

"Is she insane? Where did you find that head case?" he said in his famous growl. Once, when inspecting the aftermath of a strike on an ISIS compound, as Angriff stepped over body parts and mangled corpses, a reporter from Al-Jazeera stuck a microphone in his face and asked whether it had been necessary to kill all the 'insurgents.' The video that followed got a close-up of Nick the A chomping a cigar and sounding like an angry bear.

"I could've kissed 'em," he said. "But I'm thinking they'd rather be dead."

The video went viral and briefly trended on Twitter. Angriff became a folk hero to those sick of fighting interminable politically-correct wars. Although gruff, he was rarely angry with those close to him, including subordinates he considered brave and honorable, like Green Ghost. But *rarely* was not the same as *never*.

"I found her where you would expect." Ghost had seen Angriff pissed off before and seemed to have developed partial immunity, like a mongoose with a cobra. "I smuggled her out of a psych ward."

"So she's insane?"

"Clinically speaking, that's never been determined. But if I had to guess, I'd say... no. I knew a voodoo priest who claimed she's possessed by a demon. Somebody else described her as being sketched in black ink."

"What does that mean?"

"That she's somebody you don't forget. She's dangerous as shit, loyal like a German shepherd, and nothing scares her. She'll grow on you."

"So will melanoma. I have to admit there's something familiar about her. She looks... I'm not sure, just familiar."

"Oh?" Green Ghost watched him intently. "Any idea what?"

"No, I can't put a finger on it. But when she's not acting psychotic, she's a lovely young woman."

"Don't ever tell her that. She'll really go nuts."

"Why?"

"Nipple once described herself as thin, tense and angular."

"She's definitely not angular," Angriff said.

"If she hears you say that, I can't predict how she'll react. Be careful what you say to her."

"You need to ditch her. We can find something for her to do."

"I can't." For the first time since Angriff had known him, Ghost smiled, just a little. "I promised Mom I'd look after her."

"You're not going, Saint," Green Ghost said.

Angriff wondered if the acoustics in the tunnel had interfered with his hearing. "Would you care to repeat that?"

"I'm tactical on this and I say you're not going."

"And I run this place and I say that I am."

"That's exactly why you're not going. You run this place. You are the one and only irreplaceable person here. If I die, if Vapor dies, or we all do, this place keeps going because you didn't. But if you take a bullet to the heart, everything goes to shit. We all signed on for a mission we believe in and that mission is more important than any one of us, except you. I hate to break it to you, General Angriff, but you have to be immortal."

Green Ghost had never addressed him by his rank before.

"Damn you," he said.

Once they found the target room, Angriff insisted on waiting in the hallway close by. The team had climbed down a laddered shaft to the floor below. Like the entire complex, tunnels of sculptured stone ran off in various directions. Their target was on the main corridor and they found it without trouble. For people used to operating in complete darkness, the ubiquitous LED lighting seemed like bright daylight.

There were ten people in the strike team. Green Ghost's platoon had sixteen members, including the two headquarters sentries. However, he sent six of them exploring the base to discover what other secrets it might hold. Two more were ordered to find a way outside.

As Ghost and his team approached the target Angriff waited for gunfire, one Desert Eagle at the ready. Prisoners were a priority, but staying alive was a higher one. After ten minutes of silence, he wondered what had gone wrong. Had they gone in yet? Why were they waiting?

"All clear, Saint." Green Ghost's voice echoed down the granite tunnel. Angriff almost ran toward the room and Ghost met him at the door.

"They knew we were coming. Or assumed it."

Five bodies lay around the room. The scent of almonds hung in the air like a heavy fog, and Angriff recognized the physical effects of hydrogen cyanide, from the foam on their lips to the cherry red and purple tints to their skin.

"Cyanide? Damn, they were true believers... but weren't there supposed to be ten?"

"Yeah, we're missing five."

"So we've got five assassins running around loose?"

"I don't think so. Not unless they've been gone a while. I had men stationed at either end of the hall; there was nowhere for them to go without being seen. These five are all older, and that guy over there has a swollen ankle. There's a trap door in the far corner and I've got two of my guys seeing where it goes, but I'll lay odds it leads outside."

"You mean outside the base, onto the mountain?"

"Yes."

"What if they run into the five who got away?"

"Their orders are to take prisoners, but I sent Nipple and Wingnut, so..." He shrugged.

"There aren't supposed to be any exits except the main ones," Angriff said.

"I hate to tell you this, but that's not the first one we've found. The good news is, I think we're done with these people for a while. There're some notes and journals here, names and shit that we've got to sift through. The uptake seems to be they were planning a straight-out coup. Kill you, Socrates, and anybody else who got in the way. With any luck the answer is in these papers."

"They targeted General Fleming, too?"

"Oh, yeah. And Colonel Walling got in the way when you named him to head up deployment. I don't know if you realized it or not, but that put him fourth in command, after General Tompkins."

"No, I didn't. And Tompkins too… but you think we're good for now?"

"I do, Saint. I think we're good to go."

"What about that other group Nipple mentioned?"

"About that… you can't always take her seriously. There's an art to deciphering her."

"And you can translate everything she says?"

"I didn't say that."

Norm Fleming rose from Angriff's desk chair and beckoned him to sit down. The anxiety of waiting for news showed on Walling, Schiller, and Tompkins' faces, but not Fleming's.

"Nick goes off like this all the time," Fleming had explained while they waited. "I assume that on one of these excursions, he's going to get killed and that will be that. Worrying about it won't stop it."

Once seated behind his desk, Angriff relit a half-smoked cigar. "I know you all want details, but that's going to have to wait until we go public. Suffice it to say the threat has been eliminated and we're good to go. Norm, Dennis, do whatever you need to do, then meet me back here in half an hour. Schiller, round us up dinner and plenty of coffee, and make sure I'm not disturbed. I've got a speech to write."

Chapter 30

My family died because of me,
My friends all turned to dust;
But the ruins of the land I see
Are from your broken trust.
    Nick Angriff

June 20th, 1552 hours

Green Ghost dispersed ten of his team at strategic points to watch the crowd, handguns ready. He was taking no chances.

Dark wood paneling gave the amphitheater a soothing ambiance. One thousand stadium seats terraced upward from the stage in twenty-five rows, divided by a main aisle, with twenty seats per row on each side.

Most military facilities were designed to be utilitarian at best. Form followed function. But Overtime Prime was different. Since these soldiers had nowhere else to call home, creature comforts accented the base wherever practical. Large stadium seats and thick carpeting made sure even lengthy presentations would be comfortable. An elaborate and adjustable lighting system allowed for multiple purposes, and superior acoustics meant a speaker on stage could be heard throughout the hall without using a microphone.

The concept intended it for cultural and recreational activities, as well as for large gatherings, such as the commanding officer giving his first address. Every officer whose duties allowed waited in the audience, although the speech would be broadcast throughout the base. Everyone wanted to see the new CO.

Nick Angriff scowled. He loved being in the Army. He loved everything about it, from the oily machine-smell inside an armored vehicle to the often lousy chow. The camaraderie forged by shared privations and dangers did not exist outside the military. When people are shooting at you, and the soldier next to you stands his or her ground and helps keep you alive, it no longer matters whether you two hate each other's guts or not. You know when it really counts you can trust that person with your life. Angriff learned early in his career that, while friendship is a wonderful thing, comradeship is better.

He and Fleming stood out of sight on the side of the stage.

"It's a packed house," Fleming said.

Angriff shrugged. "It's not like I'm competing with a new movie opening."

"I know. You looked thoughtful, that's all."

"I was just thinking how much I love being the CO. Not for egotistical reasons."

"Oh, no, not you. You just have a powerful sense of self."

"Go ahead and laugh. But who would you rather lead you into battle? Tom Steeple?"

"I'm giving you a hard time, Nick, trying to loosen you up. You're the best combat commander I've ever served with, and I think you know I feel that way."

"Yeah, I do. And I appreciate it. But beyond all that, being the CO means I can make the rules. I can mold my people as I think best. I can make them killers and survivors. And now I can do it without the bullshit political correctness we've had to live with the past twenty years... you know what I mean."

"I do," Fleming said. "Before we went cold."

"Right. Those miserable bastards in DC didn't give a damn about the soldier in the field. They weighed us down with rules and regs and ROEs that got people killed. JAG got perverted from enforcing the UCMJ to imposing a social agenda that had nothing to do with military effectiveness. Armies have always existed to kill people and break things. Using them as a social experiment for political reasons left us weak and vulnerable.

"We appeared strong because of weaponry, but the core of our morale had begun to rot. It was like watching the French Army of 1940. They had more and better tanks than the Germans, and fought on the defensive, but superior equipment meant nothing compared to low morale and incompetent generalship.

"But those days are gone. Political correctness was idiotic and now it's defunct. As long as I'm in command, the Seventh United States Cavalry Brigade will operate on a strictly military basis, where merit is all that counts and political considerations don't exist. All that matters is our mission. I've never suffered fools gladly, and now I don't have to suffer them at all."

"Is that your speech?" Fleming flashed a sardonic grin.

"Don't I wish. This is one duty I don't relish. But I'll be damned if I'm going to be like the DC crowd and use speech writers and coaches to make me sound erudite. Some of those guys rehearsed endlessly and used teleprompters like a lifeline. They were more politician than military officer. My speeches might not be very good, but they're all mine. I did ask Sergeant Schiller to look it over for me."

"And what did the good sergeant have to say about it?"

"He told me not to change a word."

As Norm Fleming walked toward the podium, his posture could not have been straighter had a broom had been stuck down his shirt. The crisp uniform fit his tall frame in tailored perfection, and the decorations on his left breast gleamed in the focused lights. A perfectly knotted tie rested upon the snowy field of his shirt. Gun-metal gray hair was cropped close to his dark skin. He might have stepped right from an Army recruiting pamphlet.

"Good afternoon, ladies and gentlemen, I am Lieutenant General Norman Fleming, executive officer of the Seventh Cavalry Brigade." he said. His voice was a deep baritone. Some called it musical, being well modulated and with distinct enunciation of each word.

"As we embark on the most extraordinary journey ever taken by the armed forces of the United States of America, we should thank God we are led by a man whose courage and judgment are legendary, a man whose leadership encompasses every quality that a soldier wants in his commanding officer. He is a man for whom nothing matters except the achievement of his assigned mission in the fastest, most efficient manner possible, with the well being of those he commands foremost in his mind.

"As a soldier, I can only ask of my commander than he or she not put me in harm's way recklessly, but also not to hesitate to do so in pursuit of completing the mission. If my life is to be spent in pursuit of our goal, then make sure the goal is worthwhile and then fight to win. Hold nothing back. We all volunteered for this assignment, some without knowing who their commander would be, but whether you did or did not know in advance who would lead this command, I think we are all agreed that there could not have been a better choice than the man I am now proud to introduce.

"Ladies and gentlemen, officers, non-commissioned officers, enlisted personnel, and our civilian partners, it is my singular honor to introduce our commander, General of the Army Nicholas Trajanus Angriff!"

Angriff inspected his audience as they applauded him. Some rose from their seats, clapping and cheering, while others were more reserved. He stopped at the edge of the stage, craning his neck to see all the way to the back, then to either side of the standing room only crowd. He locked eyes with a number of people, and then came to Terry Bettison, who was one of those applauding the most. Their gazes locked for two seconds before Angriff saw Green Ghost standing at the rear of the room, watching the audience for any signs of aggression. He found it comforting.

Unlike his XO, Angriff never looked like his uniform fit. His thick legs and deep chest simply defied tailoring. He made up for it by spit-polished boots, insignia with a mirror-like sheen, and the twin fifty-caliber Desert Eagles. In the field he wore shoulder holsters, but for formal occasions he used a waist holster as a direct homage to George Patton.

Motioning for the audience to sit down, Angriff made his way to the lectern and shook hands with Fleming, who left the stage.

"Fifteen thousand years ago..." His voice had a gruff, raspy quality. When coupled with the driving personality behind it, people could not help but pay attention. "...along the border of what are now Egypt and Sudan, the first battle for which there is archeological evidence seems to have taken place at a location called Cemetery 117. Historians argued about whether it was really a battle site or not, but a large number of skeletons were dug up with arrowheads that were the obvious cause of death, and anybody who wasn't trying to sell a book believed it was the first known battle.

"No one knows anything about the people who engaged in this lethal combat, except that organized armed conflict pre-dates the historical record. Of the bodies found, many were female. Those prehistoric warriors were not concerned if you were a man or a woman. They only cared if you could fight."

Angriff's voice began to rise both in volume and urgency. "Armies have existed since men first gathered together for collective security. Fifteen farmers who picked up slings and spears to defend their village from raiders were just as much an army as the legions that conquered Dacia under my namesake, Marcus Ulpius Trajanus, or the barefoot veterans of the Army of Northern Virginia who whipped twice their number at Chancellorsville, or the panzer divisions that overran Russia... or the

Seventh Cavalry Brigade that is going to liberate our homeland, the United States of America!"

As the last note ended the crowd jumped to their feet and applauded. Throughout the mountain shouts of "Fuck, yeah!" and "Let's go!" rang through the tunnels and echoed in the hangars. Angriff let it go on for twenty seconds before motioning for quiet.

"Make no mistake, ladies and gentlemen—we are an army. We may be officially designated as a brigade, but we are an army. We are THE army, probably the only one on the entire North American continent. Possibly even the last one on the face of the earth. You and I volunteered to be here today.

"Before we go further, I want to remember our sixty-eight fellow patriots who went into Long Sleep fully expecting to reawaken and join us in our holy mission, but who, for one reason or another, did not survive the process. They knew the risks, but felt the mission was worth it. We honor them today. Their names will be inscribed in the Hall of Heroes so their sacrifice will never be forgotten. May God have mercy on their souls.

"As we transition from the deployment phase of operations to that of an active combat command, I want to make clear the exact nature of our mission. I want every member of this brigade to understand that we have not been given the task of resurrecting our country. That implies that America no longer exists and must be brought back from the ash heap of history.

"That is simply not true. This base operates under the Stars and Stripes. Wherever we set foot, the United States of America exists and holds sway. You were born a citizen of the United States of America and you are still a citizen of the USA. The borders of our nation that existed on the day you were born are still the borders of our nation.

"All that's changed is that in some places lawlessness has broken out in the void of authority after the events we call The Collapse. Other places may be occupied by foreign invaders. And while we do not yet know the details of what we face, those details are just obstacles to be overcome, not roadblocks that stop us moving forward.

"Our mission is to restore justice and hope to those living in tyranny, whether that oppression comes from criminals, warlords, or invaders. From sea to shining sea, we are going to restore the righteous authority of the Constitution of the United States of America, and woe unto anyone stupid enough to get in our way!"

Once again a standing ovation interrupted him, but this time he did not wait for them to stop before continuing.

"To say that I am outraged at the fate of our nation is to downplay my rage. I am angry, and I am vengeful. Already the liberation has begun, with the salvation of twenty-three innocent women and children who were held as slaves. The valley just outside this mountain is now under our direct supervision. Thanks to the bravery and skill of our Ready Response Team, we have inflicted several hundred casualties on an enemy, with no losses of our own.

"This is a good start, but it is only a start. I want each of you to spend the next few days familiarizing yourself with your new surroundings, and to begin the process of forging a highly skilled team with others in your department, company, or platoon. We must each of us be better than we ever thought we could be.

"As of this moment, we are on a war footing, and will stay that way as long as necessary. In the territory we liberate, martial law will be in effect. As for this command, as members of the armed forces of the United States, you are governed by the Uniform Code of Military Justice. If you have questions about something, bring it to my office.

"Regardless of your duties, you are all vital to the success of this command. Once I am satisfied as to our state of readiness, we will begin active operations, moving into the countryside, where we will meet our enemies, and with the help of Almighty God, kill them all."

"General, Private Dupree needs to speak with you right away," Schiller said.

With Walling, Fleming, and Tompkins at his elbow, Angriff was headed down the ramp when the sergeant met him. Dupree hovered nearby.

"I'm late for the staff meeting," Angriff said. "Slot time for him after."

"If you think that's best, General," Schiller said, in that way sergeants used to convey their disapproval of the answer.

Angriff stopped and studied first the sergeant, then Dupree. He nodded once and handed some file folders to Walling. "Tell them I'll be there shortly. Dupree, you've got three minutes."

Once back in his office, he pointed at the private. "Go."

"Ummm... I..."

"We don't have time for you to be nervous, son. You just got three minutes of my time while all of my officers wait on you, and that shows how much confidence I have in you. Now, say what you came to say."

"I found the tap. One of the mainframes has a hard line running into the floor below it, then through a ceramic pipe sideways, until it comes to this shaft going straight down. It goes down a long way, General. The entrance is in a little maintenance room on the twelfth level and there's this ladder along the side. I'm scared of small places, but I figured it was important so I followed it as long as I could. I was scared, sir. The air was really stale and all I had for light was the little flashlight I use for computer repairs."

"Why didn't you take a bigger flashlight?"

"I didn't think about it until I was in the shaft, and I knew if I climbed out to get a better one, I'd never go back in. There were a couple of places where you could get off, and I really wanted to, but I kept going anyway. I climbed way, way down, General. Finally I couldn't take it any more, so I climbed back up a ways and crawled out this little side tunnel. It ended in a closed door, but that swung open when I pushed it and I found myself inside some kind of storage cabinet. There wasn't a handle on the inside, so I kind of finagled with the latch until it popped open and I crawled out.

"I was in this old storeroom—just a bunch of junk, glass bottles, a bunch more filing cabinets, an old clock, nothing important. It opened onto a lit hallway and I found the elevators. That's where it showed me I was on sub-floor eleven. It's restricted access so I got out of there really quick. I didn't want to get in trouble. I hope I'm not."

"No, Dupree, you're not in trouble. Did this tapline run down that shaft past the door?"

"Yes, General, it kept going, I couldn't see how deep. But when I was way down, I found this switch on the side, with nothing else around it. There was no writing or anything, no symbols, just the switch. I figure that's how the tap got triggered on."

"Did you touch it?"

"No, sir. I didn't figure that was my place."

"But this line kept going down, right? Let me ask you this. How far could a line like that run without too much data loss?"

"A long way, if you're using top notch fiber optic cables."

"I don't know what that means, Dupree. A mile, ten miles?"

"I would think hundreds, sir."

Chapter 31

Better to fight for something than live for nothing.
  George S. Patton, Jr.

June 20th, 1728 hours

The long oaken table had twenty-two chairs, all occupied by the senior officers and department heads. Aides lined the walls on either end, but some had to wait outside the conference room. Huge flat-panel monitors flanked the table on both walls. Cork walls and carpeted floors deadened sound.

Angriff sat at the head of the table, with Norman Fleming at the opposite end. To Angriff's right sat the third-highest ranking officer, Dennis Tompkins, then the brigade's command staff, in order starting with the S-1 through the S-9. Most surprising was the man in civilian clothes sitting in the spot between the S4, Supply, and the S6, Communications. The S5 position, Security, was usually incorporated into the S2, Intelligence. To have a separate S5 was unusual, for it to be a civilian was unheard of, and for it to be Terry Bettison was unacceptable. Angriff said nothing yet, however.

On his left were the department heads and specialized commanders, starting with Agriculture and followed by Research and Development, Medical, Construction and Maintenance, Energy, Agriculture, Education and Recreation, Elite Forces, Deployment and, finally, the Judge Advocate General.

Water pitchers and glasses lined the center of the table. So many bodies in such a small space overtaxed the air circulators, and the temperature had risen almost ten degrees in half an hour.

Angriff stood and the small talk ended. Sweat ran down his back and chest, but he did not remove his jacket nor loosen his tie. Discipline started at the top, and that included self-discipline. Despite the room's sound-damping qualities, when he spoke his voice carried to the far end without need of a microphone.

"Good evening, ladies and gentlemen. Welcome to our brave new world. Most of us don't know each other yet, but that will change in the coming months and years. We've got one hell of a job staring us in the face and there's going to be a lot of trial and error for all of us, including me. The U.S. Army has liberated lots of other countries, but we've never before had to liberate our own. I have no doubt whatsoever we are up to the task.

"I think the best use of our time in this meeting is to hear from our deployment officer, Colonel Walling, on where Overtime stands regarding mobilization of assets and what those assets are. But before that, I've got a few things to say first.

"We are all products of the same corrupt and morally bankrupt system that led our country to disaster." He stopped, letting those words sink in. Most of the people in the room had served in Washington, and flourished, which meant they were part of the very system he condemned. When he met their eyes most of them looked away, with Bettison being an exception.

"As a people," Angriff continued, "we let politics and self-aggrandizement ruin our armed forces. This was driven by civilian leaders who cared more about their own careers than the well-being of their country. These narcissists then promoted and favored military officers who felt the same way, and who furthered their careers by pandering to these self-serving politicians. We all know this is true, and we all know that excuses can't explain it away."

There was an immediate shuffling from some officers, while others glanced at Bettison. With that, Angriff found out what he needed to know.

"We very much were the Roman Empire in the fourth and fifth centuries A.D.," he continued. "But understand this. I'm not talking about a particular political party or movement. Everyone shares this blame. And we, as military leaders, have all developed bad habits to survive in that atmosphere. I understand this, and as far as I'm concerned, those days are gone. What you may or may not have done then is irrelevant.

"But what happened yesterday with General Tompkins is a dangerous example of the kind of sloppy thinking that can get you and your people killed. You civilians, Colonel Schiller, and Mr. Bettison are exempt from this, but the rest of you all assumed that the major who walked into my office was still a major on the way out. That was a test. I wanted to see which of my staff had their heads up their asses and which didn't. Unfortunately, one hundred percent of you were sniffing your own shit.

"That must never, never happen again. Conditions on the battlefield change fast and you'd better be ready to adapt to them instantly. Each of you is in the chain of succession for this brigade. If something happens to me, General Fleming takes over command, then General Tompkins, and so on. Not paying attention to detail could endanger everything we have all sacrificed for. There are three things I will not tolerate—disloyalty, inattention to detail, and hesitance to act. We are America and our margin for error is nonexistent. Do not let me down again.

"Lastly, and by far most important, there is no place for politics on this base or in this brigade. There is only one political party, mine. I had better not hear about barracks lawyers creating problems, talking about rules or fairness or any of that shit. Let your people know that we are at war and that I will consider such distractions as insubordination. Since we are at war, insubordination in the face of the enemy could be considered a capital offense.

"The only law is me. The only judge and jury is me and whoever I appoint to that duty. There will be no mercy for anyone who gets in the way of carrying out our mission. I cannot and will not allow dissension in this command. If I tell you that a hamster can pull an Abrams, you'd better be looking for a harness small enough to fit a rodent, is that clear?"

"Yes, sir!" they said in unison, some louder than others.

But Angriff was not done. "This risen America has a blueprint called the Constitution and the Bill of Rights. The extraneous political bullshit that left us fractured will not be tolerated. Is there anyone here who does not understand that? Whatever power you possessed before we went cold, whatever influence you had in Washington, that is gone for good. There is a job for every man and woman. But whether that job is what you're currently assigned to do, or you wind up digging latrines, will be based solely on the performance of your duties. All that matters is your performance.

"That does not mean I will make decisions in a vacuum. I want your input and expertise, and I don't want you to be afraid to tell me anything, whether you think I want to hear it or not. I value your opinions. But once we reach a decision, I expect arguments and discussion to end and uniformity of purpose to take over. Fair enough?"

"Yes, sir."

"Good. I'm glad we're all on the same page. And if you and your people perform to my standards, there is no one, before, now, or in the future, who will be more loyal to you than me. If you're a warrior, then I'll stand shoulder to shoulder beside you regardless of the odds, even unto death.

"All right, enough of that. Colonel Walling, could you please bring us up to date on how deployment is going?"

Chapter 32

Never take the counsel of your fears.
  Lt. General Thomas J. "Stonewall" Jackson

June 20th 1747 hours

Ben Walling had been a colonel for less than four days. He had attended countless staff meetings in his career, but had never been the center of attention for so many high-ranking officers. Before starting he cleared his throat and drank some water, and tried to keep his hand from shaking.

"Thank you, General Angriff."

The chewing-out had left some of his audience surly. He held the report papers close and tried to project confidence.

"Operation Overtime was declared active at 0135 hours four days ago, in turn activating the Seventh United States Cavalry Brigade, Reinforced. This unit is unique in concept, composition and deployment. Although most of its combat components are Army, there is also a Marine recon battalion, Air Force anti-aircraft batteries and forward observers, and a SEAL team, except with nine platoons instead of the usual six. There are also assorted attached specialists from the various branches, including MARSOC Marines and experts on inland rivers from the Coast Guard.

"I want to begin by outlining the brigade's order of battle in general terms. I will answer any organizational questions that I can, but for some decisions I simply have no information and would refer you to the office of the CO. For example, this brigade has several regiments, whereas the army organization tables when I went cold had switched to the brigade system for three or more battalions. I cannot answer why we are organized in regiments."

Angriff interrupted. "The thinking appears to have been that regiments give more flexibility. A regiment can operate over a large area but only commit two battalions, while keeping a higher headquarters in direct command. With a brigade, if you only needed two battalions for the mission you would have at least one battalion operating outside the direct command of their parent headquarters. This appears to have been foremost in the minds of those who planned this whole shebang."

Walling waited to make sure Angriff had finished, then nodded. "Thank you, sir. In terms of combat strength, the Seventh Cavalry has two fully-equipped mechanized infantry regiments, each with two battalions. There is an armored battalion with four platoons of the last production model M1s, the M1A-3B, and it should be noted one of those platoons is designed for conversion to hydrogen fuel cells should that be desired. I note in passing that we possess the technology to build such fuel cells, but the details are outside the scope of this report.

"Field artillery is completely self-propelled, with two battalions of three batteries. Two of those batteries in each battalion are M109A6 Paladins, with the third being M270A1 MLRSs. All of these batteries contain eight tubes.

"It seems this concentration on heavy self-propelled guns and rockets was intentional, and that the mortar components of the infantry regiments have a higher-than-usual preponderance of eighty-one and one-hundred-twenty millimeter mortars, at the expense of sixty millimeter tubes. The one-hundred-twenty millimeters are exclusively Soltam K6s.

"I also want to mention here, without going into detail, that apparently we have a number of EXACTO rounds for not only our infantry weapons, but for tanks, artillery, and perhaps the mini-guns on the helicopter gunships. Those are mentioned in the inventory, but must have been one of the last items loaded, if they exist at all."

"Colonel Walling, for those who went cold early in the game, could you give a brief description of what an EXACTO round is?"

"Certainly, General. EXACTO rounds are self-steering bullets or shells that were developed by DARPA over the course of twenty years. In essence, it turns a shell or bullet into a can't-miss homing missile. You shoot, you hit."

"What kind of quantities are we talking about?" asked the S4, Colonel Schiller.

"Unknown at this point. Limited, but probably enough for short-term high-priority use. I suppose if we ever fight a pitched battle against a similarly equipped enemy, they could be the deciding factor in that one engagement. But that's just a guess based on what we see in the manifests.

"Getting back to the order of battle, for long-range patrols and reconnaissance we have one Army and one Marine recon battalion. The Marine battalion follows standard order of battle, but the Army is a special-purpose unit with a heavy emphasis on firepower, so there is a greater ratio of LAV25s to Humvees. And while it's not active, I have only just discovered that we have one full regiment of horse cavalry."

"What?" Angriff said. "Horse cavalry? With swords and saddles and manure, that kind of horse cavalry?"

"Yes, sir, although we haven't found any swords," Walling said. "More accurately, a regiment of horses are still in Long Sleep. Their cryogenic bays were built next to the cattle and nobody noticed it right away. I found it when matching numbers of livestock. There are over six hundred cavalry horses, and we seem to have all the equipment necessary for them to be ridden, except for riders. There are no personnel assigned to this regiment. I'm not sure where they came from, General. They're definitely not in our authorized order of battle."

"Horses," Angriff said. "You know, that may not be as crazy as it sounds. Horses don't need fuel, although they do need feed. Good job finding them, Colonel. This regiment could turn out to be very useful. Please continue."

"Thank you, sir. Moving on, our air component is quite strong. The attack helicopter battalion has four squadrons, each with twelve machines and almost twice that number of pilots. Two of the squadrons are armed with the last production model of the Apache AH-64, while the other two have the much larger AH-72 Comanche. The helicopter reconnaissance battalion contains both recon and transport helicopters, and those aircraft will have to do double duty in the event of a large airborne operation.

"We have one squadron of medical evacuation helicopters as well, flying the UH-72C, with a variety of mission-variable equipment available. I think that I should also mention that we have twenty-four Air Force F-35 pilots on staff, although we have no F-35s or fixed wing aircraft of any type."

"Did I hear that right, Colonel?" Angriff said. "We have fighter pilots but no planes? Do we have an explanation?"

"General, the men were told before they went cold that planes would be awaiting them. They are as surprised as we are that the F-35s are not here."

"Can any of them ride horses?"

The lingering tension from Angriff's butt-chewing exploded in laughter from most attendees. Bettison was a pointed exception.

Walling smiled when he answered, grateful for the release the joke had given them. "I don't know, General, but I'll be sure to find out."

"And I'm just a ground pounder, but even I know the F-35 was a piece of politically motivated crap. Why would they freeze pilots for a plane that's not any good?"

"Surplus?" Walling shrugged.

"That makes as much sense as horse cavalry... thank you, Colonel, please continue." Angriff leaned forward and perched his chin between thumb and forefinger.

Despite the joke, he had not overlooked the fact that not one, but two anomalies had cropped up in his command. Horses without riders and pilots without planes did not make sense. The horses he could explain away, since riding is a learned skill and horses could be useful on long-range patrolling.

But U.S. fighter pilots took years to train at great expense. Siphoning off twenty-four of them for a long-term project without being sure they had planes to fly made no sense. In fact, it was so ridiculous that he knew it did not happen, which meant somewhere out there was a squadron of F-35s waiting to be found.

Walling rattled his papers, and Angriff returned his attention to the briefing.

"Regarding other assets, such as energy, logistics, and fuel, I can only say where they are now. Those in charge of each department will have a much better grasp on our situation within a week or two. For now, it appears that we are about three months from the first fresh vegetables, much longer for fruit, and much, much longer for fresh meat or fish. Once the hydroponic farm is operating at full capacity, we should have plenty of produce for the entire base. But for now, it's LSL-MREs, and at full consumption, three meals per day per person, we have a three-year supply of those."

Angriff spoke up again. "Is that a threat?"

The same people laughed again, not as loud this time, which helped offset the numbing sensation from hearing so many statistics, model numbers, and topics.

"Some might see it that way, General," Walling said. "As for fuel, we have enough stabilized gasoline for at least two years full operations, with further stores for five more years in long-term storage, the fuel needing only to be chemically restored.

"Electrical energy for the entire base is provided in multiple ways. Running beneath this mountain is a large river with a strong current, from which two generators supply enough power for the entire base. This supply is adequate unless there is a higher-than-average demand, such as times of maximum effort, or if we are locked in without access to fresh air and the scrubbers have to run at full capacity.

"There is an array of solar collectors at the crest of the mountain, with this reserve power stored in the battery room near the top of base. There are wind turbines available for deployment if we have the need. Further, there are two small nuclear power plants, currently online at minimum power, but they can be ramped up to half power within three hours if you decide it's necessary, and to full power within six hours.

"Ammunition stores are large. The inventory is ongoing, so I don't have exact figures for each round or shell size, but with judicious usage we should have enough for years of operations. There are also plans for rapid construction of an organic ammo manufacturing system, modest in scope and size but capable of producing all needed ordnance short of guided missiles. Exact numbers should be available at the next briefing.

"In the miscellaneous category, we have discovered one hundred twelve large crates containing something called a 'Self-Sustaining Housing Pod. They were just discovered before this briefing and I don't have any details about what these are exactly, although we did open one. They look like a giant metal egg, with windows. The men on the spot nicknamed it an eggshell. Colonel Schiller, were you able to discover their purpose?"

The trim colonel stood, nodding at his fellow officers before responding. "I brought the manual with me," he said, holding up a thick document. "Their function is straightforward and, I might add, ingenious. Let me read from a description on Army letterhead laid into the manual... 'this SSHP is a low-energy, portable dwelling that allows users to live anywhere in the world where there is a reasonable supply of sunlight. The approximately twenty-five foot long by twelve foot wide shelter is powered by a one thousand fifty watt wind turbine, a forty-eight square foot array of high-efficiency solar cells, and for good measure, a thirteen thousand five hundred watt-hour battery. The interior living space includes a kitchenette, shower and composting toilet, built-in storage, folding bed, and some all-purpose counter space. This model also includes a rainwater collection and filtration system. Thermal buffering of the skin has been added for additional protection from the elements.'

"What these allow is for two people to live outside normal logistics zones for a prolonged period, providing there is sufficient sunlight to power the unit and either a ready source of water or enough rainfall to support their needs. It seems the SSHP was made in the USA under license from the Czech firm that invented it. That's all we know at this point."

Angriff shook his head in wonder. "My God, whoever thought of that was a genius. I'd heard such things were being planned, but to see them brought to fruition is brilliant. Thank you, Colonel. On a practical level, as I understand it, then, we could cluster a group of these around an FOB and would have no need for permanent structures, other than perhaps walls and bunkers?"

"I would think that's their intended function, General, or even for distant OPs, an early warning network far advanced from other forces," Colonel Schiller said.

"Yes," Angriff said. "Like the picket destroyers around Okinawa. Good idea, Colonel... General Fleming, I suggest you incorporate these into your planning and brainstorm their best uses, including ways in which these eggshells might be transported."

"Will do, General."

"Is there anything else, Colonel Walling?"

"Lastly, our personal effects are to be distributed within the next two days. Sir, I'll need a decision on what to do with the effects of the sixty-eight crew members who did not wake up."

"Thank you, Colonel Walling." Angriff leaned back in his overstuffed swivel chair and surveyed his new command staff. "I think we will hold off on questions until next meeting, when everyone will be more familiar with their own department. Write your questions down and give them to Sergeant Major Schiller beforehand. We'll use the first part to go through them, so unless there is something urgent, our next meeting will be day after tomorrow." He stood and stretched, and withdrew a cigar from the inside breast pocket of his jacket.

"General, may I have a moment?" Bettison said.

Angriff nodded and stepped away from the cluster of officers in the hallway outside the conference room. "What do you want, Bettison?"

"I'm your S5, General Angriff. I think we should go over the security concerns and objectives so that I can begin planning."

Angriff pointed at him and did not try to hide his distaste. "I don't know how you weaseled your way into this project and I don't care. You are not my S5 and you're not in charge of security for this brigade. Do you understand that? You have no authority until I assign you a duty.

Since you're here, when I find the time I'll think of something useful for you to do. We all have a part to play in rebuilding the country and I know you have talents we can use. Until then, you are to stand down and stay out of the way."

"That is not the case," Bettison said. "I'm a civilian and I don't take orders from you, General Angriff. I was appointed by General Steeple and my authority stems from that appointment, not from you. I'm sorry if that disturbs you, but that's the reality of the situation."

"Here's the reality, Bettison. If you attempt to interfere with this command in any way I will have you arrested. If you attempt to undermine my authority, I will have you shot. Is this clear to you?"

Bettison's face burned with anger. "You can't do this."

Angriff leaned in close. "I don't know why, but you sabotaged the investigation into the death of my family. If I had proof you did it on purpose, I'd shoot you myself, right now. I might do it anyway. As for this brigade, I can do any damned thing I want."

"I told Steeple you were the wrong man for the job."

"And yet here I am."

"This isn't the end of it." Bettison jabbed his finger at Angriff's face. "You don't know who or what you're fucking with."

"I hope you're stupid enough to cross me, Bettison. I really do. And if you ever stick your finger in my face again, I'll rip off your arm and beat you to death with the bloody stump."

SECTION 5

Chapter 33

Discretion is the better part of stupidity.
   Nick Angriff

June 20th, 2000 hours

Only three people showed up for the meeting, and he was not surprised at which three. None of them had hope of mercy or sanctuary if their identities became known.

Bettison had expected some officers would back out, but not all. But they had. Many of those missing people had helped conceive and design Project Overtime, long before it became Operation Overtime. But Bettison was determined to see it through. Long-standing plans could still work, regardless of Nick Angriff or Norm Fleming, if they had the guts to see them through.

But the one thing they not taken into account was the effect of Nick Angriff himself. Bettison had tried to warn Steeple that nobody could control Angriff, and being right gave him no comfort.

"The son of bitch gives one speech and they all cave like a bunch of little girls," Bettison said. "For decades I've listened to these same spineless idiots tell me how tough they are, how all they want is a chance to do things their way, and now one, one fucking man, has them all shitting in their pants. Damn him."

"What do we do now?" the smallest of the three men said. He spoke with a distinct New England accent. "One of those officers is bound to blab—you know they will—which puts all of us under the gun. I say we get the hell out of here, take our chances on the outside."

"No," Bettison said. "We wouldn't last a week out there without supplies. Plus Angriff would come looking for us, and they've got helicopters. No, if we're going to survive, it has to be here. Let me think..."

Bettison went quiet for a few minutes, and then snapped his fingers. "All right, here's the plan. We've still got a lot of support among the brigade's command staff. They would fall in line if we got rid of Angriff and Fleming—"

"What about that Tompkins character?"

"That old man doesn't pose any threat. Nobody knows him like they do Fleming and Angriff. He can bleat like a sheep, but we'll kill him and nobody will say a thing. No, it's just those two we've got to take out. So what we're going to do is this. We're going to lure them to sub-floor eleven and kill them. The chaos from that will give our supporters the chance to seize command. We can follow the shaft down to the outside if something goes wrong."

"That's insane," the small man answered. "How do we get Angriff down to SF eleven? The man is not stupid. It's not like you can invite him to have a drink."

"No, but I can invite him to sacrifice himself for his daughter."

"That's not our mission, boss. We can hump it to safety. It's not that far."

"Our mission is whatever I say it is," Bettison answered, angry at the challenge. "I'm the one who knows our full mission parameters, not you. I haven't told you this before, but there is no fail built into our future. If we don't succeed here at Overtime, we don't get a second chance. We'll never be part of the elite if we fail here. We'll forever be stuck below our rightful stations. And I don't know about you, but I'd rather die than go back to serving under idiots again."

Chapter 34

Gory, gory, what a helluva way to die.
   "Blood on the Risers," traditional song of the United States Paratroops

June 20th, 2210 hours

"Is that a mortar round in your pants or are you glad to see me?" Morgan Randall said, wrapping her leg around his waist while she licked his neck.

"Wait 'til that round goes off."

Erotic word play had always been part of their lovemaking, but they were usually slow and gentle with foreplay. Hiding in a shadowed corner of a small side tunnel, at that moment they were neither. Even on a base the size of Overtime, privacy was a rare commodity, so when they saw the chance, they took it.

Someone passing in the main corridor might have heard the rustle of clothing, but no one could see the entwined pair without stepping their way a few paces. Randall assumed he would hear such a voyeur coming. He did not.

The first inkling of trouble was a thin cord wrapped around his neck. Someone pulled him backward, away from his wife, and threw him against the wall face first. The cord cut into his neck and blood ran into his shirt.

Another set of hands pulled Morgan forward and wrapped her in a bear hug, while a small man started to throw a hood over her head.

Using the man behind her as a brace, she lifted her right leg and kicked the smaller man in the mouth, aiming at a mole on his upper lip. He staggered back and put his hand into his mouth. It came out bloody.

"You fuckin' bitch!" He balled his fist and swung. The blow landed square on her chin and she went limp. The two men lifted her by the shoulders and feet and took off.

Randall relied on surprise and reflexes when flying, and those same traits served him in a fight. Like all pilots he carried weapons on his person, but not just during combat; he always carried two knives. Using his right hand, he struggled to reach the small, all-purpose dagger strapped to his left wrist. With the blood to his brain shut off, his vision began to deteriorate into red and yellow sparkles. Peripheral vision narrowed. He sucked for air but nothing came.

His hands began to go numb as he tried to slide out the knife. Panic closed in and his most primitive instincts screamed for him to flail and thrash. Instead, he maintained focus long enough for the blade to come free into his grasp. While shifting it for the thrust, he almost dropped it twice. Then as he was blacking out, he shoved upward with all his remaining strength.

The three-inch blade sliced into his attacker's neck. Randall pulled it to the side as hard as he could. Blood spurted and sprayed Randall's back. He reeled aside and fell to his knees, clawing at his ruptured throat.

Randall pulled the cord away and felt the blood running down his own neck. He bent over, hands on knees, until his vision cleared. He had a pounding headache and no wife. Panting, he inspected his attacker, whose breathing through his slashed throat was rapid and shallow. A huge pool of blood made it clear he had only seconds left to live.

"Where... where did they take my wife?" Randall gasped.

The man's lips moved. In those last seconds of his life, Randall thought he might be crying, but no sounds emerged, only bloody coughs.

Angriff fidgeted with his silver Zippo lighter, the one engraved with the large A on the front, a sure sign he wanted to light his cigar. Out of deference to Fleming, however, he mouthed it, clicked the lighter open and closed, and smelled the tobacco. Fleming knew Angriff wanted his permission to light up, but he did not care. The sneezing and coughing from his allergy to tobacco smoke overrode his accommodating nature.

"You made your points clearly." Fleming continued their after-lunch analysis of the staff meeting. "If anybody's confused about how this is going to work, it's on them, not you."

"A lot of them didn't like it."

"Sometimes you get the glory, sometimes the cane. Political officers are nothing if not survivors."

"I hope that's not just your relentless optimism talking. They believed this would be command by committee, just like it was in D.C., and they don't like my approach even a little bit. The polyoffs, *political officers,* wanted to do what they do best, politick, kiss my ass, and tell me my shit smells like roses. I'd can 'em all if I could, but we need every one of them."

A commotion erupted in the corridor outside the main doors of Central Command. Peering down the ramp and through the milling people, Angriff could not see what was wrong, but within seconds two sentries came into view holding a man between them. Angriff rose and walked to the head of the ramp, where Schiller also watched.

The man in the middle wasn't being dragged, but supported. He had a shirt wrapped around his neck and the front of his own shirt had bloodstreaks running down to his waist. Schiller made to help but the sentries waved him away. That was when Angriff recognized his son in law.

"Put him in my office." Nausea welled into his throat. He knew what had to be coming next. "How bad is it?"

"That doesn't matter, General. They kidnapped Morgan." Randall gave a quick rundown of the attack. By the end, he was crying. "I tried to save her, sir, I tried, and they got her anyway."

Angriff had seen many battle wounds and could visualize the cord around Randall's neck. Getting out of that took guts and presence of mind, and Randall killed one of the kidnappers despite being surprised.

"It's not your fault, son. Remember that. It's not your fault."

He met Fleming's eyes. "Bettison. It has to be him. I should have killed him while I had the chance. I knew he was going to try something like this."

"You can't just go around shooting people for no reason," Fleming said.

"Wanna bet? I lost my little girl once. I'm not going to lose her again."

"He'll make contact. He wants a ransom. Guys like Bettison don't kill unless it serves their purpose."

"Overtime is on lockdown. Schiller, find Walling. Call General Tompkins and get me Green Ghost."

An engineer on his way to repair a leaking latrine found the ransom note in an elevator. Because it was written on an MRE wrapper in purple permanent marker, Angriff found it hard to read. He handed it to Walling.

"Angriff, Fleming to SF eleven," Walling said, reading it. "No guns. Quick. Alone or... well, you can guess, sir."

Angriff stood with hands clenched behind his back, looking down at the Clam Shell. "Read what it says, Colonel."

"General—"

"Read it!"

Walling licked his lips. "...alone or the cunt dies."

Five people had gathered in the office besides Angriff and Walling. Schiller, Tompkins, Fleming, and Green Ghost all stood, while Nipple sat on the love seat and played with her hair. Nobody knew who she was and nobody asked. She was with Green Ghost, and even those who did not know him gave him a wide berth.

"I told you this would happen." She didn't look at anyone.

Angriff wanted to slap her.

"I'll go alone," Fleming said. "See if I can bargain with them."

"Let me go with you," Tompkins said. "If something happens to me, I'm expendable. And if it comes down to it, I'm still a good shot."

He and Fleming started debating and Walling joined in. Green Ghost watched for a minute before walking over to Angriff.

"It's gotta be you, Saint."

"I know."

"If it's Bettison behind this—"

"It is." Using his thumb, he pointed at Nipple. "I don't like her, but she did warn us."

"Bettison wants you dead. He'll probably shoot you as soon as he sees you."

"Probably. But he said quick. I don't have much choice."

"Dying's not much of a plan."

"The objective is to save my daughter's life. If it costs mine in the process, I'll pay that price."

"At least give me time to suit you guys up in some armor."

"If Bettison sees body armor, I'm not sure how he'll react. He might just start shooting."

"He won't see this. It's experimental. We stole it from a DARPA supplier before the shit fell in. Some new type of ceramic mesh, very thin. It's supposed to absorb the energy from a bullet and disperse it over a wide area. You wind up with a really big bruise, but they say it stops pistol rounds. It also has nanotech camouflage, meaning it blends with its background. I'll bring one for Socrates, too."

"Sounds good to me. Let's do it."

"And you're gonna need a weapon. Ever shot a Walther PPS- M2?"

"Nine mil?"

"Forty caliber."

"No, but I'm a fast learner," Angriff said.

"Good gun, very small and thin. We'll put in on your side, but if you get frisked it's over; there's nowhere to hide it. And even if they don't find it, Bettison still holds all the cards. The minute you step off the elevator he'll have you covered. While I'm getting this stuff I'll talk to my guys, see if there might be another way down there."

That tripped a memory. Angriff paused, and there below him, typing at his work station, was Private Dupree.

"I'll be damned," he said. "I've got a plan."

"We need to get going," Fleming said. "It's been almost two hours since we got the note. I'm not anxious to be a target, but if we're going to do this, we need to do it."

"I know," Angriff said. "Damn the network. I can't be sure Ghost has had time to get in place."

"Nick, these pouches are slipping into my crotch. If we don't go now we're going to have to undress and retie them. I'm also worried they're going to leak."

"All right, let's go rescue my daughter."

They had to move slowly to make sure the decoy pouches did not slip. Given their anxiety, the elevator seemed particularly slow. When it got to the final stop, sub-floor eleven, the doors slid open and a small man with an M16 covered them. Using the gun, he motioned them out.

"Over there." His accent made it sound like *ova theya*.

Angriff stopped. He knew that voice from somewhere.

Taking measured steps, they entered a wide corridor with long shadows thrown by the dim lighting. Nothing was visible until they came to a bend, and there, standing to one side and pointing a pistol at them, stood Terry Bettison. Darkness gave his angular face a demonic aspect Angriff had never noticed. In the middle of the tunnel sat a metal chair, with a sheet of paper and pen on the seat.

"All right, Bettison, I'm here. Where's Morgan?"

"I'm surprised, Angriff. It doesn't look like you're armed, you're not wearing body armor—don't tell me you actually showed some brains for once. I'm proud of you."

"You want me to pat him down?" the small man said.

Angriff and Fleming wore standard pullover shirts that lay flat against their chests. There were no bulges to indicate body armor or guns. "No. Stay away from him. He's probably planning on you doing just that. That's your style, isn't it Angriff? Direct action?"

"Are you sure you don't want me to clear him?" the man said. "Just have him lie down."

Annoyed, Bettison snapped, "Do you see any guns?"

"Not from here, but that don't mean shit."

"Armor? Do you see any armor?"

"No armor, but something ain't right."

"The only way he can hurt us is if you get in range for whatever they've got planned. He wants his precious girl back and won't do anything to jeopardize that."

The small man retreated a few steps, unhappy. "This ain't very professional."

Best not to give them time to work it out. Angriff cleared his throat. "I did what you said. Where's my daughter?"

Bettison pointed to his hatchet man. "Go tell the slut to yell so he can hear her."

Angriff did not react to hearing his daughter insulted. He stood still, buying time.

A few seconds later Morgan yelled, "Run, Daddy!"

"What's your endgame, Bettison? So you kill us. What does that get you?"

"I'm not sure why you care. This isn't a movie where I reveal my plans while you figure out how to escape. I've got plans; there's just no reason to tell you what they are."

"Don't you want to gloat?"

The small man came back out, leveling his M16 in their direction. "Let's hurry it up. I'm getting that jumpy feeling."

"You heard the man, Angriff. We need to speed this up. I want you and General Fleming to sign that paper. It's your resignation as commander of the brigade and hands over power to your command staff. They will then pick the most appropriate commander. There's no need to waste time reading it. Just sign."

"And my daughter?"

"Your daughter is a highly decorated tank commander. We need all the good soldiers we can get. As long as she doesn't cause trouble, no harm will come to her."

"What if I don't believe you?"

Bettison chuckled. "I didn't realize you had a choice."

When the small guy left the room, Morgan Randall lay alone, watched by the guard she had labeled Smelly because he stank of garlic and mold. Not his breath; him. The odor seeped out of his body. When she'd first awakened and he'd slid his hand under her shirt and cupped her breast, she'd gagged at his reek. She'd almost vomited until the small man had said no, they had to wait. Then the middle-aged one they called Bettison had showed up and nixed the idea for good. Smelly had growled.

Her jaw ached from getting slugged and her shoulders burned from having her hands tied so long behind her back. The rag stuffed in her mouth made it hard to breathe. Dumped like a bag of laundry on the dusty floor, she was surrounded by the store room's junk, strange shapes in the dim light. A clock on a shelf was stopped at six o'clock.

The voices outside were loud enough to hear but not to distinguish words. She recognized her father's voice and wanted to cry, but didn't. Bettison had promised not to harm either her father or Norm Fleming, and she prayed he kept his word. She didn't count on it, however, and it seemed more likely he would just shoot them. It was the safe thing to do. If that happened, if she died in that ill-lit dungeon, she asked God to help Joe not blame himself for what happened. They'd been taken by surprise and it was nobody's fault except her kidnapper's.

Smelly leaned out the doorway, staring into the hall. Morgan stretched her neck to relieve the stress in her shoulders. Movement caught her eye, and bizarrely, the door of the cabinet against the wall opened. A young woman with blonde hair and freckles put a finger to her lips. The lean face of a man appeared beside her.

Then the shooting started.

Angriff put the pen down and stepped back, hands in the air.

"We've done what you said. Now let my daughter go."

Bettison collected the paper, held it up until he could read the signatures, and seemed satisfied. "Good job, generals. For once, you weren't a pain in my ass."

At a distance of twenty feet, he raised the pistol and fired two shots into Fleming's chest, then Angriff's. Both men staggered under the impact of the rounds as red liquid drenched their clothes. Fleming fell backward immediately, while Angriff dropped to one knee, swayed, and rolled over on his side, facing away from Bettison.

"Nice shooting," the small man said. "Stay or go?"

"Let's play it safe and go. Kill the girl."

"I might play a little first."

"Damn, you guys are sick. Hurry it up if you have to. We need to be outta here before they figure out Uncle Sam isn't coming back up. Five minutes and we're gone."

It had been a close-run thing. Angriff was a tough bastard, Bettison gave him that much, but in the end it had all worked out. He had every confidence Overtime would soon be theirs. He eased slowly toward the two fallen men. Time for the coup de grace. He stood over Angriff and aimed at his head, avoiding the red puddle surrounding the body.

But something round and cold pushed against the back of his head and a hand slapped the gun from his grasp.

"I wouldn't move if I was you," Green Ghost said.

Morgan had dubbed the last of her kidnappers Mole Man because of the brown mole on his upper lip. When he returned, she still lay on the floor, hands behind her and the rag in her mouth.

"Lendy! Lendy, where you at, man?" He stood in the store room's center, staring around, and did not notice the blood leaking from the big storage cabinet or the lean man slipping out the door behind him.

He leaned his gun against the wall and unzipped his pants, letting them drop. "Time for fun. If Lendy gets back, he can have sloppy seconds. I think you'd like that, wouldn't you?"

Something sharp touched the shaft of his penis. He looked down. A petite hand held a large knife with the blade turned downward. His erection faded.

"I like sloppy things, too," said a young-sounding female voice. Another hand shoved a dirty rag into his mouth.

Morgan Randall took the rag from her own mouth and jumped up. Mole Man's eyes widened. Maybe Lendy wasn't coming back.

From the tunnel outside, Green Ghost yelled, "We're good out here. Saint Nick is fine."

"Daddy?" Morgan shouted. "You okay?"

"I'm fine, sweetie."

"You wanna do the honors?" Nipple smiled.

Morgan leaned in close, staring at the jagged rip in Mole Man's lower lip from her earlier kick. "First you tried to kill my husband, then my dad, and that really pissed me off."

"No try about it, bitch. We did kill your husband." But the quaver in Mole Man's voice undermined the attempt at bravado.

"No, you didn't. These nice people talked with him. So if you want to keep your dick, you should do the same."

Bettison turned his head carefully. A killer in dark camo pressed the muzzle of an M16 against his temple. Three feet in front of him, the gory wraith of Nick Angriff extended a small handgun aimed at his chest. There was nowhere to run.

"I guess you win after all." Bettison reached into a jacket pocket.

"Don't do anything stupid," Ghost said.

Angriff wanted nothing more than to empty the magazine into Bettison's chest, but the needs of his brigade came first. "You talk to us, you live."

"That's not going to happen." Bettison reached into both jacket pockets.

"Keep your hands where I can see them!" Ghost warned.

"Or what? You going to kill me? Good, go ahead and do it. See what your fool commander has to say about that."

"You don't have to die, Bettison. You know I'm not a liar. If I say I'll spare your life, I will."

"You're not a liar, you're something worse, you're an idiot. You still haven't put it all together, and without me you never will... well, not in time, anyway."

He jerked his hands out of his pockets, holding something round and green in each one. The tops were red. Crossing his arms, he used the index finger of the opposite hand to pull the safety pins from each one, then let go of the lever.

"Grenade!" Green Ghost lunged at Angriff. Fleming dove for the ground.

Bettison raised his arms and flung the grenades. Fitted with electrical impact fuses, they detonated on the hard stone floor. The fragmentation explosives blew Bettison backward and shredded him, almost ripping off his lower jaw and spraying small red chunks of him in a circle. Angriff felt the stings of jagged metal slicing into his skin.

Before the last shrapnel quit rattling against the distant stone floor, Angriff scrambled up and knelt beside the mangled body of Terry Bettison. Somehow the former FBI agent was still alive.

Blood foamed on his lips. "You... have no idea... what's headed your way."

"Tell me, Bettison. Get it off your chest before you go to meet God. It's not too late."

"God..." He giggled, coughed blood, and died.

At the loud *whang* of the grenades exploding, Morgan dashed into the hallway. She could still hear shrapnel ricocheting from the granite walls and floor. Acrid smoke hung over four prone figures. The closest, Bettison, was a gory mess. A second later the bulky figure of her father pushed to his feet, aided by the lean man in camo. As he knelt beside Bettison, she ran to his side.

Angriff felt a hand on his back. He reached for her and pulled Morgan close. "I'm okay, princess. Any of them left alive?"

"Mole Man," she said. "The short one with the mole on his lip. I left him with that other woman."

"Other woman?" Angriff glanced at Green Ghost.

"She means Nipple." It took most of a second for Ghost to realize the flaw in that plan. "Shit..." He sprinted back into the room where his sister held Mole Man prisoner.

She stood over his body, holding the knife. "Not me, bro. I didn't do it. The guy foamed at the mouth and started flopping around."

Angriff nudged the little man's body with his boot. Something about the man triggered a feeling of familiarity... had he met him somewhere? It was too vague to recall.

"Cyanide again." Ghost crouched beside the corpse.

"With a rag in his mouth?" Fleming said. "It's nearly impossible to bite down hard enough to break a glass capsule with your mouth full of cotton."

Opening the man's mouth, Green Ghost pulled out the rag and used a bright penlight to look for glass shards.

"Son of a bitch," he whispered to himself. He spoke louder to the group. "This wasn't an ampule of cyanide. The guy had a false tooth."

Nobody spoke. Only professionals had false teeth filled with cyanide.

"Assassin?" Fleming said.

"Most likely," Green Ghost said. "His tongue had to be able to trigger it; otherwise the gag would have stopped this just like it would an ampoule. This is sophisticated shit."

"Can you get those filled with absinthe instead of cyanide?" Nipple said.

The acrid stench of blood and gunpowder filled the hallway.

"We're heading out," Green Ghost said. "I've got Vapor and some of the others following those RSVS people, and me and Nipple are gonna follow that shaft and see where it goes."

"How long do you think you'll be gone?" Angriff said. "I need you here. I'm making you head of security."

"I'll only be gone a few days. I'm not worried about you now that you're on alert. Then we can talk about this security thing."

"I owe you."

"No, you don't."

"I need one more favor. There's supposed to be a switch down that shaft, maybe eighty or a hundred feet down. I need it turned on, but only for about twenty minutes. Then I need it turned off again. I know that's a pain in the ass, but can you do it?"

"Done."

Morgan, Fleming, and Angriff emerged from the elevator. Three of the headquarters sentries stood covering the octagon with weapons trained and ready to fire.

Walling stood behind the guards and exhaled with relief. Although Angriff was drenched in red, which looked surprisingly similar to blood, Walling didn't blink. "It worked?" There had been an uncomfortable chance that the decoy pouches filled with red paint would slip from their taped positions, especially once the two generals had begun moving and sweating.

Angriff stalked off in the direction of Central Command. As he entered through the massive doors, some of the soldiers working the consoles stood and applauded, including Howard Wilson Dupree. The general had no time for such things and waved his hands for silence. He kept moving straight for Dupree's station, and the young private's expression reflected a flood of panic.

"I need to get a message out," Angriff said. "Now. There's no time to waste."

"The system is still down, General."

"This is for whoever is reading our mail. Can we send a message to whoever tapped our mainframes? Is that possible?"

"I suppose it is, sir. If they're reading every keystroke, they should get it. Whether they notice it or not in the flood of data, I can't say."

"Label it as critically important or something. Tell me when you're ready."

"Ready now, sir."

"Quote me verbatim... all right, here we go. From General of the Army Nicholas T. Angriff to whatever coward infiltrated my command and tried to have me assassinated. I'm sorry to tell you this, but your plan didn't work. I'm not that easy to kill. I don't know who you are, but I'm going to find out. And when I do, I'm coming for you. You fucked with the wrong guy this time, and when I find you—and I will find you—I'm going to kill you. That's not a promise. That's a fact. End of message."

"Done, General."

"Thank you, son. Let's hope somebody just wet themselves."

June 21, 0332 hours

Angriff held up his hands, still caked with red. The crowded conference room fell to dead silence as his command staff digested the image of their commander covered in blood from head to toe. A few of the officers had seen Nick the A at his worst before. Most had not. The creases in his wide face were deeper and darker under the legendary scowl.

"In the past three days," Angriff snarled, "two assassins have tried to murder your commanding officer. Me. Our best helicopter gunship pilot is in the infirmary with a serious wound from an attempt on his life, while a lieutenant in the armored battalion was kidnapped and threatened with rape and death. The blood of those perpetrators is here, on my hands." He displayed them as if holding his twin Desert Eagles. "This is the blood of Terry Bettison. He and all of the other would-be murderers are dead."

Nobody moved or cut their eyes away from Angriff's measuring stare. The danger in the room was palpable and glancing away might have been interpreted as a guilty plea.

"This brigade exists for one purpose and one purpose only—to bring our country back to life. It is now obvious that others saw an opportunity to advance their own agendas, just as they did before The Collapse. I am now going to tell you, for the very last time, that is not going to happen.

"We have crushed two plots centered on those selfish ends. We have killed the plotters, but we know there are more. So listen very closely. If you were in league with Terry Bettison, if you thought this brigade could be used for your own purposes, then you were wrong, and you have a choice.

"From this moment forward, you can loyally serve the Seventh Cavalry and help us with our mission. If you do that, there will be no further repercussions. However, if you do not, if you choose to put yourself before the needs of your country, then I will by God shoot you myself. Is there anyone who does not understand this?"

If possible, the silence was even more complete than before.

"Dismissed."

Chapter 35

After the dead have fallen,
When the living have left the field;
The Valkyries come calling,
To harvest their grisly yield.
    Traditional Norse battle song

June 23rd, 0722 hours

The enormous window flooding Central Command with natural light had a metal mesh catwalk running its length, with flights of stairs at either end. On the far right, unseen in the shadows, a small door led into a series of three bulkheads. Each bulkhead, by itself, was enough to proof the portal against attacks by any known gasses or radiation.

Passing through those bulkheads led to a private viewing platform high up the side of the mountain. Framed in titanium, the platform had its own large window, eight feet long and six feet high. This was manually raised or lowered to allow for an unobstructed view of the valley below, and allowed the viewer to breathe fresh air. A steel grate five feet high prevented anyone from falling off. Access was limited to the CO, XO, anyone with them, and critical maintenance personnel.

"How's your chest?" Angriff said.

Norm Fleming stood upwind of Angriff's cigar, although swirls of wind sometimes brought the smoke his way. "Better. It doesn't hurt to breathe as much. What about you?"

"Looks like I got kicked by a mule, but yeah, better. That's some damned fine armor. I wish we had it for the entire command. But all these damned distractions... I wish I could shoot Bettison."

"You could, you know. It wouldn't accomplish anything, but you could do it."

"Don't be a smartass. We're way behind where I hoped we'd be. If we knew who'd accessed our data I'd feel better about moving out. One of the computer techs, a kid named Dupree, thinks he can rig some sort of trap for whoever it was, but we can't wait. We need to see what's out there, Norm. Tompkins' report was better intel than I dreamed we'd ever get, but it's still just one small piece of a huge puzzle.

"Green Ghost wants me to wait until he can scout the immediate areas, but he's not back yet and I can't risk waiting any longer. I'm thinking about ordering lurps to the west and north. We can put OPs on those mountains to the east and on the ridgeline north and south, but ground to the west doesn't look good for that. That needs recon."

"Do you think it's too soon? There's no real unit cohesion yet, and we can't be sure of who to trust and who not to."

"I know, but we're going to have to take some chances. We'll just have to be vigilant."

"Be quick but don't hurry," Fleming said.

Angriff prided himself on both his knowledge of military history and leaders, but had not heard that one. "Clausewitz?"

"John Wooden."

"Oh. Well, a good plan well executed now is better than a perfect plan later."

"Patton?"

"I'm paraphrasing, but yes."

"Then why send a lurp north if we're going to put an OP up there?"

"I want to scout that plateau where we shot up that jimbang battalion, see if anybody's been there, pick up whatever intel we can from the wreckage."

"What's a jimbang?"

"My son-in-law picked that up from his ground crew. It's Malaysian for ugly fuckers, or something like that."

"I'll stick with burps," Fleming said. "How's he doing?"

"He's good. The doctor was afraid the garrote might have damaged his vocal cords, but he got lucky. Morgan got lucky, too. At least her jaw wasn't broken, although she has to eat soft food for a few more days."

"Those bastards. Anyway, that's a long way out for an OP right now. I think we should leave that for secondary expansion, maybe in a month. Let's get some OPs closer in first. Maybe set up that plateau as a FOB."

"You're the S3; whatever you think is best. I like that FOB idea. I was also thinking that plateau could be a landing pad for ferrying men or supplies, so a FOB might even be necessary and that seems like the perfect spot to fortify. But we need to know about lines of sight and local water supplies."

Taking a long pull on the cigar, Angriff lowered his voice to add gravitas to his words. "We don't have endless supplies of anything, so the sooner we get going, the sooner we find out what is possible. I want to know who my enemies are, how strong they are, and the best way to kill them. I can't do that by having my people sitting on their ass inside this mountain."

Fleming sighed. "Most of these people have never served together, never trained together. Most of them don't even know each other's names. They've just come out of Long Sleep in a world they don't understand, and if we then go sending them into potential combat situations before they've had a chance to train with their units... I don't know. That seems like asking for trouble to me."

"You may be right. Hell, you probably are right. That's why I value you so much as my XO—you keep my more reckless impulses in check. But this time, I've got a gut feeling that something is coming our way, something we need to know about. I can't explain it. But even if our lurps don't find anything, the mission itself will be the best possible training. You know, if everybody is thinking alike, then somebody isn't thinking."

"Patton again?"

"It's not Gandhi. So thank you for making me think this through, but I want lurps out starting tomorrow."

"You're the boss," Fleming said. "Any directives on size, recon range, equipment?"

"Ops are your department. There's nobody better. But I'm thinking we need to at least go out a hundred clicks, maybe two hundred even, if we can support that far. And now that I think about it, since we're going to do it, let's go in all directions. OPs out as we discussed, lurps in all four directions. Have backup ready to go."

"What about an air component?"

"Well, that's up to you," Angriff said. "But I think we're better off holding the gunships in reserve. We can have reinforcements to any lurp within thirty minutes, an hour if they're two hundred clicks out. No reason to burn fuel or tip off a potential enemy that we own the skies. Let's kick off pre-dawn, have everybody back by dark."

"That's moving, Nick. No need for FAOs, and I assume no Fisters?"

"No need for artillery that I can see, not if it's a lurp. The FAOs I'm not so sure. That's your call."

"Maybe I will send one with each task force. They could use the experience. The OPs will have to be radio only, though, because we haven't found much wire yet. There's supposed to be hundreds of miles of it, but so far we can't find it."

"Hmmm... I don't like that. Let Walling know that I consider finding that wire a priority. No unnecessary chatter, then, and coded only. I want radio discipline enforced. Now that our network is up, I don't want anybody listening in."

"Roger that." Fleming patted Angriff's shoulder.

For several minutes Angriff smoked and stared at the landscape beneath him, lost in thought. Patches of agave, yellow sunflowers, and sedge carpeted the desert floor, interspersed with mesquite and ironwood trees. Pastel green saguaro cacti contrasted with red stones tinged with pink in the fading light, while low on the horizon the sky faded from cobalt blue to light purple. Such vibrant colors gave the panorama a fairy-tale feel, too perfect to be real.

"How can anybody see that and deny there's a God?" he said.

"You're preaching to the choir, Nick."

"How did it come to this?" Angriff mused. "How did the greatest civilization in the history of mankind crash into ruins?"

Fleming answered as if it were an actual question, not a rhetorical one. "You know, I've been thinking about that very thing. How could this happen? And I think the answer is simpler than we might have guessed."

"What do you mean?"

"There was nobody to fire the warning shot."

Angriff drew in smoke. "Help me out."

"Think about it. Our society became so sensitive to every little detail of daily life that it fractured. Did you ever hear about micro-aggressions?"

"Is that like a skirmish?"

Fleming chuckled. "In a manner of speaking. Micro-aggressions were offensive messages built into everyday speech. Not overtly, but a slight or insult you probably weren't even aware of. These were usually directed at some marginalized group with an axe to grind who got the attention of the media."

"That doesn't even make sense. How can you insult somebody without intending to insult them?"

"The offended party wanted a reason to complain, and our society had decayed to the point where the media paid attention to them. Anyway, the country became so fractured that our enemies poured through the cracks, and the few patriots who tried to warn everybody were shouted down."

"So they fired the warning shot, but nobody listened?"

"That's a good way of putting it," Fleming said.

"Makes as much sense as anything else. The people on the wall when the barbarians launched their final assault tried to rally the defense, but the rest of the country ignored them."

"Except in our case, the walls were gone. Everybody was too absorbed with their own agendas to notice their enemies had torn them down."

"From the inside out," Angriff said. "And now we're standing watch in the ruins."

"That's about it. We're standing the final watch. After us, there's nobody left."

"Standing the final watch... Are we kidding ourselves, Norm? On the surface of it, this mission looks impossible. Before The Collapse there were nearly four hundred million U.S. citizens. How many can possibly still be alive? One percent? Less? Our mission is to restore the nation, and while we've got some impressive firepower for a unit our size, there are less than thirteen thousand of us. That's not even a good sized town.

"We have no idea what infrastructure can be salvaged, if any, or who is on our side and who isn't, although we do know that there is some sort of Islamic state set up throughout the southwest. I don't want to sound like a pessimist, but I don't want to buy into a fantasy, either. I can't say these things around anybody else, but you need to tell me if I'm being delusional. You need to promise me that."

Fleming smiled. "I've never minded telling you when you were wrong before. Why would I start now? As for the mission, hell, how should I know? Nobody has ever tried anything like this. We might as well be Lewis and Clark. But I don't think we can afford to worry about those kinds of things right now. All we can do is plow forward, do what we think is best, and see what happens."

"Well, beyond that horizon, there are a whole lot of windmills just waiting to be jousted with. Maybe you're right. Maybe that's all we can do."

Fleming stepped back and inspected his friend: scuffed black boots, green fatigues, and a brown bomber jacket. He could have passed as a sergeant. "If you're going for the medieval Spanish look you might want to work on it. You don't look much like Don Quixote to me. Maybe we need to thaw out one of those horses."

"Thank you, Sancho, but that's not necessary," Angriff said. "I wish that was all we really had to worry about, though, a few damned windmills. I can't get over my own people kidnapping my daughter, assaulting my XO, and trying to kill me. Who would have thought it possible? And a caliphate, a fucking Islamic kingdom set up in my country... what next?"

He paused so long Fleming thought him finished and started back inside. But as he turned away Angriff stopped him. "As XO, there's something you need to know. This stays between us. We have nukes."

Fleming's jaw dropped, without words.

"Not the big ones, although presumably those are still in their silos. We have tacticals, more than ten. I have no intention of using them, but they're an option and if something happens to me you need to be prepared."

"They're just different ordnance," Fleming said. "Nothing more, nothing less."

"Keep telling yourself that. It might make it easier if you ever have to use them. What a mission we've been given. We were trained to destroy, but after that we have to learn how to build."

Angriff went silent again, brooding, staring off into the distance. Long minutes passed, and Fleming shuffled his feet before Angriff spoke again. "Can you smell that, Norm?"

Fleming shook his head. "Smell what?"

Angriff tilted his head back and sniffed. "Vegetation. Plants. Things growing in the ground. I think I even smell sage. That's the smell of America, the smell of home. It inspires me."

I might agree if I could smell anything other than cigar smoke, Fleming thought. "Sure, Nick. It's inspirational."

Angriff, however, was too absorbed to hear him. "One good thing came out of all this, anyway. The bastards who brought all this on are dead and gone. It's like killing cancer—sometimes you almost kill the body getting rid of it, but until the cancer is gone the body can't begin to heal. Anybody left in this command who might have been fellow travelers will think twice about crossing me again. And all those greedy sons of bitches who destroyed America from the inside are rotting in the ground somewhere. It might be the most they've ever contributed to this country, by fertilizing the soil."

"I hope you're right."

"What do you mean, you hope I'm right? You don't think they're still alive, do you? After fifty years?"

"They froze us," Fleming said. "Why not themselves?"

Angriff said nothing, but after a few seconds he grunted. "You don't know how much it means to me, having you here now. You see things I don't, and I see things you'd miss. Together we make a damned good team. You're the only man I can talk to on a personal level, and I need that. I'm going to lean on you a lot in the coming months, Norm."

"I'm glad I could be here."

"I know, but thanks. I really mean that. Now, before we start hugging each other, it's time we was fixin' to get on with it, as my dad would say. Time to go down the rabbit hole. Not every problem can be solved with a bomb or a bullet, but most of the ones we're facing can, so it's time to start killing the bad people and saving the good. Let's hope we don't have to use nukes to do it."

Epilogue

"That's them." Vapor sharpened the focus on his binoculars. "The dumbass shits must have thought they could whip into a drive-through for a burger and lemonade."

"They're looking pretty ragged." Green Ghost lay beside him at the crest of the little rise. "There's only four of them. We're missing one."

"Probably dead. You take off into this desert with no supplies or skills, you deserve to be part of the food chain. Maybe the others ate him."

"Her. The one missing is a female."

"How could you tell? She could've played defensive end. Why did your crazy sister have to kill the one decent-looking chick?"

"I didn't kill her," Nipple said. "She died."

"Shut up, both of you," Ghost admonished. "I'm not a fucking referee. Anybody got any ideas where they might be headed?"

"Shit if I know," Vapor said. "All I can see is cactus and rattlesnakes out to the horizon. I think they're wandering around like Joshua leading the Jews out of Egypt."

"Moses," Nipple said. "Even I know that."

"We're losing the light, so they'll be making camp soon," Ghost said. "At zero hours we move in for a snatch. Prisoners are critical; we need the intel. Got it? I want these people alive. Vapor, you and Wingnut circle behind that ridge over there. Me and Nipple will move in from here. No shooting unless you have to. The more prisoners, the better. Got your NV gear?"

"Roger that." Vapor and Wingnut took off in a crouch.

"Eat something," Ghost said. "I'll take the watch."

"They're still moving, big brother," Nipple said. "Why are you so sure they'll stop?"

"Most people are afraid of what they can't see, so they hunker down and pretend it makes them safer. It's the only way they can sleep. They're from the city. They think this desert is actually more dangerous than a place like Chicago or D.C. You watch. They'll have a fire going within twenty minutes."

Exact almost to the minute, a campfire lit the growing darkness. Green Ghost settled down for the five-hour wait, never taking his eyes off his prey. The flames of their fire rose and he could see them walking around in its flicker.

At 2345 hours he shook his sister awake from a sound sleep. By zero hours they were ready to move out, M16s loaded and ready, while third-generation night vision goggles lit the landscape an electric green.

Six hundred fifty yards across the valley, Vapor and Wingnut started moving toward their target with the precision of long practice and experience. Within minutes they had all spread out and approached from four directions. Nobody would get away.

But within the circle of firelight, they found no one. The gear remained, including two half-full plastic jugs of water. But no humans.

"This is fucked up," Vapor said. "I had the watch. I didn't see anybody leave."

"Somehow they must have spotted us," Green Ghost said. "If they saw us without us seeing them, they're damned good. Spread out, find some tracks. They can't have gotten far."

Throughout the night they searched for some clue of how their quarry escaped, or if their quarry escaped. They found nothing until dawn, when sunlight finally betrayed faint footprints leading north. Vapor was their best tracker, so Green Ghost waited as he walked back and forth, then got down on all fours and lay down beside the tracks. Whenever he did this routine, it reminded Ghost of a searching dog. After fifteen minutes he quit, satisfied.

"Flat soles, probably five individuals. The tracks leading away are deeper, so they were carrying something heavy, obviously our targets. They got them first and went north. Just over this hill are hoofprints. Ten horses, maybe nine carrying riders. Somebody beat us to the kidnapping."

"How did we not hear them?" Green Ghost said.

"I don't know, man. I'm just telling you what I found."

"If you're right about the number, that means they brought enough horses for five riders."

"What are you thinking?"

"I'm not thinking anything. I just don't understand how they could pull this off with us watching the whole time."

"Me, either. Whoever these people are, they're studs. I hope they're on our side."

"Nobody is that good. Except ghosts," Green Ghost said.

The End

About the Author

Native Memphian Bill grew up eating wild blackberries while riding his bicycle on back-country roads, day-dreaming about spaceships and devouring books. He has read *The Lord of the Rings* 32 times so far.

Grooming four acres of land east of Memphis maintains his boyish figure. Bill loves nothing more than reading (and writing!) an enthralling book, while ignoring eight barking dogs and two cranky old cats, four nests of screeching hawks bordering his property, various bobcats and coyotes, and a constant barrage of cartoons aimed at a three year old.

His indulgent wife just shakes her head and smiles.

Also from Dingbat Publishing

Chapter One

current time

Three neat entry wounds drilled through the silk of Aunt Edith's blouse, stiffened and blackened by crusted blood. The underlying color was unrecognizable. I only knew it was supposed to be green because she wore it during our unfriendly dinner the previous evening and I remembered. Lying on the sidewalk with her legs crumpled beneath her, she seemed even tinier than normal, like a toy that had been roughly played with and then pitched aside.

I dropped to my knees beside her. Her eyes were wide, staring at the dawn breaking beyond the storefronts, and her mouth gaped. She was such a private person, so contained, elegant, brilliant as gold beside the base metals of the rest of us. Death seemed an exposure, a stripping of her secrets. A humiliation.

I reached out to stroke the drifting black and silver tendrils of her hair into place. But a hand snatched my wrist and twisted it aside. I jerked my head up—

—the picture window of the Carr Gallery, just overhead, was splattered with something dark. More of it sprayed the polished maple door, the brass railing and handle and mail slot. A small hole in the door, at waist level, had been marked with chalk—

—more dark stains, lit obliquely by the dawn light, trickled down the red brick, dripped from one concrete step to the next, painted the sidewalk. I suddenly realized I could smell it—

—I ignored the background *crump* of artillery fire and panned the rifle's scope along the enemy emplacement, atop the ridge overlooking our sandbagged trench. Beneath the camouflage netting and wilting tree branches I made out one big field gun with its muzzle recoiling, another, a third—

—the enemy spotter stood contemptuously in full view, binoculars to his eyes, gazing off to my left but sweeping this way. The rangefinder showed the distance at eight hundred meters. I set the elevation turret and aligned the sight's upper chevron on his center of mass, drifting aside by one hash mark to compensate for the gentle flow of air across my right cheek. Binocular lenses flashed sunsparks. His lips moved as I took up the initial pressure on the trigger—

—flashback with visual, auditory, tactile, and olfactory hallucinations. Hadn't happened in months. It was impossible to prevent it, stop it, tone it down, or predict its arrival. But we were intimate enemies, my flashback and I, and I knew its script. I clenched every muscle I possessed, including my eyes, and froze in place, ignoring it all. It's how I'd taught myself to respond when the city street morphed into a battlefield without warning, and so far it had prevented anyone from locking me up. I was even able to fool most acquaintances into thinking I was still sane.

But nothing blocked the sights, sounds, or other manifestations. Machine gun fire hammered into the nonexistent sandbags, thuds echoing in my bones, and the dust and acrid gunpowder caught at the back of my throat. Someone screamed, a long shrill sound that climbed higher in pitch and volume, scraping across my nerves. The enemy guns chattered again and a fire of agony spurted across my back. Wavery, sick-feeling blackness rushed in behind the pain. I refused to wobble. I ignored the war zone and the adrenaline tearing me apart, and waited for the screaming in my damaged memory to stop. For several more seconds it dragged on, a horrible rising shriek, but finally it cut out in its usual abrupt manner, as if someone hit a neurological mute button.

The flashback lost. It couldn't control my actions nor force me to betray my internal damage to the civilians. I wanted to collapse with relief. I refused to do that, too.

Ambient city noises resumed. There were lots of voices around, both live ones and the scratchy overlay of radio transmissions, and in the distance someone called my name. Even with my eyes squeezed tight, popping emergency lights strobed across my retinas. I still smelled the blood.

I failed Aunt Edith. Everything inside me wrenched. I failed her and now she's dead. That particular fear, of failing someone important, always followed the flashback. Knowing it was coming never prevented the reaction. I wouldn't show that, either.

Only when I knew I was back in real time did I open my eyes.

Dawn and Boston had returned. The battlefield was gone, replaced by the street of upscale shops, converted from historic red-brick row houses. Picture windows with discreet painted logos and black wrought-iron bars alternated with concrete steps rising to entries, each landing decorated with trees or flowers in wooden barrels. Blood painted the steps and façade of the Carr Gallery, Aunt Edith lay dead and hidden beside the entryway stairs, and there on her other side was a doughy face like something a baker played with before rolling it out. Its expression was outraged and the hand attached to the equally doughy body still gripped my wrist, our arms crossing above Aunt Edith's neck.

"Don't muck up my crime scene, man," he said in pure Brooklynese.

Ice clogged my veins. My field of vision constricted until all I could see was his face before me. I could control my physical behavior during the flashback and even my awareness, once I realized its game was on; I couldn't chain the emotions, nor the adrenaline. The muscles I'd released tautened again. Flight wasn't an option, but pounding something was. "She's not a crime scene."

He glanced down, as if only then realizing Aunt Edith was, or had been, human. "She is now."

I went for him. But strong arms hauled me back and away.

One of the live voices sniggered in my ear. "What a circus."

No sense fighting. It wasn't the policemen restraining me nor the crime scene technician I wanted to pound. I wanted the spotter, the one that got away during the war. If I could find the murderer who'd dossed down my Aunt Edith, he'd do, as well.

"Charles!"

That was my cousin Patricia's voice, piercing the enshrouding mental fog. I ignored the hands gripping me and peered over my shoulder. She stood alone, makeup smeared and lipstick chewed off, in the midst of the curious bystanders behind a strip of yellow tape. Flimsy as it looked, that tape represented the boundaries of the permissible and therefore was sufficient to stop her. Had they put that up behind me? I couldn't remember seeing it, much less ducking beneath it.

Patty seemed safe, so I turned back to Aunt Edith and eased from the policemen's holds. But a man stepped between the crime scene technician and me—between Aunt Edith and me. "Mr. Ellandun?"

I looked around him and didn't bother being subtle about it. Aunt Edith stared back, the heavy emptiness of the dead replacing her usual honest and level gaze, neither judgmental nor compassionate, with something blank. One of her pumps had fallen off and a chalk circle had been drawn around it. A bit of trash; the most amazing woman I'd ever met, and she'd been tossed aside like a bit of trash. It was beyond wrong. It was obscene.

"It's captain, actually," I said. "Captain Charles Ellandun."

He kept speaking, but as usual, Aunt Edith dominated the scene without trying. Only now it wasn't her elegant vivacity accomplishing that feat, but its absence. She had been the Rock of Gibraltar in my life since I'd been eleven and meeting her had been the watershed moment of my watershed year. She'd always been vital, compelling, more alive than the city itself. It was impossible for her to be dead.

Her skirt was the same as last night, as well, woven wool in the Hunter tartan plaid, the one she'd worn the day I first met her. Likely she'd returned to the art gallery directly after dinner, then. She still wore her wedding ring, as usual her only jewelry. There was no sign of her purse.

"Captain?" It was the man who'd stepped between us, a plainclothes detective in a button-down shirt and dark slacks.

Pounding him wouldn't help, either. I forced myself to look at him. I even remembered his question, although I was too distracted to focus. "Yes, I own several handguns."

"And were you in the war?" His voice was professional, beautifully modulated, and easy to listen to, even at that moment.

Even if he was an irritant.

"Yes." Was I ever.

The long, drawn-out *skrip* of a closing zipper demolished all my good intentions. The doughy crime scene technician slowly sealed the body bag. The shadow of the canvas flaps fluttered across her blank eyes. Then she vanished inside.

The air left my lungs as if I no longer needed oxygen, either. Again tunnel vision narrowed my field of focus, this time to the gurney as it rumbled past. The technician's hand rested atop the lumpy canvas.

I yearned to go for him again and fought the flashback-induced impulse. Although the battlefield had vanished into the scattered recesses of my mind, the subconscious, primal scream of combat still goaded me. Then I caught up with what the irritant standing beside me had just said in his elegant tenor.

Where were you last night.

I stared at him while the implications of that question soaked into the corners of my damaged brain. How long that took, while we locked eyes and assessed each other, I don't know; accurately measuring time has never been one of my finer accomplishments. But the details of his perfect face—expensively styled bronze-toned hair rippling above his ears, brown eyes steady and suspicious, smooth tan that had nothing to do with working outside, not a trace of stubble on the square jaw—left an after-image on my retinas like the strobing emergency lights. How could he stand being so damned perfect? It didn't matter whether pounding him would help or not. I went for him instead.

Again hands hauled me back. And suddenly cousin Patricia was between us, grabbing handfuls of my sport shirt and shaking me, or at least it. "Charles, for God's sake, what is *wrong* with you?"

I nearly told her, nearly reminded her of my diagnosis, but couldn't see the point even if I was an Ellandun and lived for the fight. The gurney and the moment were gone and the bloody adrenaline finally snapped. I shuddered beneath her clenched fists as the aftereffects kicked in. From the way her already wide green eyes were stretching wider, she felt it, too.

"Charles?" This time, her voice was less than a whisper and it broke in the middle of my name.

If I could have stopped the shaking, to protect Patty I would have done it. I'd failed her, too, and again I closed my eyes. Whatever showed in my all-too-transparent face, she didn't need to see it.

Because I'd tried to tackle a plainclothes police detective, Boston's finest slung me into the back of a squad car to cool down, one of an armload of emergency vehicles scattered about the street. They closed the doors, too, and how the July heat that rapidly built up inside that car was supposed to help me cool down, I cannot imagine. The interior stank from the stale fast-food wrappers littering the floorboards and the stain of something I didn't want to identify on the part of the seat I avoided.

I'd put up with all of it if I could have Aunt Edith back. She couldn't possibly be dead.

Outside the patrol car and a few yards away, Patricia and Brother Perfect chatted like old friends, her eyes sliding sideways to check on me every minute or so, his never leaving her damp and smudged face. He'd positioned her so she couldn't see the blood. Her mousy brown hair strained back in a knot that looked painted on, but then so did her jeans, and with her streamlined figure, I'm certain the average male never noticed the hair. To give him credit, Brother Perfect's gaze didn't drop, not even to her green cotton camp shirt, halfway unbuttoned from the bottom and tied in a knot above her belt buckle. Perhaps the stained handkerchief she used to rearrange the sad remnants of her makeup put him off.

Finally she walked away, ducked beneath the yellow crime-scene tape, and waited outside the perimeter, staring at me in the back of the squad car with her lower lip between her teeth. Brother Perfect watched her until their eyes met for a brief glance, and then he turned, opened the squad car door, and slid into the front passenger seat.

To give him further credit, he didn't bother scolding me. "You say you have several guns. Tell me about them."

I rubbed my eyes. "I own an M-16, a Mauser sniper's rifle—"

"Handguns, Captain. Tell me about your handguns."

To hell with him. I moved over until I breathed the outside air. "I have a Colt .45, two old Walther nine millimeters and two new ones—"

"What's the smallest bore handgun you own?"

The question threw me until I realized the holes in Aunt Edith's lungs had been small. "The nine millimeters."

"No twenty-two?" he asked. "Nothing smaller than a nine?"

"No," I said.

He stared at me for a long moment. The shakes had diminished as the adrenaline ebbed away, leaving me taut and intensely aware, and the skeptical curl of his lip made his opinion of my veracity perfectly clear. Again my temper began heating—there was something about him that made that a delightful process—but I swore this time I'd hang onto my self-control.

"I've kept records," I said. "And my LTC Class A and FID are both in order. You're welcome to check them."

"Thank you." The tone of his voice left no doubt he'd do so whether I volunteered them or not. "Are you carrying now?"

"No." But I intended to rectify that as soon as possible.

"So where were you last night?"

"At home." I gave him the address of my condo on the waterfront, north of Burroughs Wharf and well away from the tourist congestion at the Aquarium and Rowe's Wharf. He didn't write anything down; perhaps he had a photographic memory. "I had dinner with Aunt Edith around seven, got home around nine thirty or a bit after, and stayed in."

She had tried to persuade me to be sociable and forgiving, get involved with her latest bloody art show, see the family while everyone was in town as if I had a particle of interest whatsoever in them. The remembrance of how little encouragement I had given her during that, our final conversation, set my insides squirming.

"Can anyone confirm that?"

I hadn't even checked email. "No."

That internal squirming had a distinctly frigid tinge to it now. He'd gun for motive next; wasn't that how they did it on those stupid cop shows?

But he surprised me by motioning me out of the car. He leaned atop the hood, his perfect face strobed by the popping emergency lights so that he seemed dipped in blood then wiped clean, over and over again. I knew that image would stay in my nightmares for a long time to come. Something else to appreciate about the man.

"Don't leave town," he said, and walked away.

***

Thanks for reading! Dingbat Publishing strives to bring you quality entertainment that doesn't take itself too seriously. I mean honestly, with a name like that, our books have to be good or we're going to be laughed at. Or maybe both.

If you enjoyed this book, the best thing you can do is buy a million more copies and give them to all your friends... erm, leave a review on the readers' website of your preference. All authors love feedback and we take reviews from readers like you seriously.

Oh, and c'mon over to our website:
www.DingbatPublishing.ninja

Who knows what other books you'll find there?

Cheers,

Gunnar Grey,
publisher, author, and Chief Dingbat

Printed in Great Britain
by Amazon